Argimou

Early Canadian Literature Series

The Early Canadian Literature Series returns to print rare texts deserving restoration to the canon of Canadian texts in English. Including novels, periodical pieces, memoirs, and creative non-fiction, the series showcases texts by Indigenous peoples and immigrants from a range of ancestral, language, and religious origins. Each volume includes an afterword by a prominent scholar providing new avenues of interpretation for all readers.

Series Editor: Benjamin Lefebvre

Series Advisory Board:
Andrea Cabajsky, Département d'anglais, Université de Moncton
Carole Gerson, Department of English, Simon Fraser University
Cynthia Sugars, Department of English, University of Ottawa

For more information please contact:

Siobhan McMenemy
Senior Editor
Wilfrid Laurier University Press
75 University Avenue West
Waterloo, ON   N2L 3C5
Canada

Phone: 519.884.0710 ext. 3782
Fax: 519.725.1399
Email: smcmenemy@wlu.ca

Argimou: A Legend of the Micmac

S. Douglass S. Huyghue (Eugene)

Afterword by Gwendolyn Davies

Early Canadian Literature

Wilfrid Laurier University Press acknowledges the support of the Canada Council for the Arts for
our publishing program. We acknowledge the financial support of the Government of Canada
through its Book Publishing Industry Development Program for our publishing activities. This
work was supported by the Research Support Fund.

Library and Archives Canada Cataloguing in Publication

Huyghue, S. Douglass S., 1816–1891, author
    Argimou : a legend of the Micmac / S. Douglass S. Huyghue ; afterword by Gwendolyn Davies.

(Early Canadian literature)
Includes bibliographical references.
Issued in print and electronic formats.
ISBN 978-1-77112-247-4 (softcover).—ISBN 978-1-77112-265-8 (PDF).—
ISBN 978-1-77112-266-5 (EPUB)

    I. Davies, Gwendolyn, writer of afterword. II. Title. III. Series: Early Canadian literature series

PS8409.U4A7 2017   C813'.3   C2017-900675-4
                                           C2017-900676-2

Cover design and text design by Blakeley Words+Pictures. Cover drawing, ca. 1845 and possibly
by a Miss Grove, depicts a scene from a Mi'kmaq settlement near Dartmouth, Nova Scotia. Library
and Archives Canada item C-117295, from the Thompson Album. The sketch appeared originally
on the cover of a children's novel, *Little Grace*, by Miss Grove, published in Halifax in 1846.

This book is printed on FSC® certified paper and is certified Ecologo. It contains post-consumer
fibre, is processed chlorine free, and is manufactured using biogas energy.

Printed in Canada.

Contents

Series Editor's Preface

S amuel Douglass Smith Huyghue was born in Charlottetown, Prince Edward Island, on 23 April 1816, and was raised and educated in Saint John, New Brunswick. In 1840, while living in Halifax, he began publishing poems in the *The Halifax Morning Post and Parliamentary Reporter* using the pseudonym "Eugene," which he continued to use when, after moving back to Saint John a year later, he began publishing his work regularly in *The Amaranth*, subtitled "A Monthly Magazine of New and Popular Tales, Poetry, History, Biography, &c. &c." This included, in five monthly installments between May and September 1842, the full text of his first novel, *Argimou: A Legend of the Micmac*. As Gwendolyn Davies notes in her entry on Huyghue in *The Oxford Companion to Canadian Literature* (1983), "Although *Argimou* purports to be a romance set in Acadia in 1755, it is in reality an impassioned novel of conscience exploring the disintegration of Mi'kmaq culture under the influence of European settlement; it is also one of the first Canadian novels to describe the Expulsion of the Acadians" (377). The full text was then republished in book form by the Morning Courier Office in Halifax in 1847; a teaching edition of the book, based on the *Amaranth* text, appeared with an introduction by Davies in 1977, a second edition following in 1979. After he moved to London, England, in 1849, he published, under his own name, a second novel, *The Nomades of the West; or, Ellen Clayton*, but it was not a financial or critical success. In 1852, he emigrated to Australia, where he held several government positions and achieved renown as a painter. He died on 24 July 1891.

This Early Canadian Literature edition uses the Morning Courier Office edition as its copy-text, the sole known copy of which is held at the Nova Scotia Archives. All footnotes are Huyghue's and appear in the Morning Courier Office edition. The present edition silently corrects obvious typographical errors but leaves intact several archaic spellings, including "carriboo," "christian" (uncapitalized), "countrol," "dependant," "discant," "ecstacy," "pourtray," and "wippoorwill." It regularizes the spelling of "warrior," which appeared sometimes as "warrier," as well as the proper nouns "Anglasheou," "Madokawando," "Milicete," "Peticodiac," "Waswetchcul," and "Wennooch."

BENJAMIN LEFEBVRE

Works Cited

Eugene (*see also* Huyghue, S. Douglass S.). "Argimou: A Legend of the Micmac." *The Amaranth*, May 1842, pp. 129–42; June 1842, pp. 161–77; July 1842, pp. 193–209; Aug. 1942, pp. 225–38; Sept. 1842, pp. 257–81.

———. *Argimou: A Legend of the Micmac*. Halifax, Morning Courier Office, 1847.

———. *Argimou: A Legend of the Micmac*. 1977. Sackville: R. P. Bell Library, 1979.

Davies, Gwendolyn. "Huyghue, Douglas Smith." *The Oxford Companion to Canadian Literature*, edited by William Toye, Oxford University Press, 1983, pp. 376–77.

———. "Huyghue, Samuel Douglass Smith." *Dictionary of Canadian Biography*, n.d., biographi.ca/en/bio/huyghue_samuel_douglass_smith_12E.html.

———. "Introduction to the Second Edition." *Argimou: A Legend of the Micmac*, by Eugene, R. P. Bell Library, 1979, pp. i–xiv.

Huyghue, S. Douglass S. (*see also* Eugene). *The Nomades of the West; or, Ellen Clayton*. 3 vols. Richard Bentley, 1850.

Argimou

Chapter I

"I love the Indian. Ere the white-man came
And taught him vice, and infamy, and shame,
His soul was noble. In the sun he saw
His God, and worshipped him with trembling awe;—
Though rude his life, his bosom never beat
With polished vices, or with dark deceit."

Argimou, the son of Pansaway, was as brave a warrior as ever bounded in the war-path of the Micmacs. The speed of his arrow was like the lightning of the Great Spirit. The eagle of the salt water screamed its death-song as it fell pierced by the strength of his arm. His foot was swifter than the carriboo when it flies from the hunter's approach; and he cried to the blue-eyed pale-faces, "see! a warrior can look at the face of the sun without shedding a tear." His voice in battle was like the storm in the forest; as the trees fall by the blast so were his enemies swept away by the tempest of his wrath. The Mohawk told his name to the tribes of the great Iroquois; and the Penobscot spread his fame in the land near the setting sun; but the warriors said to their young men, when the women trembled at the sound, "Go! wash away this big thought from our hearts in the blood of our enemies, that our mouths may not be filled with the praises of a stranger, or our dreams haunted by this Bashaba* of the Micmacs."

Such is the song which may sometimes be heard in the wigwams of the poor Micmacs, when they gather around the fire in the cold winter evenings and seek a brief forgetfulness of their poverty and degradation, in listening to the wild tales and triumphant recollections of the years that are gone. When the narrator pictures forth the secret ambuscade, the midnight attack that rooted out some plant of the invader from their fatherland; when he enters into minute details of the fierce conflict, the unyielding struggle—the number of captives taken—foeman slain, then may dark eyes be seen to flash again with their ancient fire, and heads are thrown back with the haughty bearing of warriors; while the sinewy hand grasps instinctively the knife, and the out-dashed arm plunges the weapon to and fro, as though seeking the heart of an imaginary victim in the maddening bursts of the war-song. Alas! poor remnants of a once mighty nation—ye are like the few remaining leaves on a tree from whence their companions have withered; a little while and the blast will moan a lonely dirge through the naked boughs—the voice of Nature will sigh her last farewell.

Gentle reader—the aborigines of America have always engaged the warmest interest of our hearts; excited as every natural sympathy must be by the melancholy truth, that in a little time all traces of the numerous and powerful nations, once inhabiting the great forests and plains of the New World, will be obliterated for ever from the face of the earth; their characteristic features, the simplicity of their habits, and their extraordinary intelligence, displayed in appropriating to their purposes the resources of these vast solitudes for which they seem to be especially adapted by the Creator, are rendered doubly impressive to the mind of the philosopher. There is an originality, a romantic charm about those "wanderers of the wild," which insensibly leads captive the imagination, and heightens our compassion for their undeserving fate.

* Great Chief.

Then, again, the thought, which sophistry or a guilty conscience would seek to shroud in an impenetrable veil of obscurity, will at times start up like an avenging ghost, to haunt us with the accusation of injustice and crime. Ay, these are harsh words, but the terrible truth, though it burn to the core, must not be salved over with the unction of smooth phrases. We are the sole and only cause of their overwhelming misery, their gradual extinction; directly, by lawless appropriation of their hunting grounds, to utter violation of every principle of justice, human or divine, which is supposed to influence the conduct of a christian people; indirectly, through the propagation of disease in its most harrowing forms, and the blighting introduction of that direst of all plagues—the accursed "fire-water," which metaphorical designation is most strongly illustrative of its destructive effects. What the grasping ambition and cruelty of the white man failed fully to accomplish, the wasting sword of pestilence and dissipation has fatally consummated. They are passing away from the presence of the stranger, with the groves that gave shelter to their wigwams, the woods where their fathers hunted the deer, and they frolicked in happy childhood. Every tree that bows its proud head beneath the axe of the settler is a death-knell to their vanishing tribes. Driven back as exiles from their country, and sacrificed at the shrine of an inhuman policy, with numbers fearfully diminished, the unflinching heroism of their ancestors burns brightly still within their hearts, as their republican persecutors have reluctantly proved— "with all the scorn of Death and chains." Even at the present period, the flaming hamlet and bloody deed of retaliation bear witness in their own figurative enunciation, that "the grass is not yet grown upon their war-path." In a few years the record of their names, their noble struggle, their empassioned eloquence, will live but in the cold historic page, or faintly linger in the memory of those "who linked them fast to sorrow;" and, perchance, like ourselves, many a curious mortal may hereafter intrude upon their peaceful slumbers, and recreate with fanciful enthusiasm a sylvan dwelling for the children of the red-man;

5

clothing the dishonoured hills and vales with the gorgeous mantle of primeval nature, and casting the solemn shades of dark foliage on the lakes and streams, scarce ruffled by the graceful motion of the light canoe, whose grave occupant seems a natural adjunct to the wild majesty of the scene; or touching the secret spring of those fierce passions ever dormant beneath the calmest exterior, the most unsuspicious repose, fill the sanctuaries of a fictitious wilderness with the unhallowed voice of strife, and enact again some of those dark episodes of Indian warfare, to adorn the vista of a tale. When the hunter's form is seen no more in the dismantled woods, and the song and dance are forever hushed, perhaps we may experience a tardy sensation of pity and regret for those who are beyond the aid of an impulsive charity.—We rear the germ of a great city without casting a thought upon the generation crumbling beneath, which, if it wake not a throb of sympathy, may teach, at least, a humiliating lesson to our pride—the moral of the impartial grave. Alas! we have little kindred feeling for those removed from our peculiar circle of selfish association;—should we not discard all narrow conception of moral obligation to our fellow creatures, and embrace, within the scope of a comprehensive benevolence, every individual composing the family of the human race?—And, O ye Legislators and Philanthropists! who yearly expend large means upon projects of speculative utility, if you come forward even in the last hour with generous determination to lighten in some respect the dark shadow that sullies the vaunted integrity of the national character, incalculable misery may be averted, and blessings, instead of bitter curses, your reward. Pour out, not hundreds but thousands in the furtherance of this good cause; that it is a good cause who will attempt to deny?—Have we not palpable proofs daily before our eyes of utter want and wretchedness, clothed in all the loathsomeness of abandonment and shame? Look at that shrivelled remnant of what was once a powerful, energetic man!—his ragged garments a mockery to the piercing blast; which, by implanting the seeds of moral infirmity, only hastens the inevitable result—lying in helpless intoxication at the corner of a street, an object of contempt and ridicule to the sordid wretch who administered the draft that consumes his vitals; is not *there* a fitting subject for the purposes of amelioration? It is needless to attribute his abasement to the influence of depraved propensities, why place temptation in his path?—nor is it wonderful that the poor untutored Indian should be incapable of resisting the delusive pleasure, which yields a temporary alleviation of suffering, when so many—possessing wealth and every advantage of moral and intellectual culture, are its unresisting victims.

We have been led far beyond our intended limits in the foregoing remarks, but it must be confessed, that we are apt to feel rather warm upon the subject, and could consign a volume to its serious consideration. Giving that as our best excuse for this long digression, we will now proceed to the development of our story.

Of that portion of coast which, washed by the waves of the Gulf St. Lawrence, terminates the north eastern limits of Nova Scotia, the bold promontory bearing the name of Cape Tormentine, forms a most conspicuous feature. This headland, giving existence to a beautiful bay on its southern side, forms the nearest point of connection with the adjacent Island of Prince Edward, or St. Johns, as it was then called; indeed, from the similarity of its soil with the general red colour of the opposite shores, one would fain imagine that at some distant period the latter were united at that particular spot with the main, and though a convulsive effort of Nature severed the medium of conjunction, and caused a narrow strait to flow between, the parent still advanced her giant limb to promote a re-union with her alienated child. A long line of dim coast, here distinctly visible, but receding to a deep bay to the eastward, until you might mistake it for a blue cloud resting on the horizon, appeared to run almost parallel with the main land.

Turning shoreward, the view, at the time of which we write, was enchanting in the extreme, from its glowing luxuriance, and the

refreshing contrast of the bright green foliage, clothing every eminence and hollow until it dipped into the blue water clasping point
and indent, and reflecting from its clear depths a fairy semblance of
surrounding objects; and a few pale shreds of cloud scattered over the
firmament above. The Baye Verte after stretching far inland, contracted its limits; when again expanding, it terminated in a second bay
of small extent compared with the space beyond, but far surpassing it
in materials of picturesque beauty. Several deep coves, each transmitting a slivery stream, pierced the land at the harbour's head, into the
bosom of which the Gaspereaux River also poured its tributary flood,
and lost its identity by mingling with the brine of the impatient sea.
Near this estuary the ramparts of a fort could be observed, from which
waved lazily the "tri-colour" of France, and dotting the surface of the
water numerous canoes filled with natives appeared swiftly concen-
trating toward the jutting point at the entrance of the inner bay, on its
northern side, where an animating scene was just then exhibited.

Upon a sloping plateau, which was divested of the exuberant
vegetation garnishing the landscape, and blending insensibly with the
sand of the beach, a crowd of dark skinned warriors were gathered
in various groups of a wild and fanciful character. In one place might
be seen a knot of Micmacs from the Bay Des Chaleurs, in tunics of
deer skin, confined round the waist with a sash of brilliant colours,
or merely a leather thong, and legs encased in tight leggins, in many
instances of blue cloth, embroidered with fringes of red hair down the
side; below which the moccasin displayed an instep ornamented with
figures worked in dyed moose hair, or the quills of the porcupine. Every
man carried in his girdle the *witch-bodie*, or purse, made of the skin of
some small animal, the paws and tail of which were still preserved, and
often garnished with beads and scarlet cloth; beside this depended in
its blood-soaked sheath, the long bladed knife—that ruthless weapon
which is inseparable from the war equipment of an Indian brave.

Across the knees of some lay the long French Fusee, while others held a rough bow with its store of flint headed arrows.

These men, who were of strong athletic make and lofty stature, reclined in attitudes of unconscious grace, assisted by the unfettered freedom of their costume, and the indefinable air of majesty which breathes, as it were, from the lineaments of the forest-born, and flashed in fiery glances from eyes of most intense blackness; the expression of deep determination upon each face was softened by the masses of raven hair, which, though cut short over the brows, fell in thick shades to the brawny shoulders. In another place, a party similar in general appearance to the above, but differing slightly in apparel, attracted the eye. These were Penobscot warriors from the westward, with their neighbours of the Milicete tribe; and their habiliments were more in keeping with their rude, savage aspect; for occupying a territory further removed from the European settlements, they had not caught insensibly the polite tone which was evident in the Micmacs, from their intercourse with the French; nor were they enabled to procure, thereby, the dearly prized finery of their gayer brethren. One individual, who appeared to be a subordinate chief, wore a cap made of the skin of a carriboo's head, to which was attached the branching horns—giving a fantastic appearance to the gigantic proportions of the wearer as with impressive action of the right arm he recounted his warlike exploits, or delivered some exposition of Indian policy, with all the force of gesticulation and passionate appeal, which is so conspicuous in the harangues of the natives;—while the listeners, with stolid countenances and grave attention puffed long whiffs of smoke from the variegated stems of their pipes; the bowls of which, wrought of dark stone, were ingeniously and even elegantly carved. Near at hand a more noisy set were seated on their hams, playing the game of the Bone, with a number of round flat pieces made of that substance, differently marked and coloured; which being thrown up and caught in a wooden

9

platter, denoted by their position the chances of the player. Several lookers-on were gathered round the principal parties, who by vehement exclamation and loud shouting, evinced their interest in the result; and such was the infatuation of some, that knives, guns, and all their worldly possessions, were staked upon the hazard of a throw, until they were left almost naked—for they even stripped themselves of their habiliments to allure the smiles of that "*ignis fatuus*"—Fortune.

Here and there a trio of maidens in richly figured caps of conical shape, and long gowns of foreign material, would excite observation from their showy exterior, and the peals of musical laughter which ever and anon rang, clear as a bell, from their merry lips; but they were few in proportion to the other sex, and as the small portion of leggin allowed to be seen below the upper garment proved, belonged, with one or two exceptions, to the Micmac tribe—of which were the greatest portion of the warriors there assembled.

But in remarkable contrast to the peculiar stamp of the before mentioned clusters of wild, unsophisticated savages, a number of Acadian peasantry in broad rimmed hats of straw, and half military costume, which was deemed essential to the warlike spirit of the time, conversed apart from the rest, with the vivacity common to their light-hearted nation. Among these were mingled a few French officers from the garrison of the fort, whose brilliant uniforms and martial-looking mustaches created a still greater dissimilitude to the dress and lineaments of their Indian coadjutors.

On the smooth sand that bordered the rippling tide, were upturned a number of bark canoes, which seemed objects of considerable curiosity to one or two young soldiers, lately arrived from "La belle France;" who, after minutely examining their construction, expressed by divers shrugs and facial contortions, their unqualified contempt and amazement that a human being should be so regardless of personal safety as to trust himself to the guardianship of such nut-shell fabrics. And in the wavelets that spread their store with a quiet whisper upon the strand, a few gleeful, plump-looking urchins were dipping their unshod feet, and scampering about in boisterous merriment, utterly regardless of the proximity of the *pale faces*.—Higher up and half hidden by the branches of the trees, was a large tent of square form, composed of green stakes and interlaced boughs of the fragrant fir, in which were seated, in full council, the elders of the nation, and the chiefs of the several war-parties, from the allied tribes, then gathered together to assist in the grand ceremony about to take place, namely—the inauguration of the newly elected chief to the important position and powers which he was henceforth to assume in the opinions and concerns of his nation. This envied rank, only attained by the superior acquirements and courage of the possessor; as, unlike many other tribes of this extraordinary people, it was not transferred by hereditary succession, but acquired through general suffrage alone—had become vacant by the death of the previous occupant, who was slain in a hostile expedition to the British settlements on the peninsula, from which the present bands had not long since returned.

While the various knots and stragglers of this large body of Indians, following the bent of idle caprice or personal inclination, were occupied in the manner we have described, the quick, dull taps of a drum were heard to proceed from the council tent; whereupon each warrior sprang simultaneously to his feet, and fell, as if by tacit consent, into the ranks; which were speedily ranged in the form of an open circle, the circumference of which was increased gradually by the repeated addition of row after row, till the whole assembly were gathered into its limits—appearing like a living belt of silent, immoveable figures, the innermost portion of whom were seated on the green sward, with the intention of allowing the supervision of those in the rear. On that side nearest the secret conclave, a double line of natives formed a lane leading to the door of the tent; and within the enclosure, beside the passage of communication, stood the representatives of French denomination, before alluded to. Amongst the zone of grave, stern faces clustered every where around, not a single muscle betrayed the smallest movement, or was ought betokening animation visible, save the unceasing gleam of innumerable black eyes; indeed, though the several aspects varied in feature and the exaggeration of expression, produced by the application of paint, still so little was there of life and motion in the group, that you might have imagined them carved out of solid wood. Whatever passions existed in the breasts of hundreds there,—and they were many and unquenchable—all outward manifestation was prohibited by the indomitable self-possession of the Indian character. But the most conspicuous personage was a young warrior in the prime and graceful dignity of early manhood, who leaned against a tall post in the centre of a ring—from which dangled a number of half-dried scalps—with assumed carelessness, in which might be detected a mixture of pride and joyful anticipation, or his proud glance belied the impulse of the owner's heart. His height was rather above that of his brethren, and to proportions of faultless symmetry were joined a degree of strength and agility which excited the wonder and admiration of the warlike tribes. Of his mental qualities it is related, in the simple manner of the people—"that he was never known to quail at the face of man, or to falter upon a trail; that he walked straight forward without looking another way, and carried an open palm; and, moreover, that he never let the grass grow over the memory of a good deed, but, with the unrelenting constancy of his race, an injury was never forgotten."

And now he awaits the moment of installation to that rank which for years it had been his sole object to attain; at last, the hope which had filled his dreams by night, and nerved his soul in battle to the accomplishment of the boldest deeds, was to be rewarded;—for he had been proclaimed victor by an overwhelming majority of votes over his competitors, and when he left the spot where he then stood it would be with the proud distinction of Grand Sachem of the Micmac nation.

'Ere long a stir is perceptible in the direction of the tent, and an old man with long silvery hair, so heavy with accumulated years that he is obliged to be supported by a chief on either side, advanced within the thronged circle, followed by the other elders and influential persons composing the council, each bearing some portion of the insignia appertaining to the chieftainship, which, after the young warrior had been invested with a dress of costly material, heavy with minute embroidery, and leggins of scarlet cloth, beaded and fringed, were in succession delivered into the keeping of Argimou;—for such was his name, with a brief but impressive oration from the father of the tribe. There were the *wampum belts* of woven cylindrical shells from the country of the great lakes; the symbolic pledges of alliance with the neighbouring tribes; the ornamented *to-ma-gan*, or pipe, of cemented friendship; the bright *to-ma-hawk*, or hatchet, signifying active war; and lastly, the beaded fillet, with its eagle plume—the distinguishing badge of a Bashaba. Then came forward a French officer of rank, and presented to the chief, in the name of Onanthio,* a scarf of brilliant colours together with a medallion of silver, on which was embossed a likeness of the Sovereign, and many other articles of value and esteem among the natives; which part of the ceremony concluded with a long speech from the aged warrior, pronounced with a voice clear and powerful for his years, in which he inculcated upon the mind of Argimou an imitation of the wisdom and bravery of his ancestors—their prowess in battle—their justice in peace, with the necessity of preserving the closest amity and co-operation with the generous *Wennooch*;† whose king, their great father, had sent such choice gifts as a pledge of his good intentions to the nation. When the old man concluded his address he was so exhausted that they were obliged to carry him away as helpless as a child; and then might be seen harsh features to relax with an involuntary feeling of sympathy and affection, and a low murmur rose from the multitude whose iron hearts would have defied the utmost torture to wring one groan of weakness from the body's agony, though

---

* The name by which the French king was known among the native tribes.

† Frenchman.

13

they were torn limb from limb;—for even the unrelenting savage acknowledges the potency of that spell which links in one bright chain every created thing with the heaven from whence it came to purify and bless! The love which they bore to that hoary patriarch was not as the fickle bond which a breath might sever, a passion that consumes itself away—they had listened to his eloquence in their earliest years, and even then his hair was grey; they revered the voice which preserved the deeds of their fathers like a chronicle of the past, and regarded him with that awe which sanctifies the attributes of extreme age; for to their superstitious mind he appeared a spirit from that country of blessed influences to which he was so quickly hastening.

The crowd now broke away from the circle and gathered within the banquet hall, a large shed open in front, behind the council tent, where a plentiful feast was prepared, which speedily vanished before the attacks of so many well armed mouths, and a hunger that nothing seemed to mitigate or assuage. After this pleasing and important part of the observances to which the day was devoted had been complied with, the Indians with lively gestures and many a grin of promised merriment, unbent, from the cold, dignified demeanor so general during the former ceremony. They now seized their guns, charged with powder only, or provided themselves with stout thongs of moose skin, and fell into a double line of considerable extent, through which the new chief was doomed to run the gantlet, in pursuance of custom immemorial;—as thereby the endurance and activity of the Sachem were supposed to be tested in no small degree. Divested of his state tunic and its various appurtenances, Argimou appeared at the top of the long lane, stripped to the waist, from which a piece of bear skin descended over the loins, revealing a form moulded in the purest contour of natural beauty, whose natural majesty was not unworthy a comparison with the ideals of antique sculpture. At a given signal off he darted with amazing swiftness, saluted from either side with sharp lashes on the arms and shoulders; while at the same time the repeated discharges of fire arms, the muzzles of which were pointed at his uncovered legs, occasioning a severe pricking sensation in those members, blended in loud discord with the yells and laughter of his tormentors—increasing in a burst of stronger excitement and applause as the agile Indian would avoid, by some extraordinary leap or sudden dodge, the blows and aim of his assailants.—Three times this ordeal was repeated, when the chief, having escaped with no greater injury than a few slight erasements of the integument, and a plentiful sprinkling of powder grains in his lower extremities—which were considered an honourable commemoration of his induction, was lifted in triumph upon the athletic backs of the warriors, and escorted to the palaver house, where a lighted *to-ma-gan* was presented, and he was allowed to indulge in a short period of repose after the unusual exercise and rigorous treatment he had undergone.

Chapter II

The broad disk of the sun which hung for a moment like a shield of burnished gold above the forest groves, had pressed his last kiss on the face of the western sky; ere its warm blush faded, the deep peal of a watch-gun from the ramparts of the fort rolled over the glass bay with booming reverberation, till, spreading its roar over the strait of Northumberland, the distant shores of Prince Edward's replied in a low murmur like the subdued resonance of a distant thunder growl. The first shades of evening darkened over the earth and air, while from the clear arch overhead, the sparkling beam of one glorious star gazed down upon the dim woods and their drowsy solitudes. The bear looked out of his den, and saw its ray piercing the leafy labyrinth, and glistening upon the drops of dew that fringed the moss-covered entrance of his cavern, and gazing without consciousness, upon the faint glow until his sleepy eyelid closed; with a grunt, the hermit buried his head in the pillow of his broad hairy paw. The moose, quenching his thirst at the shore of some quiet lake, starts with vague fear at the burning reflection in the depths of the dark water, and turns away with a scanty draught, to the security of his wild-wood lair. But the old grey owl uncloses an eye, and when he recognises an old friend sends a shriek of joy—a merry war-whoop, over the hills and groves; for he knows that star, though the herald of darkness and repose to the rest of creation, is to him the harbinger of an opening, busy day. The Micmacs lighted a large fire, which shed a ruddy glow upon the adjacent foliage, and poured a lengthened stream of brilliancy far across the surface of the bay. Around the flame a ring of natives of both sexes moved with slow unvaried tread to the cadence of a guttural chant, and the monotonous "cush! cush!" sound of the rattle,* which the singer beat untiringly upon his bended knee. Then the figure was changed, and in the snake dance they strove to imitate the movements of that reptile in a series of graceful convolutions, which was kept up with much spirit until the performers were completely exhausted. They lit them each a birchen torch, and hurrying to the beach embarked in their canoes, at the prows of which the ignited brands were secured on elevated poles, the chief leading in advance with a double flambeau. When the miniature flotilla was ready to proceed, a simultaneous yell, terrible and unearthly, seemed to burst from the bosom of the bay, and was wafted from shore to shore, from point to inlet by the startled echoes, until it died away in the far forest glades. The sentinel, pausing in his lonely walk, felt a thrill of dread creep through every limb, and exude in moisture from the roots of his hair, as he listened to that tremendous cry; then the paddle blades dipped noiselessly into the stream, and the whole mass moved onward over the liquid expanse, like a galaxy of flaming meteors, to the deep measured intonation of a war-song.

The bark cones of several wigwams on the outskirts of an encampment, soon appeared in bright relief through the reflected torch-light, from the dim obscurity of the shore they were approaching. Then groups of females were seen clustered at the water's edge, to welcome the returning warriors. As Argimou stepped from the canoe he threw a searching glance toward the maidens, and his eye wandered in its scrutiny over their bright intelligent features until it rested upon the

---

* This is made by filling the shell of a tortoise—the scull of any small animal, or, simply, a cow horn, with fine shot: and is used to mark time in the dance.

half-averted countenance of a beautiful Milicete girl, whose slight fawn-like figure and picturesque costume, were partially visible in the fitful illumination. And, in truth, that young squaw might well agitate the thoughts of a bolder hunter than Argimou. The fiercest brave that ever leaped upon the track of an enemy could not meet with steady look the fascinating glance of that soft, dark eye, with its lurking laughter ever ready to sparkle forth and wreath the features, otherwise reposing in a sweet, plaintive expression, with a sunny smile of innocence and joy. Indeed, the prevailing character of the face was pathetic tenderness; so very—very enchanting, that you almost disliked the beam of warm sunlight which at once passed over it. Her complexion was exceedingly clear and almost as light as a European's; and the pale cheek, in moments of animation or impulsive feeling, would glow with a rich suffusion like the petals of the wild rose. This gentle creature, whose unstudied graces and unaffected delicacy would have shamed the artificial allurements of many a fashionable belle, if the symmetry of her round unshackled limbs—the surpassing beauty of the small hand and foot, did not create a sensation of mingled wonder and envy, answered to the euphonious name of Waswetchcul, by interpretation—"*the flower of the wilderness.*"—As the chief passed on he caught the speaking expression of one quick glance, darted timidly from beneath the fringed lid, and the world of sympathy and kindness that dwelt in the greeting was more grateful to his heart than even the exulting consciousness of a successful ambition. When is that all-powerful principle conveyed in the electric flashing of an eye, which thrills through every particle of our being, making each fibre tremble with an unknown sensation which we in vain seek to analyze, but have, most of us, experienced at some period of our lives; which, even as a memory, when the cooling blood and blunted nerves hasten on the torpidity of age, warms, with a sudden, involuntary flame, the expiring embers of the freezing heart?

The interesting female whom we have introduced to the reader, was a descendant of Baron St. Castine, whose romantic residence among the aborigines, forms so novel an episode in the early history of Acadia. This nobleman abandoning the luxuries and pursuits of refined life, after serving as a soldier, sojourned for upwards of twenty years with the Abenaquis Indians, among whom he married and had several children; finally, he became Grand Sachem of the western tribes, and rendered powerful assistance to the French in their contentions with the subjects of the British crown. Dearly beloved by the natives for his integrity and benevolence, they gave to his son, at his death, the same rank which the father had so equitably sustained among the people of his adoption. The parents of Waswetchcul had died when she was a mere child, and left her to the care of an uncle, a proud, gloomy savage of avaricious propensities, and his wife, an aged squaw, whose whithered aspect and sharp grating voice, presented a painful contrast to the fresh budding charms and musical tones of the wild flower, doomed to languish within the precincts of her cankering influence. Madokawando, as her husband was called, though the Milicete were not on the best of terms with the tribe among whom he now tarried, had joined with a numerous party of warriors, for the sake, chiefly, of partaking in the expeditions sent from time to time into the enemy's country as they offered manifold opportunities for indulging his love of plunder and again, which was the ruling passion of his selfish nature; as a proof of which, he had promised the daughter of his dead brother to an old crippled chief of the Penobscot, who had been inflamed with a desire of possessing the beautiful girl, and, being wealthy, had offered large bribes to her guardian, which the cupidity of the savage could not withstand; and so the unalterable pledge had been given, that, ere the lapse of many moons, Waswetchcul would be conveyed a helpless victim into the wigwam of her shrivelled admirer. But a powerful, unlooked-for impediment, of which he was not aware had arisen, that bid fair to overturn the sordid scheme of her uncle. Argimou, the first time he beheld the maiden, was struck with her exceeding loveliness, and secretly resolved to devote his energies to the possession of her affections, but he was prompted by as pure and deep a passion as ever sprung within the breast of man. What he would have aided in thwarting for the sake of justice alone, the excusable selfishness of love rendered infinitely more onerous and desirable; and when many a furtive glance had indicated that mutual interest which a stolen interview fully ripened into the glow of reciprocal attachment, Argimou made a deep vow that his Flower should never be sent to wither in the country of the Penobscot, and he only awaited a favourable opportunity to fan the spark of animosity which he well knew only smouldered in the bosoms of the Milicete and his own nation; ever ready to burst the temporary restraint which policy had enjoined: their confederacy with the French alone preventing it from raging with all the malignancy and stern unsparing hostility that characterizes an Indian feud.

The warriors betook themselves to their several cabins, on their arrival, where round the social fire their voices might be heard chatting and laughing about the occurrences of the day. 'Twas with mingled sensations, from each of which, as from many sources, a bright stream of pleasure arose and united in one broad current of happiness, giving an elasticity to the thoughts and bearing, that Argimou put aside the blanket curtain over the door of his wigwam and responded to the affectionate congratulations of his father, a middle aged warrior of a grave, commanding appearance, whose bold, aquiline features were reflected in a softer outline on the noble profile of his son. A slight indisposition had prevented him from witnessing those observances associated with the dearest aspirations of a parent, namely the exaltation of his child, and now he beheld the decorated figure of his proud boy with undisguised triumph and an emotion of tenderness that brought an unaccustomed moisture to his unwavering eye. During the earnest conversation which followed, the father impressed upon his offspring the serious nature of the duties incumbent upon him in his future career, and in conclusion, alluded with mournful pathos to the companion of his youth, the mother of Argimou, who had gone to the Great Spirit when the strong and intrepid warrior before him now, was a little helpless child, with the fond memories of long years busy within his breast, unfolding the half obliterated scroll of the past and its hopes and sorrows venerable with the dust of time, Pansaway enveloped his body, silently in the skin of a deer, and stretching himself upon the pine branches matting the tent, was soon wandering in those mysterious regions which an Indian supposes to be swayed by the prophet— Manitou of dreams.

But it is not to prepare for slumber that Argimou divests himself of his newly acquired and somewhat cumbersome ornaments, nor is it to look at the stars that he peers out into the night. His head is turned in a listening attitude, but no sound escapes from the pyramidal dwellings around, and even the incessant bark of the irritable watch cur has ceased to trouble the drowsy woods with its sharp querulous sound. With noiseless tread he steals from the birchen canopy, threading his way among the trees until he reached a solitary dell, through the midst of which an unseen rivulet prattled in a low whisper, with the flags and entangled shrubbery hiding its devious track. Here Argimou paused, and applying his concaved hand to his mouth, emitted a correct imitation of the distant hoot of an owl, which was repeated after a short interval, when every sense of the utterer was directed to catch some expected signal of reply, ere long the acute ear detected a slight rustle of the leaves such as a rabbit would occasion in his tiny path, and before the vision was conscious of a darker shade in the gloom of the foliage, the quick pulsation of a soft, warm breast, was felt against the ample chest of Argimou, and a voice whose faintest tones thrilled to the listener's soul, breathed in accents of most intoxicating melody beside his burning cheek.

"My sweet flower still keeps its perfume for the son of Pansaway," said he, as the maiden released herself from the close embrace of her lover, yet allowed an arm still to encircle her lithe form, and a hand to smooth and part with trembling caress the long silky hair which shaded a face lovely as was ever worshipped beneath the starlit heaven.

"Love," she replied, with all the tenderness of her sex, and the low, musical enunciation of her people, "Waswetchcul is only too happy if she fills the thoughts of Argimou when he wears the wampum belt of a Sagamou; so very—very joyful is she, that she almost forgets the crooked path in which she must travel. The moons will come and wane, that will sever our hearts for ever, before she awakes from this pleasant dream—speak—young brave!—that this fearful mist may pass away from my eyes like the haze of the morn, and my heart be refreshed by the dew of your kind words, like the spring-rain which maketh the young grass green."

"Fear not, O maiden! whose voice is sweeter than the honey of the forest bee, the arm of Argimou is strong. The flower will blossom beneath the shelter of the wigwam; who is he that cometh like a hungry snake from the sunset to seek for prey? 'ere the poisonous breath of the old Penobscot fool sullies its purity, Argimou will tear it away with a fierce grasp and plant it again where no evil eye will dare to look upon its beauty. Listen Waswetchcul," continued he, while his voice gathered strength with the tenor of his words, "beneath our tribes the chain of friendship is dim, for the Milicete encroached upon our hunting grounds, and when we sent messengers to make them see clear that they might not wander in a wrong path, they drove them back without listening to their words, with laughter and scorn, yea! even the sacred bearer of the pipe and wampum was treated like a dog in their wigwams; so that the proud warriors of the Micmac burn to wash away the wrong in the blood of thy nation, and they know well that when we enter the Milicetejik country it will be in the war paint of an enemy. But the tribes have sworn to preserve ever bright, the belt of alliance which they wove with the Wennooch* when they first came to visit their red brethren, and taught them the use of their big thunder in the chase and in battle. Hear me, Waswetchcul! The tree of peace which we have planted on the highest mountain of our country, spreads its arms over the generous stranger, until we are in our graves its leaves must never wither, and therefore have we buried our vengeance until another time, for a dark cloud is gathering over the setting sun—it draws near!—it covers the whole sky with its black shadow; but the hatchet of the Wennooch is flung into its bosom, and I see it flashing there like the hate of a warrior; 'ere it falls to the ground, the blood of the Anglasheou† will be poured in torrents upon the thirsty ground! Hear me, Waswetchcul! When the sun grows bright again, and the sky is clear over the nations, then will Argimou lead his young men into the Milicetejik country and seek his love by the banks of the Ouangondy‡ that the small roots of her heart may entwine themselves with the fibers of Argimou's breast so that no wind can ever tear them asunder."

With such soothing language did the Sachem strive to banish the apprehensions of his mistress, until the time of parting arrived; when, clasped in each other's arms, and lips united in one long, long kiss, the lovers faultered forth their passionate farewell.

* Frenchman.

† Englishman.

‡ The Indian name of the river St. John.

Chapter III

Acadia—under which name was included all that country now composing the provinces of Nova-Scotia and New-Brunswick, presents a history of varied and exciting interest. From the first landing of the French, in the year 1605, until the date at which our story commences, its progress toward cultivation and agricultural improvement, had been continually retarded by the successive struggles of the French and English governments for its possession, which resulted in the permanent establishment of British rule; but still the peninsula of Nova-Scotia was the only portion of this territory that could be considered within the actual jurisdiction of the crown, for the enemy driven from their original strong hold, retired upon the neck of land which unites the former with the adjoining continent, and having there fortified themselves with considerable strength, continued to harass the infant colony by fitting out hostile expeditions against the several villages in the interior in which they were generally successful, from the insidious manner of their approach, and the small means of protection at the command of the early settlers, separated from each other by intervals of dreary forests and numerous intersections of lake and river.—In these enterprises, the French derived important assistance from their close alliance with the native tribes, and to the facility which the nature of the country presented for the practice of their desultory mode of warfare, may be chiefly attributed the almost invariable result.

The French inhabitants of Acadia, after its conquest, occupied a rather anomalous position, as they steadily refused to take the oath of allegiance to a foreign power, and maintained a sullen neutrality, which was ever ready to merge in acts of secret hostility, perhaps excited and nourished by the narrow policy pursued towards a subjugated people. These peasants, or *Neutrals*, as they were then designated, were a simple, virtuous race, gentle and unassuming in their manners, primitive in habits, and deeply attached to their country and possessions; assimilating themselves in feeling and custom to the powerful nations that held a right—undisputed while the stranger needed their assistance in his utter helplessness, but soon forgotten when the hand which sued for protection turned viper-like with base ingratitude against its benefactors, in the perpetration of unholy fraud—to the wilderness regions in which were reared their peaceful habitations, they secured the affections of the Indians with that singular ease and tact for which the French nation have been always remarkable. Thus cementing the bonds of a friendship that never faultered or ceased its protecting influence, while their wigwams could afford shelter to the persecuted peasantry, or their aid was required in those fierce schemes of retaliation which wasted like a whirlwind the plantations of their mutual oppressors, whose harsh measures converted a people, naturally peaceful and inoffensive, into a material of stern and ruthless aggression, and, perchance, a community of interests and misfortunes tended still more to strengthen that fellowship existing between these two very distinct but equally doomed races. So inveterate were they in the prosecution of their system of depredation, that the town of Halifax, then lately built, was enclosed in a strong fence of palisades for its greater security, and the residents prohibited from straying beyond their protecting limits; as a short time previous, they made a night attack upon the small village of Dartmouth, opposite the former place, and with their allies, carried off or scalped its inhabitants. The French government, still in possession of Cape Breton, with its strong fortress of Louisburg, and the isle of St. John, alluded to in our first chapter, offered every aid and encouragement to the designs of these marauders, by supplying arms and stores, offering at the same time, a high premium for scalps and prisoners. Moreover, to give a bolder impulse to the disaffected peasantry, with a view to the reconquest of the country, M. La Corne was dispatched from Canada with a strong force and munitions of war, to Bay Verte, where he built the fort before mentioned, and shortly afterwards, another was erected on the western side of the isthmus, which was named Beau Sejour, situated at the head of Chicgnecto, or Cumberland Bay, as it is now denominated; and a third at the mouth of the river St. John, on the north side of the Bay of Fundy.

The province of New-Brunswick at this period was a wild unappropriated region, covered with dense forests, only traversed by the wandering Indian, or affording an asylum in its almost impervious solitudes, to a few scattered remnants of the proscribed Acadians.—This territory, though claimed by the British, was virtually in possession of the Canadian government, and the early adventurers sailing up the St. John, had established a strong hold called Fort Jemseg, celebrated afterwards for the heroic defence of Madam La Tour, and the melancholy fate of her brave followers; which, with the additional redoubt at the river's mouth, were the only significant symbols of European prerogative as yet observable upon its soil.—This portion of North America was peopled by several independent tribes of Indians, which, speaking a different dialect, and confined to the limits of their own hunting grounds, held little intercourse with one another, except in forming an occasional alliance for purposes of hostility or mutual protection. The Mareachite, or Milicete, occupied the territory bordering on the St. John, and extending as far westward as the country of the Penobscot, about the river of that name, who appear to have originally sprung from the same stock, as the similarity of their languages would indicate.* These again were bounded by the tribes of the great Abenaqui, who were in force near Trois-Rivieres in Canada; while the Micmacs confined themselves chiefly to the peninsula of Nova-Scotia, although a branch, the Richibucto tribe, extended along the north eastern coast of the Gulf of St. Lawrence as far as the Bay Des Chaleurs, touching the lands of the brave and powerful Mohawk, one of the five confederated nations of the Iroquois, so famous in the early history of the Canadian wars.

Having made these general remarks upon the country in which our tale is laid, for the purpose of rendering it more intelligible to the reader, we will briefly state that the authorities of Massachusetts, then an appendage to the British Empire, urged by the repeated encroachments of the French, determined to expel them from the frontiers of her eastern possessions, for which purpose, an expedition was fitted out in the spring of the year 1755, composed of two regiments of Provincials, raised in New England, with three frigates and a sloop under the command of Captain Rous.—This force after rendezvousing at Annapolis, proceeded up the Bay of Fundy in a fleet of forty one vessels, to attack the enemy's position at Chicgnecto; to the principal point of which, Beau Sejour, we will now revert.

This Fortress, placed on an elevated promontory of the narrow neck that connects Nova Scotia with the main, commanded an extensive view of the country around; and from the ramparts, on a fine summer's day, in truth it was a refreshing thing to let the eye wander over the wide prospect, spread out on either side, like a map of diversified colouring. To the northward would be seen the great prairie of Cumberland waving its broad sheet of grass like the billows of a troubled sea, through which the waters of the Au Lac wound its silver thread, a veritable "*anguis in herba*," until it was lost in the prospective of the plain, which at the distance of six miles, terminated

* See Drake's History of the North American Indians—page 137.

27

its breadth in a ridge of upland, indistinct and blue, above which was faintly visible, the far summit of the Shepody mountain; while to the southward, was beheld a marsh of much less extent, but like its overgrown neighbour, also possessing a permeating stream, which, like a deep trench between two belligerents, at that time divided the territories of the conflicting powers, as at the present moment it affords a line of demarcation between the sister provinces. At the entrance of this river, the Massaquash by name, a blockhouse was erected, with a strong breast-work of timber, whose cannon commanded the passage of the stream, and garrisoned with a strong body of Acadians, and Micmacs. On the high ground beyond the valley, where the village of Amherst now stands, and in a direct line with Beau Sejour, from which it was distant about one mile and a half, might be descried the outline of Fort Lawrence, the most interesting feature in the landscape to the inhabitants of the former place, for, waving over its battlements in proud rivalry, was displayed the "red cross flag" of England—this fortress being purposely intended as a check upon the movements of her active adversary. To the westward the view terminated in the Bay of Chicgnecto, which, when the tide was low, presented an unvaried flat of mud with low meadows on its southwest extremity. But the connoisseur, perchance, turns away in disgust from its sombre lifeless expanse, to revel in the verdure of the plains, or the luxuriant foliage of the adjacent trees, until enchanted with the vivid contrast, he glances mockingly back at the waterless bay, when—"Presto change!" does he dream? or is it but a cheat of the disordered vision? scarce a minute has elapsed, and now a wide sea of dark, tumultuous waves is tumbling and rushing in towards him with the swiftness of a race horse, as though it would overwhelm every thing in its progress; roaring upward through the mouths of the river, like a solid wall, and swelling their floods to the height of 60 feet above the level of the ocean; phenomenon which has but one or two parallels in the known world. Thus some years since on paying a visit to this remarkable spot, while musing upon the stirring scenes once enacted beneath the grassy ramparts, fast crumbling away by the touch of remorseless time, we witnessed with unfeigned astonishment, the transition above described.

From the palisades of the fort, the glacis sloped gradually until it reached the water side, and clustered about its skirts without any attempt at regularity, were visible a number of log cabins, interspersed with the simple, but picturesque wigwams of the natives, made of the white bark of the birch tree. This straggling hamlet stretched its dimensions far back to the confines of the great marsh, in one place dotting the green lawn with habitations, then again only indicated by the wreaths of thin grey smoke that ascended slowly from different points among the willow groves, and blended peacefully with the calm, blue air. Beneath the shade of an aged tree, a knot of Micmacs were playing the game of the bone, with vehement action and vociferous exclamation; while others with lazy attitude, more in keeping with the quiet repose that seemed to consecrate the hour, were stretched upon the soft turf, puffing light clouds from the beloved tomagan, and seemingly occupied with their individual reflections, or listening perchance, to the clear laughter of the French maidens mingled with the mellow lowings of the herds, borne betimes, from the meadows, on the bosom of some drowsy breeze. Yet over this rural scene was fated to pass, like the scorching simoon of the desert, the lightning breath of strife. 'Ere the lapse of many days, the groan of anguish, the grasp of the dying will resound through the startled groves in unaccustomed murmurs, blended with the sharp whistle of the ball, and the crash of the deadly shell. Even so are the lights and shadows ever chastening each other over the current of our lives; to-day we rest beneath the shelter of some wide spreading tree and dream of happiness and peace, the storm of the morrow comes—the tree is blighted—the illusion is gone; and alas! the dew and sunshine can never fully obliterate the traces of the tempest, or make the heart put forth green leaves, as in "that first and only time." But the spirit that never tires nor slumbers, shrouds the record of man's ravages from the eye of offended heaven, with visions of regenerated beauty, and "smiling amid the ruin he had made," woos him to spare!

Why doth yonder sentry stand, as if in deep abstraction, upon the bastion's top? are the stern duties of his calling forgotten in a revery of his native land, and the endearing memories ever associated with the absorbing spell of home? And yet methinks, his posture savours more of earnest watchfulness than listless contemplation: his suspicious eye is intently scrutinizing an object on the verge of the horizon, a mere speck upon the division line of sea and sky—'tis the loom of a gull, or the fragment of a cloud resting on the waters. But behold! that sunbeam has tinged it with a snowy gleam, too brilliant for a cloud, and too steadfast for a bird's wing.

"Ha!" exclaimed the soldier with sudden emphasis, "I am right after all. See there are two, three, yet another, by the blessed virgin, 'tis the enemy at last!"

And now arose within the fort, the hum and bustle of preparation, the confusion of many voices, and curious faces gazed with disquietude at the fleet gathering like a flock of ill-omened birds in the south-west. An alarm gun thundered from the ramparts its grave warning, which was quickly repeated from the post on the river. The warriors under the old tree sprang from the ground with a joyous cry and elastic bound, to gird themselves for battle; but the peasant girls turn pale at the inauspicious sound, and hurry homeward with trembling limbs, to sorrow and to weep.

Before night-fall, the scouts sent out to watch the movements of the enemy, returned with the intelligence that their whole force was landed above five miles from Fort Lawrence, and had bivouacked; for the day had been spent in the disembarkment of stores and baggage, and no demonstration of immediate approach was observable, so that the repose of the garrison, would be most probably undisturbed for one night longer, 'ere they awoke to the stirring business of a beleaguered fortress.

When the sun went down, a large fire was kindled upon the bank of the Massiquash; for the Indians were about to celebrate the custom, which from time immemorial, they have always observed on the eve of a great conflict. By the flickering light, was gathered a motley crew of agile savages in warlike array, and faces rendered terrible by the expression of ferocity which the war paint alone can create.—Their bared limbs and bodies, unclothed to the waist, developed their muscular proportions in the glory of strength and manhood, while the bronzed skin shone with a clear polish as they moved within the glow of the flame. At length it burnt upward with a steady blaze, shedding a wild and ruddy gleam, that gave an unearthly character to the objects around, and revealing a scene where human passion revelled in very drunkenness of unrestraint, wholly devoid of that check which usually prevents all manifestation of natural feeling in the mien of the savage. At first, with linked hands and grave gestures, the warriors moved round the hissing pile in solemn measure to the cadence of a low melancholy chant, uniting, at intervals, in the sudden ejaculation which burst in full chorus from each throat, and then as quickly relapsing in the clear tones of a single voice, protracting the song. Now they sever and recede with quickened movements, or advance toward the centre, beating incessantly their buskined feet upon the hard ground; then, as the accelerated blood bounds and swells in their arteries, with the excitement of the war-dance, the dread whoop rings over the valley, curdling the life-blood of the listener's heart. Faster and faster, with giddy speed, they whirl around the pyre, until the stars seem to join in the frantic reel, and then fell dizzy and exhausted, into inexplicable confusion. Then by virtue of his rank, a lofty warrior steps forth into the area, with features hidden beneath a mask of colours, traced in bands of fiery red around the piercing eyes, and shading the lower part

31

of his face in a streak of the densest black, but the beauty of his form, and the proud majesty of his mien sufficiently denoted the presence of the Micmac Sachem. Three times he encompassed the pile with a bright tomahawk flashing in his waving hand; then with empassioned utterance he harangued an imaginary foe, in the metaphorical spirit of his race, ever seeking to embody their ideas, for the purpose of illustration, in the likeness of familiar objects; and seizing a burning brand, dashed his axe against it with action suited to the vehemence of his words—scattering the sparks like red rain on every side, and cleaving it with repeated blows, until nought remained but a few splintered fragments, which were regarded with a triumphant look, as if a real combatant had fallen by his prowess in the field of battle. Another chief then took the place of Argimou, and enacted with still greater energy the pantomimic combat, who was in turn succeeded by a third, and so on, till the chiefs of the different tribes had each borne a part in the violent exhibition. At last the gigantic leader of the Milicete party burst into the ring with a cap upon his head crowned with the branching horns of a deer, and a shaggy bear skin depending from his broad shoulders. You might have deemed him one of the satyrs of old, engaged in the performance of his unhallowed orgies, so uncouth and barbarous was his appearance. He leaped with superhuman strength and distorted action from side to side, sometimes even into the scorching embers. He shrieked as with intolerable agony, every sinew stretched to its utmost tension, as though the slightest touch would snap them asunder like an overstrained cord, and the starting eyeballs seemed consuming with the fire of madness that blazed within. Fiendish yells poured forth "fast and furious" from the retracted jaws, until wrought into ungovernable rage by the sight, the whole band rushed with shouts and brandished weapons into the flames; every vesture of which was soon obliterated by the redoubled strokes and trampling of a phrenzied multitude, inflicting, in the *melee*, severe wounds upon each other with their keen knives, for the darkness gathered thick over the smouldering ashes of the extinguished fire. But the voice of Argimou was heard above the din, commanding them to desist, else the anger of the Great Spirit would be kindled against his people.—"See!" said he, as he pointed upward with outstretched arm, "behold, brethren!—The shades of our fathers look down from the land of dreams—they have sent a token that the red man must prepare for the battle which comes!" and a feeling of awe passed over those fearless but superstitious warriors; for amongst the stars that thronged the western sky, the new moon was suspended in the semblance of a bended bow.

At the dawn of the fourth of May, 1755, the British provincials, whose strength was increased by a detachment of regular troops and a small train of field artillery, commenced their march across the country to attack the French position, under the command of Lt. Colonel Monckton; while the naval force under Captain Rous, sailed up the bay to render assistance by sea. Upon reaching the Massiquash river their progress was impeded by the breastwork and blockhouse, now swarming with defenders, who received them with a galling fire from loophole and embrasure, while the cannon swept the surface of the river, rendering any attempt to cross extremely hazardous and uncertain.—However, the repeated assaults of the enemy and their superior numbers soon began to make an impression upon the wooden defences, and the well directed fire of the artillery created great havoc among the crowded peasantry—annoying them exceedingly by striking large splinters from the surrounding parapet. Volley after volley sent its leaden shower, and before the smoke cleared away the British with a loud cheer rushed forward. One moment the Acadians with their Indian allies stood firm—the next beheld them in full retreat from the out-works, which were instantly in possession of their foes; and then the garrison of the block-house, struck with panic at the rout of their friends, abandoned it and fled, leaving the passage of the river unde-fended. But Argimou and a body of his bravest warriors scorn to turn their backs upon their enemy, and are resolved to yield their station only with their lives.

A crash is heard at the entrance—the red-jackets are bursting the door with the butts of their muskets—it falls inward, and the foremost assailants drop dead before the scathing fire, poured from within, while at the same time, a whoop of defiance arrests, like a knell, the rush of fresh combatants to the opening. But the stern command of their leader, to "charge with the bayonet," is instantly succeeded by an impetuous onset, and though many a bright knife and tomahawk was reddened with warm blood, and a heap of victims marked the unflinching bravery with which they fought; still overpowering numbers, and the fearful diminution of the heroic band, told plainly that they must perish at last. It was a gallant sight to see a mere handful of warriors keeping the whole force of the enemy at bay; and among these, conspicuous from his stature, and the wampum band with its simple plume adorning his brow, nor less by the lightning thrust of his long blade, Argimou stood encircled by his followers.—His voice was distinguishable amidst the clashing of steel, the execrations of the soldiery, and the cries of the wounded, exhorting his brethren to repel the ceaseless onset of the foe, and shouting aloud as another warrior fell by his side, the rallying words—"be strong! be strong!" Yet resistance was in vain; one by one the Micmacs are pierced with the bayonet, and the interior of the blockhouse is filled with eager enemies pressing each other forward in the crowded space. Argimou alone remains, like a grim tiger, with a wall of corses around him, and bleeding from numerous wounds. A row of glittering bayonets is presented at his breast—another instant and they would have clashed in his heart, but a young officer threw himself in front, and beating down the muskets of the soldiers with his sword, forbade them, on their lives, to harm the Indian, "comrades!" he exclaimed, "let us take him alive, he is far too brave to die!" and before Argimou had ceased to struggle, he was a disarmed prisoner at the mercy of his enemies.

Chapter IV

After having made the necessary preparations, Colonel Monckton advanced towards Beau Sejour, which he proceeded to invest without delay. In the night, the troops worked hard at an entrenchment, commenced close under the guns of the fort; the remains of which may still be seen on its north-eastern side. This was effected, though the French kept up a continual fire from the ramparts, and the besiegers were not enabled to bring a single cannon to the assault. But important assistance was rendered by a heavy bombardment of the enemy's position, from Fort Lawrence; and to those engaged in the business of that night, it indeed was a stirring sight. The glacis of the fort was lit up with an incessant flash of musquetry and the broader glare of artillery, whose roar reverberated over the wide marshes and among the distant hills. Then again a ghastly blue light would throw its spectral illumination over the whole scene, disclosing for a time the operations of the sappers, and then leaving the stupefied vision unable to penetrate the thick mantle of darkness that succeeded. At intervals, a shell could be observed, its lighted fuse traversing the air in elliptical curve, until it fell, with admirable precision and a hissing sound, into the French redoubt; scattering death and devastation around. Sometimes one of these missiles would explode before it reached its destination, wasting its deadly contents upon the sky; in which it seemed as if a meteor had burst, throwing its red fragments among the stars, whose lesser ray was suddenly obscured by the power of the lurid gleam.—The deserted habitations of the Acadians were soon enveloped in flames, and a cry of anguish rose within the fort as the peasantry witnessed the destruction of their beloved homes. But in the meantime their Indian allies were not idle, for in large bodies they hovered continually around the skirts of the foe, like troops of famished wolves; and many a loud shout of triumph, and reeking scalps attested the fearful work of retaliation carried on; though the victims were few, comparatively speaking, yet the terror they inspired was very great, for there seemed to be no certain security from their revenge, they struck so secretly, suddenly and home, for four days the besieged withstood the efforts of the English, when, reduced to a state of misery and ruin by the harassing bombardment, they offered terms of capitulation, which were acceded to; upon which the British troops marched into the fortress, and the French laid down their arms. It will be unnecessary to dwell upon this part of the story, suffice it that twenty pieces of cannon, with quantities of ammunition, were found in the place, which rendered its easy reduction the more extraordinary, for the besiegers had not planted any guns under their batteries; but the dilapidated state of the buildings proved the extremity to which the garrison had been brought previous to their surrender.

The victors slept soundly that night within the captured fort, except those whose wounds denied them the blessings of repose. When the first streak of grey light appeared in the east, and the lingering ray of one pale star alone remained to herald the approach of day, a figure, wrapped in a watch-cloak, stood upon the rampart, seemingly the only being abroad at that early hour. His face was turned in the direction of the distant fort, which was enveloped in the veil of white mist, rolling in heavy volumes from the marshy grounds below. Presently the dim clouds were tinged with a slight bordering of rosy light; it warmed, it brightened, when, bursting from his rest like a fierce warrior, the blood-red disk of the sun rose from the hills and penetrated the dense fog which, the ratified by its beams, was slowly wafted up the valley before the fresh breeze from the bay, leaving the landscape in all its summer beauty, open to the enraptured view. A smile passed over the handsome features of the soldier, as he descried the object of his search embosomed in the foliage of the opposite hill, and his lip murmured with half-suppressed utterance, that appeared to be addressed to the heart of the speaker, as if engaged in earnest self-commune. That the reader may conjecture the origin and nature of the reflections, we have ascertained the following.

Edward Molesworth was a young Englishman of good family and prospects, who had entered the army when only a boy, and after serving for some years in various parts of the United Kingdom, received with enthusiastic joy the intelligence that the regiment to which he belonged was ordered to the American provinces; for he had a strong desire, common to the adventurous spirit of his age and nation, to visit foreign lands, and realize some of those romantic dreams which, excited by the eager perusal of travel and wild tales of the New World, had become indelibly impressed upon his youthful imagination. And, verily, he had scarcely landed upon its shores before there was every reason to justify the assumption that one passage of romance in the history of his life was about to be fulfilled; for ere he was a fortnight at Annapolis Royal he had become as devout a votary as ever worshipped at the shrine of passionate love. And, O Clarence! wert thou not well worthy the homage of one true heart? when all who ever looked upon thy angel face felt themselves humbled before the divine purity, breathing like a sweet perfume from its every feature, and blessed the God who created that being in his image to teach them charity and kindness to every living creature. And thus is beauty not unworthy of that admiration which the heart of man involuntarily lavishes upon its possessor. If the eloquence of a flower lifts the mind to the contemplation of Him who is an incarnation of all good—if the glorious rainbow is a pledge of hope to the benighted world, why should the lovely face of woman be less expressive than the lovely flower, or less hopeful than the evanescent bow? Like the one, it speaks of a clime where bright and fadeless forms are gliding in an atmosphere of love and happiness, so ineffable, that the fading imagination offers, as the only fitting emblem of such beatitude, the most beautiful of created things. Like the other, it says to the sceptic, that harmony which streams like sweet music from every line, that eye which beams responsive to the soul's emotion—which melts and burns—can never be the offspring of undirected chance; nor doth the spirit whose outpouring is thus made manifest, sleep in that beauty's grave!

Among the officers attached to the garrison of the place, was a Captain Forbes, who had been quartered there for some time with an only daughter—the sole living relic of a partner, long since removed from this transitory scene. Edward, attracted by the uncommon loveliness of Clarence Forbes, and thrown in continual contact with her father, soon became an intimate in the family; and the old veteran beheld with feelings of unmixed pleasure the mutual attachment that appeared daily to root itself with deeper power in the hearts of both. Admiring as he did the frank, generous character of the young soldier, he hailed with parental gratification, the prospect of obtaining so desirable a protector for his darling child; for with the engrossing partiality of advancing age, heightened by the resemblance which she bore to the object of his first affection, and the surpassing measure of her own goodness and grace, did the old man love that daughter. The time glided imperceptibly with golden wings, and Edward was ever at the side of Clarence, drinking intoxicating draughts of delight from her deep blue eyes, and listening to the soft melody of her silvery voice, until a new world of thought and sensation had started into existence at the touch of the great magician's wand. Little did he imagine, before he himself experienced its truth, the awakening power, the elevating tendency of that mightiest of human sentiments, stirring up the latent qualities of the soul, which expands beneath its ray as the buried seed by the warmth of the new-born spring bursts forth in foliage of bright and stainless dye. As the glow of passion spread itself over every portion of his being, making the heart throb with a sense of tumultuous joy, strange and indefinable, his spirit caught a higher aspiration for the noble, and the exalted. Turning from that loved face, radiant with affection's light, his mind instinctively dwelt, by association, upon whatever was most excellent in the natural and moral world. And so from the love of woman springs a desire for the beautiful and the good.

An avowal of feeling on the part of Edward met with no impediment to his happiness, and the moment which would unite forever the destinies of two fond hearts was drawing nigh, when the harsh trumpet-call to arms first woke them from their tranquil dream, and brought them suddenly back to the stern demands and realities of life. A blow was about to be struck, and lovers saw with regret, that a delay would inevitably occur in the completion of their hopes: for both Edward and the father of Clarence were among the number destined to accompany the expedition then about to prepare for active service on the frontier. Captain Forbes would have wished his child to remain behind while he was engaged in the precarious struggle which would inevitably follow, but no persuasion or apprehension of the peril and privation inseparable from the nature of the undertaking, were sufficiently strong to overcome the force of filial solicitude; and—for who can unravel, even in his own breast, the intricate threads that form the web of every fixed purpose—perhaps the desire of being still near the idol of her young heart, was an additional inducement for Clarence to insist upon accompanying her father.

Upon the arrival of the troops at Chignecto, she was placed within the protecting walls of Fort Lawrence, as a secure asylum during the progress of those hostilities which had terminated so successfully for the honor of the British arms. But poor Clarence was fated to undergo all the terror and disquietude which the danger of those most dear awakens so wildly in the bosom of her sex, which, however, received a terrible increase as soon as she learned that her father had received a wound while employed in the trenches; which, though not attended with fatal consequences, still occasioned great pain and debility, while the advanced years of the sufferer precluded any hope being entertained of other than a protracted recovery. It was then that the old man missed the unwearied attentions, the compassionate tenderness of his child, and upon the capitulation of Beau Sejour it was arranged that Edward should conduct the maiden to her father, with a sufficiently strong escort, enjoined rather from motives of prudence than necessity, as soon as the principal force of the English, which were about marching to attack the sole remaining post of the enemy upon the Gaspereaux, had taken their departure from the fort. Therefore is it, that the lover leaves his restless couch to welcome the approach of dawn, counting the sluggish hours that intervene ere he can behold the features of his betrothed once more, and vowing in his heart that nothing shall cause a further procrastination of an indissoluble union with one so necessary to his very existence. "O Clarence!" said he fervently, "wert thou mine forever, unalterably linked by the force of human bonds, as thou art already entwined with every feeling of my soul, perchance this vague disquietude, this fearful shadow of some unknown evil, would not haunt me with such melancholy fancies. Away, absurd delusion! is the hope that never faltered in the hour of battle to sicken with despondency when there is nought but happiness before me, unclouded as the prospect of glorious beauty upon which I gaze. Let me banish all thought save delightful anticipation of meeting the beloved object of so much solicitude again. Is not the brightest jewel that can reward the ambition of man, the possession of a pure and confiding heart? That boon is mine; and it may be that the priceless value of the treasure is the cause of these groundless apprehensions for its safety, which force themselves so unaccountably upon my mind." Here the foreboding reflections of the lover were interrupted by the quick rattle of a drum, rolling aloud the reville amid the deep silence of the morn, which speedily aroused the garrison from its slumbers, and caused the soldier to retreat from his lofty station towards his quarters beneath, as the sound of various voices began to issue from the shattered tenements of the fort.

In one of the upper rooms of the dismantled barracks, the windows of which being knocked into one, afforded rather more air than has at all agreeable to the feeling of the inmates, who, to remedy the work of their friends, had made shift to supply the deficiency by placing a few rough boards across the breach in the front wall, several half-dressed soldiers were busily engaged cleaning their arms and accoutrements, while the rude jest and hearty laugh kept equal pace with their not overburdensome labours.

"Tim," said a robust Emeralder with red hair and face to match,— the natural ugliness of the latter, enhanced by a broad patch over the left cheek, who was furbishing a bayonet with the rapid friction of a soft leather rag—"Tim, a bouchal, win d'ye march for the Bay o',— what's this they call it? Those d——d French lingoes stick 'til yer mouth like a pratie skin, an' not half as swate."

This was addressed to an individual who presented an appearance the very reverse of the former. His face was pale and emaciated, the ghastliness of which, was rendered more apparent from the black curling hair by which it was surmounted, terminating in a queue of regimental proportions behind. The two might have afforded a good example of the effects of dissipation upon different temperaments. The one lusty, warm, and sanguine, unnatural stimulation appearing only to create more energy in the man; the other shrunken, cold, and colourless, his hand tremulous the while, with the influence of nervous reaction upon the debilitated system, and looking as though you could not find one drop of blood in his placid, lifeless veins.

"The Bay of Verte, perhaps you mean, Dennis?" was the reply to the foregoing question, "we have orders to start in an hour's time, and the Colonel, you know, is not the man to lag when there's work to be done."

Appearing satisfied with this information, the Irishman approached the other, and, in a hoarse whisper, said—"Comrid, have yis a dhrap left in the canteen? the air is raw an' pearcin the morning, and the stomach widin me is a grownin wid the could I tuck in the trenches."

"Not a lap, not a squeeze!" exclaimed the first, petulantly, "you sucked it like a leech the last time I gave you the can, and didn't leave what would wet the lips of a baby, leave alone enough to give one an appetite for his breakfast before a long march."

Here the speaker cast an indignant look at the applicant, which, with the reproof was equally disregarded, as he shouted—

"St. Patrick presarve us! I must have a dhrink, or maybe I'll drive mad wid the impression and the hunger that's a tearing inside o' me, och! och!" And here he forced a fit of coughing, to excite the compassion of his auditors. "Och! och! see that now, it's fairly fetchin the breath out o' me, it is."

"Dennis," asked one, "who gave you the mark under the left eye, my boy, was it the enemy?"

"No, Jack, wan o' thim black ducks we skivered in the blockhouse beyont. By the crass—though I say it that shouldn't, Dennis Sherron was a haporth too much for the likes of he, anny way, and so I tould the devil, as I shoved my fark intil his mate basket."

"But the cut, Dennis?" resumed the questioner, "what'll Biddy say when we go back with such a slash upon your handsome mug?"

"By St. George! you're right there," struck in Tim, "depend upon it man, she'll give him a far unkinder cut than the knife of an Ingen, and more severer and indelible."

A burst of merriment succeeded to this sally, but Dennis looked around disdainfully without vouchsafing any direct reply, quietly remarking, in allusion to the original subject of his discourse, namely—the movement of the troops.

"Twelve miles, is it, through the woods?—And an aisy an a pleasant walk yees'll all have, wid the mosquitoes, an the shkamin salvages a stringin an scalpin of yees."

"Be me shoul! its sorry I am that I cant kape yer company barring the hate and the drought. Why, Tim!" and here he put his hand on the curly pate of the person addressed, "I say, Tim! The imps ud make a fortin with that poll o' yourn, its the very moral of a Frenchman's wig, so it is."

"Hands off!" exclaimed the other, no way relishing the joke, and letting the butt of his firelock fall heavily upon the toe of his tormentor—"Take your paws off, you blackguard! and thank the Lord that your own is safe, for I'll wager, there's not a thievish finger among the Aborigines, would meddle with thy carotty top, for fear of being singed."

"Bravo!" "Fire away, Tim!" "Can you answer that, Dennis?" shouted several voices, while the old barrack room roared with laughter. But the ire of the Irishman was roused by the retort and its painful accompaniment, which sent him hopping about the floor, and deepened the hue of his cheeks, as he replied quickly and with emphasis:—

"Then be the piper that played afore Moses, and the holy saints to the fore! It's yourself ud be sorriful for that same, you spalpeen; an faith, wor yer hair the shade o' mine, what wid the dhrink ye tuck an the imptiness that's within, ye'd blaze up like a sky rocket, and lave hus, may be, yer two outlandish legs for a parable of muzzy Tim Patterson."

How far the rising cholor of the parties would have proceeded it is impossible to say, for at that moment the first bugle sounded, and an orderly enquired at the door, if Mr. Molesworth's servant was within, as he had been asking for him below. Upon which, the dispute terminated, as Dennis, acting in that capacity, hurried away to obey the summons of his master.

Chapter V

At the appointed time, the troops, with the exception of that portion which was intended as a permanent garrison, were drawn up on the parade in the centre of the fort. In front on their respective chargers, sat Colonel Monckton, the chief in command, and the Honourable Colonel Winslow, who was in charge of the New England corps, surrounded by a number of officers in the uniform of their several regiments, and further distinguished by the different degrees of that high, martial demeanour, only to be acquired by long and active participation in the practices of war; of which they were possessed. But, if, to the eye, the dashing equipments and soldier-like air of those holding commissions in the king's service presented a more showy and chivalrous exterior, the simple and unpretending appointments and bearing of the Provincial officers were equally indicative of physical capability and stern determination to brave and endure whatever duty required or hardship imposed, in the prosecution of the present undertaking. While the group conversed gaily and without reserve, the roll was being called and the men told off. When the preliminary arrangements were concluded, the commander looked at his watch.

"Gentlemen," said he, "we must be moving now, the sun is getting up already, and there is a lengthy road before us. Remember the orders—there are to be no stragglers from the column, and keep a sharp eye about you: an Indian ambushment would be no child's play in these woods. To your places—one more blow for his Majesty and merry England, and the campaign is finished!"

Colonel Monckton bent low in courtesy to his colleague as they separated, while the rest took their respective stations in the ranks. The word was given, the troops wheeled into column, and to the inspiring sound of martial music, the gallant array moved out of the fortress, in compact order and animated spirits. In a few minutes the bayonets of the front files and a white plume were seen to glance for a moment ere they were hidden among the dark foliage that formed a rich belt beyond the glacis; the main body slowly followed, and finally the rearward files also disappeared behind the trees, while the roll of the drums grew fainter, and at last ceased altogether to woo the listener's ear, as the warlike column penetrated deeper into the bosom of the interminable forest.

Some time after the departure of the British force from the defences of Beau Sejour, or Fort Cumberland, as it was henceforth to be designated—having experienced a change of both name and masters at the same time—a party much more scanty in numbers and display, pursued the same route for a short space, when turning aside into a by-road which ran at right angles with the former, they descended gradually into the valley of the Massiquash, and struck across the open marsh in the direction of some earthen mounds, the salient angles of which were visible upon the eminence beyond. These consisted of Edward Molesworth, mounted on horseback, while his servant Dennis, though fully accoutred, led another steed by the bridle, whose caparison sufficiently showed that it was intended for a lady's use; and a guard of twenty men in the scarlet uniform of the king's troops. As the young officer conducted his small force over the river by means of a rude bridge that had been hastily thrown across to facilitate the transportation of guns and munitions, and also for the purpose of establishing a communication between the two forts, his thoughts were naturally engrossed with the object of the present excursion, and his heart bounded joyfully at the prospect of meeting his beloved. The beauty of the day, and the cheerful scene around, added to the healthful tone of his mind, no longer a prey to the anxiety which so strongly pervaded it in the morning, while every sense was conscious of an invigorating influence. The eye turned from the fair blue vault of heaven, to become dazzled with the sun-light that glittered over the warm meadows, the grass of which rustled and waved in the soft breeze from the sea that sparkled like a zone of moving diamonds beyond the fields. The ear drank the mingled music of a thousand living voices, keeping jubilee in the sunbeam, appearing to gladden the face of old mother Nature, as she smiled to see her children so happy, and decked herself in the choicest garlands to do the summer honor. The grasshopper chirped a merry treble from the ground, while the boblincoln, swinging on the top of some long reed, bore the burthen betimes of his clear flute-like song; and anon the robber bee would rush like a ball athwart the track, blowing blithely on his wild buglehorn, as he carried his spoils homewards; and the balmy odours of innumerable flowers and sweet shrubs, almost intoxicated with their fragrance. The tall grass reached the girths of the horses, and half hid the bodies of the soldiers, who kept close together, and cast suspicious glances on either side, as if expecting to detect an Indian foe lurking beneath its ample cover; though, to all appearance, every trace of their subtile enemy had departed from the neighbourhood. But bitter experience of the fallacy of trusting to what under other circumstances would be deemed a position of most perfect security, made them cautious and doubtful, even in a spot where peace seemed to have set its seal. That their fears were not without sufficient reason will be apparent, when it is related that the party had scarcely reached the rising ground at the termination of the valley, when the painted serpent-like head of a crawling savage was protruded into the trampled trail they had left behind. He took a long scrutinizing look at the retiring soldiers, and a malignant gleam shot from his eyes, while his parted lips showed the white teeth in a triumphant grin, as he adjusted the wisp of grass which was secured to the back of his head by means of a withe passed round the swarthy brow. At the same time the meadow in the vicinity appeared to move, as if a number of converging breezes were playing over its surface. Meanwhile the unconscious party arrived at Fort Lawrence, within the palisades of which they were speedily admitted and their commander ushered into an apartment, the arrangement of which indicated the presiding influence of female taste, speaking eloquently to the exalted fancy of the lover. A door at the further end suddenly opened, and the next moment the sweet, child-like Clarence was weeping on his shoulder, while she muttered in broken accents, "Dear Edward—my father!"

Kissing the tears that bedewed her soft cheek, the youth sought to relieve the anxiety of his beloved, by those endearing expressions which affection knows so well how to employ, allaying her overwrought fears for the safety of her parent. As the arrangements of Clarence had been previously completed, she hastened her departure with that promptness which an eager desire to visit the bedside of her father and a sense of duty seemed to demand on the part of his gentle daughter.

Bidding farewell to her friendly protectors, who regretted her departure, she left the fort under the guidance of Edward and the armed escort. With the consciousness that her best loved was at her side, the feeling of the maiden warmed with the elasticity of youth, and the loveliness of the scene and the hour, as they wended down the descent among the trees that whispered with their countless leaves overhead and around them; while the shrill drums of the cicada,

"Those people of the pine,"

47

filled the groves with incessant music, that seemed to follow the travellers until they emerged upon the plain. When the wild luxuriant landscape first presented itself to the gaze of Clarence, she exclaimed with enthusiasm:

"Look, Edward, how very, *very* beautiful!"

Her companion turned, not in the implied direction, but towards the animated glowing countenance at his side, and smiled as he replied—

"Yes, dearest, but methinks, the face of earth has received an additional lustre, since I traversed this same path, but a short hour since. There is a brighter tint to the yellow sunbeam, and the green leaves; the very heaven seems purer than heretofore. Whence comes this spell, this surprising witchcraft? perhaps mine own love can explain the mystery?"

And the lover sought to read an answer in the half veiled eyes of Clarence, whose blushes gave sufficient evidence that she felt the compliment conveyed in his words.

Ah, Edward, did your betrothed ever appear so beautiful in your sight, as at that moment? The soft bloom under her cheek, heightened by a flutter of pleasurable excitement; the light brown curls playing in the warm breeze, and tinged with gold in the sunshine; the clear expressive blue eye, now turned in the fulness of confiding love upon thine, then seeking the shelter of the dark fringed lid, with a diffidence irresistibly sweet. Look at that slight, graceful figure just rounding into womanhood, and think of the dove-like heart whose every throb is quickened by a feeling of tenderness for thee. Ah, what happiness is still vouchsafed to those within the enchanted circle of "Love's young dream." 'Tis sad, to think that the charm can ever break, and that, as the weary years roll on, and the heart grows old in the pursuits of shadows, we should turn not to the false hope which we trusted, but to the memory—perchance, disregarded; wondering to see how bright and pure one solitary vision shines amid the painful and less blameless records of a later period. 'Tis very sad to find that retrospection cannot afford, after our vain search for happiness aught that might ally itself with that blessing,—save the memento of a broken dream. As earthly objects grow dim to the mental eye, and a truer hope points upward to the calm heaven, the old man finds, as the light breaks amid the darkness, that the love of his youth and age are, in their effect, the same. Also! that in this world of ours, the fairest joys are the most fleeting: even as the beauty which, while we behold its glory, and acknowledge its power, is passing unconsciously away.

But to return. We left our lovers wending their slow course over the valley, and communing with each other in the confidence of mutual affection, nor thought they, that each moment they were approaching the brink of unknown danger—it might be destruction.

After indulging in one of those visions of felicity, which we are so apt to cherish, when like the soldier, our hearts are young and our hope undimmed, and which he painted in all those glowing tints with which love delights to clothe its creations; in conclusion, Edward said to his companion, just as the hoofs of their horses trod simultaneously upon the echoing planks of the bridge—

"Then, my own, will we make our happy home in the abode of my ancestors, and I will show you all my old haunts; the river where I used to fish—far clearer and more undisturbed than this beneath us; the woodland walk, the quiet dell, so dear to my childhood, but never, no, never half so much appreciated as when with sweet Clarence, I shall revisit those scenes, which I have often thought the most beautiful in all England."

The whole party were now upon the narrow bridge which trembled with the heavy tread of the soldiery, when, suddenly, as if from the bowels of the earth, a terrific yell burst forth, and while it was yet lingering in the ears of the astonished listeners, a number of armed savages sprang from the grass that had concealed them, and rushed in a body to intercept their progress, and 'ere they could think of retreating, or, in fact, before their faculties had recovered from the shock of surprise, another band of enemies on the opposite side of the river had cut off the passage in the rear. Edward, as soon as his first alarm had given place to the instinct of preservation, gave one look behind, and seeing that their only hope of safety lay in the success of a bold effort to force their way to the bank in front, he shouted aloud in the energy of desperation—

"Forward, men—for your lives!" And, grasping the reins of the half-fainting Clarence, he dashed into the midst of the ferocious throng just as the Indians poured their irregular fire among the crowded soldiery, who were confined upon the scanty bridge, with deadly effect; for the swift plunge of several bodies into the dark water was heard to follow, which was hailed by a whoop of exultation from the remorseless foe. For a time nought could be distinguished amidst the smoke and confusion save the glancing bayonets and the gleam of uplifted knives and tomahawks around the spot where Edward disappeared. But he was soon seen cleaving his way out of the dusky circle, with the rapid sweep of his long blade, striking his opponents right and left, and warding off the blows aimed at his helpless charge. Yet his life must have been sacrificed had it not been for Dennis, who followed close behind his master and beat back his numerous adversaries with his bayonet's point, making deadly work upon the exposed bodies of the Indians, and accompanying each thrust with an Irish howl, which made an equal impression on their breasts. It was a fearful scene. The woodwork of the bridge became slippery with blood, which occasioned the death of some, whom the ball and hatchet had as yet spared; for in the frenzied rush of the soldiers to the front, many were precipitated into the flood below, who added to the screams and yells of their foes the sharper cry of horror and despair, as they sank grasping beneath its turbid surface, or were carried away by the rapid current before the eyes of their comrades, who were incapable of rendering them any assistance, and so they perished.

"Push on—push on!" shouted Edward, disengaging himself from the throng of natives, and followed by the remnant of his small party, who fought, back to back, against the numbers hemming them in on every side. But before the horses' heads could be turned from the conflict to effect a rapid retreat, a gigantic warrior was seen making swift bounds towards them. When within a few paces the Indian flung his hatchet with a fierce whoop, which, cutting the air with great force and a whirring sound buried itself in the chest of Edward's charger. Making a tremendous spring forward, that tore his hand from its grasp of Clarence's bridle, the wounded animal bounded with frantic speed over the plain, and after several plunges at random, fell heavily to the earth with his rider; but not until Edward had seen, with a pang of agony, the horse of his betrothed led away among a crowd of savages, and he heard a shriek which made his very heart cease to beat. Then all sense failed him, as he was dashed to the ground by the fall of his expiring steed. His fate would have been quickly sealed, had not the faithful Dennis bestrode his lifeless body, and clubbing his firelock, kept the enemy at bay. But succour was at hand. A gun from fort Cumberland roared over the valley, and the harassed soldiers beheld a detachment advancing up the marsh at double time to their assistance. Cheered by the sight, with a shout of defiance, they rushed again upon their foes, when, as if by magic, the latter suddenly disappeared beneath the thick grass, and they were left apparently alone with the unequivocal traces of the conflict, which were presented by the tramplet and corse-strewed meadow around.

Chapter VI

When Edward awakened to consciousness, his eyes gradually recognized the walls of his own barrack room, upon the bed of which he was lying, and from thence wandered to the figure of the garrison surgeon, who was busily engaged in fastening a bandage on his arm— upon which the operation of venesection had just been performed; and the earnest face of Dennis, also occupied in the execution of various duties connected therewith.

. Slowly the bewildered senses of the patient were restored, and with their reviving perception came the appalling memory of the bloody onslaught at the bridge, and the capture of Clarence. With tumultuous violence, the crimson torrent rushed from its source, swelling every vein and artery upon his face, previously so cold and pale. Starting up in the bed, Edward grasped the doctor's arm with impulsive strength, and asked with emotion—

"Is *she*—is Miss Forbes?" He could not finish the sentence, but his arm trembled, and his countenance assumed an expression of intense agony that frightened the medico so, that he could not immediately reply.

"My dear Molesworth, I—I—really you are exceedingly irritable. I am not made of wood or iron, that you should use my member so unmercifully; besides, allow me to remark, you will cause the vein to bleed afresh, if your transports are not controlled. Dear me, I thought so—Dennis, the basin again, and another bandage."

Poor Edward pressed his hand upon his brow, through which a throb of pain suddenly darted, and sank back upon the pillow with a deep groan. A few minutes elapsed 'ere he again spoke, and then it was with an altered look and tone.

"Dickson,—which was the doctor's name—for God's sake, tell me unreservedly what is the result, or do my own thoughts too truly anticipate the tale?"

"My boy," answered the other, "now that you are more responsible, I will relate all that I know about the affair you mention." Here the doctor applied himself to the contents of a capacious snuff-box, with much formality and self-gratification, before he resumed the thread of his discourse.

"It might have been noon, or perhaps a half hour later, while engaged in an interesting discussion upon the chemical affinities, with my coadjutor from Massachusetts, which was rapidly approaching a climax, whence unquestionably I should have borne off the victor's wreath '*vincit veritas*,' for, between us, these provincials are lamentably deficient in natural philosophy—just as I was about advancing in support of my hypothesis, a most remarkable instance of complex attraction between bodies in solution, that the abrupt explosion of a gun estranged our minds from the subject under consideration. On hurrying to the ramparts, we were quickly informed of the alarming cause, which you can imagine affected me in no small degree, as, upon occasions of such nature, I was well aware that professional services were indispensable. Therefore, after the men had left the fort to render assistance in your extremity, I followed with the operators, *et cetera*; and on reaching the field commenced an immediate examination of the bodies, for the enemy was no where to be seen, but unfortunately, though many could not have at first received mortal injuries, yet, yourself excepted, I found them all *in articulo mortis*, for with that barbarous, and, I may say, unscientific propensity, inherent in the savage mind, the integument covering the head and to which the hair is attached had been stripped entirely off; literally, they were scalped—therefore any effect of intellectual skill was useless. So true is it, that *litera emollit mores, &c.*" Here the doctor, with a look expressive of contemptuous pity for those unsophisticated essayists in the science of anatomy, paused awhile to indulge in another modicum from his capacious box, 'ere he rolled on again the river of his words.

"But," asked Edward, almost exhausted with overstrained attention to the torturing prolixity of his companion, "what of Miss Forbes? 'Tis of her I spoke."

"Very good," continued the doctor, "I was coming to that point. When it was found that the lady had been taken prisoner a party instantly went off in pursuit, and for some time they were guided by the prints of her horse's feet, until the course of her captors deviated from the valley, assuming a western inclination over the high grounds, when all further traces were lost, doubtless from the unyielding nature of the soil, which is more indurated than the alluvial deposition of the marshes."

Here the speaker was interrupted by a faint cry from his patient, who he found had fainted. After the usual application had succeeded in recovering him from the swoon into which he had fallen, upon the confirmation of his worst fears, Edward remained a long time silent and seemingly apathetic. At last he said:

"Dickson, do you believe that 'coming events cast their shadows before?'"

"No such thing," answered the doctor, who was not much given to sentiment or superstition; "the fact is, the human mind, influenced by cerebral excitement, is apt to give a feverish colouring to the suggestions of fancy, ever ready to draw irrational conclusions, and discerning amongst its visionary jumble, a vague prophesy of the future."

But the patient shook his head, as if unconvinced by the metaphysical argument of the other.

"The nerves," resumed the doctor, enlarging with the loquacity of his profession, while he wiped the point of his lancet with a silk handkerchief, "the nerves, to employ a vulgar figure, bear the same relation to the body as one's creditors do to the individual. As long as the vital power can afford a sufficient recompense for their labours in its behalf, and is capable of discharging its obligations with punctuality, a mutual understanding exists between the two, which induces a cordial interchange of favours. Thus the nerves enable the body to carry on its various functions comfortably and correctly, and in return receives a tone, an elasticity, which is indispensable to health. But mark the change, the moment that, from sudden prostration, imprudent outlay, or a variety of causes, the supply ceases, or is irregularly transmitted; then these medullary cords, like a legion of vipers, start up to annoy and persecute the poor wretch, already a sufficient object of commiseration." The doctor took another pinch. "What is to be done in such a case?"—he spoke feelingly.

"Thrash the dirty blackguards widin a hair's bridth o' th' divil," muttered Dennis, who was examining his master's soiled trappings at the other end of the room.

"Again I repeat," continued the doctor, "what is the *modus operandi* in such a crisis? The alternative is obvious, *ex necessitate rei*. You apply to a friend, who steps in with generous intention, and arranges matters—restoring the confidence, allaying the irritation of the parties, by the application of those remedies which are capable of effecting the best and quickest compromise. Now, in this position, my young friend," and here the speaker's heart swelled with the thought, for with all his faults he was a kind man—"in this glorious relation stands the sublime profession of which I am a humble member. 'Tis our day, *deo juvante*, to bind the broken reed, to administer to the wants of the bankrupt body, to correct the morbid irritability, the vitiated qualities of the arterial and nervous systems by means of emollients, sudorifics, refrigerants, sedative narcotics, and counter irritants, *cum multis aliis*," ("the dead languages," quoth Dennis,) "which the science of ages hath bequeathed as a priceless legacy to her disciples."

The doctor looked up as he finished his discourse with a warm glow upon his pleasant countenance, while, at the same time, he tapped, in a peculiar manner, the side of his box with the third finger of his right hand, as a prelude to the refreshing of his olfactories, after his laboured and voluminous illustration. But the complacent smile quickly vanished, and the suffusion faded when he noted the abstraction of his patient's thoughts; and leaving a few directions with Dennis, he took a rather precipitate leave, in no very enviable mood; for he very much doubted whether Edward had listened to one word he had uttered.

Who could picture to himself the lover's anguish, as hour after hour he lay upon his pallet watching the shadows creeping imperceptibly on the wall, and wondering at the deep silence around, when his heart and brain seemed bursting with intolerable agony. He thought till "thought grew almost madness," of his blighted hope, his sudden bereavement. The face of the loved and gentle Clarence seemed at one moment to beam before him in all its radiant beauty, then, like the change of a hideous dream, he beheld her in the grasp of ruthless savages, borne away, away, into the lairs of the wilderness; and that wild cry for help—will it ever cease to haunt his memory; O God! why is he here? Is there no aid, no power to save his own—his betrothed, from the horrors of captivity, or a violent death. Then, as the consciousness of his own helplessness, and the utter folly of attempting to track the savages in their native woods, forced itself upon his mind, his head would drop again on the pillow; and, as though mental suffering had destroyed itself with its own intensity, or existed as a thing distinct from perception, leaving the faculties prone to receive an impression of, and attach unusual importance to, the most trivial objects. With strange inconsistency, and the interest of a little child, he noticed again the creeping shadow, and the very spot whence it had advanced since he looked before, thinking how dim and sluggish it seemed, and that no power on earth could make it move faster; but if it did, it would be a relief. Then some long forgotten scene that occurred years ago, when he was a boy, would be constantly recurring to his thoughts with wonderful distinctness;—though why, or how it referred or associated itself in any way with the present, he could not tell—but so it was. And the very air seemed stagnated and lifeless, and he would have welcomed the smallest breath of wind or noise as a blessing; any thing to break the dreadful spell that bound his senses in an unnatural mood—half apathetic, half distractive. And hard by, in the French chapel, an old, venerable man lay, pale and emaciated from suffering. The long, thin, iron-grey hair falls neglectfully beside the worn hands that are spread over his face to conceal its emotion from the eye of the stranger. But no movement is observable in the limbs of the sufferer, nor doth any murmur escape from his lips, save, occasionally, a low, half-suppressed moan. Yet deeper and more blighting is the silent woe that wrings the father's heart for the loss of his child, than the wild phrenzy of the lover's grief. The green sapling, though bruised by the tempest, will be restored in time to its pristine vigour, but the aged tree retains evermore the scarred traces of the storm, which severed its last bough. The young plant bends to the blast that destroys its less pliable neighbour.

Chapter VII

I t was on the morning of the second day after the event, narrated in the previous chapter, that Dennis entered his master's room, with the joyful intelligence, that the expedition to the Bay Verte, had been successful, the last strong hold of the French having yielded, followed by a general disarmament of the peasantry in that part of the country, to the number of 1,500. When Dennis had delivered this important piece of information, which elicited a cold "'tis well," from Edward, who was sitting by the bed-side, with a thoughtful and dejected air, the faithful fellow subdued the natural liveliness of his manner, as he added—

"But there's more—yer honor, and may be it 'ud ase the trouble an' th' sorrey, that same."

"What is it, Dennis?" inquired Edward, without altering his listless position, as in doubt whether any thing was capable of yielding him the slightest interest now.

"As I was sayin," continued Dennis, "it wor crassing the parade I wor, maybe a minute agone, whin, who shud I mate but Sergeant Gallagher, of ours, on guard the day. And, says he, 'Dennis,' he says, 'there's a Frencher, or Neuthral,' yer honor, though that's nather here nor there, for aint they our nateral born inemies? An, says he, there's a black duck, no, a Frencher, who tould him that a black duck, in the bombproof—though by the same token, it was proved and found wanting, and says he, as I wor sayin, botheration, where wor I, yer honor?" Here Dennis, having twisted the thread of his discourse into an inexplicable tangle, stopped abruptly, and stood scratching his auburn head, with an expression of stupid bewilderment on the face, ludicrous to behold. Edward who was possessed, merely, with an idea that his servant wished to tell him something, though what it was, he could not imagine, raised his head with a severe reproof, that, at any other time, would have ended in a fit of laughter, as he witnessed his confusion. At last, at the command of his superior, Dennis managed to say. "The long an short of it is this, yer honor. There's an Ingen prisoner in the bombproof, wanting to get word wid yerself, plase yer honor, respectin the scrimmage at the bridge, beyant, and Miss Clarence—God be kind to her."

"Ha!" exclaimed Edward, starting up with sudden animation, for hope began to dawn again within him, and partially dissipated the gloom that overshadowed his soul. "There may be some thing in this. I will at once to the prisoner. Heaven grant one ray of hope, and what ever human fortitude can dare, that will I, even where it a thousand deaths, if it lead to the rescue of my beloved."

Such were the half-muttered reflections of the lover, as he left the staff barracks, where he was quartered, and crossing the open court, reached the entrance of the low bombproof, which afforded sufficient ground for the remark of Dennis, for it was much shattered by the shells thrown into the fort, during its investment, and failed in yielding that shelter to the besieged, which, from its name, it would seem to insure. He was immediately admitted into the interior, where, unseen at first, in the dark vaulted chamber, he found the prisoner whom he sought, leaning with folded arms against the damp wall. Upon questioning the Indian, Edward discovered to his regret, that he could not understand the English language, however, it occurred to him, that the natives were familiar with the patois of the Acadians, and as he spoke French fluently himself, through its means they might be enable to converse. Nor was he deceived, for upon the interrogation, "who art thou?" a beam of intelligence flitted over the face of the Indian, and erecting himself with an air of pride, he answered in tolerable French—

"Argimou, the son of Pansaway."

"What wouldst thou with me?" rejoined the soldier.

"Listen," was the pithy reply. "The *Anglasheou* are great warriors. The *Wennooch* fought. They were driven away like dry leaves in the wind, but the red man never knew fear, nor showed his back to his enemies. His warriors were pierced by the long knives and spears of the stranger—like grass by the lightning, yet the eye of the *Sagamou* drooped not;—he never knew fear. But the thirsty spears were at his heart, ready to drink the blood, when a young brave spoke, and at the sound of his voice, death vanished away—like a ghost in a sick man's dream. Does my brother know who that lone warrior was?—look! or has he changed since he became a captive among the pale faces?"

As the Indian ceased speaking, he approached nearer the ray of light that issued from the half-open door, and, to his surprise, Edward recognised the striking features of the gallant chief, whose life he had been instrumental in preserving at the taking of the blockhouse, and whom he had not thought of since, supposing that he was liberated with the Acadians found in arms at the capture of the fort. With generous enthusiasm, the young Englishman proffered his hand in friendship, which was as warmly clasped by the other,—while he resumed—

"Hear me, my brother. The same spirit made us both, and to each, though of a different skin, he gave the same heart to teach him what is good. Our fathers have said, the memory of a kindness is like the sun, it never grows cold or wanes; an Indian never forgets. Argimou's eyes are weary, for he sees nothing here to make them glad; he would look upon the great hunting grounds of his nation, the faces of his kindred;

the air of a dungeon makes a warrior very sick, and pale as the blue
eyed stranger. But Argimou did not forget, and when he saw the young
brave carried home like a man asleep, and was told that his heart was
dark with grief, for its *sunbeam* had departed, then he said, I will speak
to my brother, and we will go hence and follow the sun' beam, that he
may smile again and be happy."

"Generous being," replied Edward, with emotion, "I believe what
you have said, for my own breast tells me it is true. Guide me to the
lost one, and freedom and all that wealth can procure shall be yours."
But with a look of proud disdain, the chief drew himself up to his full
height, and answered with emphatic enunciation,

"Argimou is a warrior. He is not greedy, nor would he tell a lie to
save his life."

Edward, observing with ready tact, that an idea of any prospect of
reward having prompted his proposal appeared to wound the feelings of
the Indian, forbore all allusion to the subject, asking when they should
commence the pursuit of Clarence, and what force would be required
for the service. To which, Argimou replied—

"Does my brother dream, or is his hair painful to his head, that
he talks of marching a drove of palefaces through the forest—like
blind owls? Their scalps would be hanging dry, in the council hall of
Onanthio, at Louisburg, 'ere the moon is full. Listen my brother. The
Milicetejik have stolen the daughter of the stranger, for their Sagamou
is a thief, and only *he* would be outlying when the warpath leads to
the village of the Micmac. So that there is a long train before us, and
we must go along, for a Milicete is a fox in cunning—and a serpent in
deceit;" and here the warrior threw himself into an attitude of great
dignity, 'ere he concluded, impressively, "but the Micmac is a moose,
in the sharpest of his scent—a carriboo, in swiftness—a beaver, in
wisdom."

After seeing that every comfort which the nature of his situation would admit of, was afforded his grateful friend, Edward, with

an elasticity of thought and feeling, to which he had been for some time a stranger, proceeded to the quarters of the commanding officer, where he met with a hearty participation in all his plans and prospects in achieving the deliverance of the captive maiden. Unlimited leave was granted to him, and unconditional liberty to his Indian guide. While every assistance in providing the contingencies necessary for the undertaking, was cordially rendered by his brother officers, among whom he was much esteemed for his acquirements and amiable disposition.

In one respect, only, was Edward at a loss to decide. It was his wish that his servant Dennis, who had proved himself so valorous, and, above all, so strongly attached to his master, should accompany them on the expedition, as he might be of valuable service in case of a recourse to violence being requisite. Yet, when he mentioned the subject to Argimou, it met, at first, with the decided disapproval of the chief. But after endeavouring to point out the many ways in which he could be useful on their journey, a reluctant assent was yielded, though evidently, rather in courtesy, than from a conviction of the chief's judgment, as he regarded the son of Hibernia, as a nondescript species of animal, of whose habits and propensities he was entirely ignorant; therefore both experience and sagacity told him to beware how he risked the safety of his scheme by such an uncertain accession to the party.—However, it was arranged that Dennis should go, and having provided every thing needful, the principal of which was a complete suit of Indian costume and its appurtenances for each individual, being adopted at the instance of Argimou, as most favourable for purposes of convenience and concealment, in case they should meet with any of the bands of armed peasants, known to be scattered about the country through which they would be obliged to travel; it was proposed to commence the journey at sunrise on the following morning.

Chapter VIII

Leaving now the lover absorbed in the contemplation of the prospect that had so unexpectedly presented itself to his despairing mind, let us return to the wretched object of all this solicitude.

When Clarence was borne off in the possession of the Indians, after witnessing, as she supposed, the death of her lover in the bloody onslaught at the Massiquash, the transition was so instantaneous, and the speed with which her captors hurried her away, so great, that she had no time to comprehend in its fullest sense, the horrors of her situation. After the utterance of that one cry of terror, all further appeal to the commiseration of her friends was prevented by the ferocious menaces of the savages, who held her by main force on either side of the horse, and brandished their knives and tomahawks in the maiden's face with significant gestures, which conveyed to the victim's understanding, the impression that they would enforce obedience with instant death, if she attempted to struggle or remonstrate. So that acquiescence was the natural consequence of extreme fear, for Clarence knew not at what moment they might put their bloody threats into execution.

For some miles, the Indians held a direct course up the valley, 'till at length, being joined by the rest of the warriors, the whole party, whose actions seemed to be guided by the same gigantic native that had flung the fatal hatchet, apparently the cause of all her misfortunes, left the low, marshy tract, using all those precautions which their sagacity and the rocky nature of the place where they made the upland suggested, to prevent pursuit; with what success, has been already related. Then winding for a time through the trees, in a line parallel with the river they had left; they crossed the road traversed by the troops that morning, and dipping down into the great prairie, struck directly to the westward, passing the Au Lac and Tantemar rivers, at their upper part, by means of floats and canoes, for which there appeared to be no scarcity. Being joined by another party, with prisoners, also on their return to the west, they again traversed an elevated country, undulating in hills and covered with broad luxuriant groves, untouched by the axe of the settler, through which the war-party advanced without effort or an instant's delay, though to the weeping Clarence, there seemed no path or sign of any kind to indicate the route. A halt was not made until they reached the bank of a river, of greater extent than those they had passed, watering a beautiful valley bordered on its further side, by lofty hills which were partially cultivated, while here and there, where the dark forests had been cleared away, might be seen a few huts of the Acadians, clustered peacefully beneath the shade of the gigantic trees. Here the Indians took a hurried meal of dried moose meat, and obliged Clarence to dismount, which was a relief to her fatigued limbs. But there was little time given to rest, for, ere long they were moving again, and having embarked in canoes they crossed the stream, making the horse of Clarence swim over. Which being done, the band passed on, without relaxing their speed, until their progress was stopped by the waters of a larger river than any they had previously encountered. Yet, after waiting an hour, they were enabled to ford it, as the tide then was at its lowest ebb. By the time that the passage was accomplished, the day was swiftly declining—the sun having sunk long since behind the lofty mountain in their front. Therefore, preparations for a bivouac were commenced, fires being lighted and packs thrown from the shoulders of the carriers, and divers rude utensils extracted therefrom. While some collected fuel from the quantities of decayed trees around, or filled dingy kettles with water at the river side; others, again, cleared the underwood from the place, lopping off the lower branches from the fir trees, which were placed on the ground as a bed to rest upon. In the mean time, Clarence was deposited in a rude shed, hastily formed of green boughs, and with her arms bound, left to the misery of her thoughts, and the physical exhaustion that resulted from the harsh treatment and fatigue to which she had been subjected during the forced retreat of the savages. And then, in the comparative stillness and solitude which succeeded, did the gentle girl reflect upon the occurrences of that eventful day. She shuddered when she thought of the harrowing scene she had witnessed—that fatal blight that had fallen upon her promised happiness. The tones of Edward's voice seemed still like sweet music, to linger in her ear, as he expatiated upon the blessings which would accompany their union—the return to the home of his fathers with his own Clarence—the delight of visiting again the beloved spots so sacred to his memory, in the company of one still more sacred and loved than even they; those words seemed but a moment since, breathed in the warmth and eloquence of passion at her side, and now, what an unforeseen change had swept over the current of thought—life—even the face of nature itself. Her lover dead, herself in the power of unrelenting savages, separated forever from the familiar faces of friends, the endearments of home and her poor father—would he survive the loss of his Clarence? Where would they take her? could help ever reach the captive through the fearful, trackless forest? and then—her fate? O God! who would attempt to pourtray the unutterable thoughts that weighed like a horrid phantom upon the soul of the wretched girl? And she, the tender—the child-like—nursed like a delicate flower with all those nameless attentions which, though unknown to herself, had their origin in the delight and pleasure every heart felt in contributing to the happiness of one, who made all that ever gazed upon her sweet face, themselves conscious of the same feeling—was fain in her desolation, to throw her wearied frame upon the cold earth, in the careless abandonment of grief. And while she lay, scarcely sensible of aught but her own sorrow, the shades of night gathered around, and condensed, as it were, in deeper gloom within the coverts of the dismal woods.

The thronging stars began to appear in the gray heaven, and as Clarence saw them twinkling palely through the fissures of the imperfect roof, she turned towards them, as to the only familiar things among the strange objects by which she was surrounded, wondering if there was no intelligence in their fitful, yet penetrating look, that they might take pity on her, for they seemed to her like so many eyes gazing down upon the world, and bearing witness to the deeds of wicked men. And, straightway, she thought of that *All-seeing Eye* which never slumbers, and breathed a prayer, pure and earnest as the heart from whence it arose, to the disposer of all things, the good and bad, the just and unjust, for mercy and protection. Was it not heard? Surely, never went there up a more fervent appeal to the throne of heaven, than that of the friendless girl, from the depths of the dreary wilderness. And she experienced a relief from the commune, for a feeling of composure shed a soothing balm upon her mind, as she became more trustful in the guidance of an inscrutable Providence. After a while, some person with a lighted torch approached the place where the maiden lay, and set a bark dish containing food, by her side, saying, at the same time, a few words in the Indian language. Clarence, surprised at the musical tones of the voice, so very different from the uncouth guttural sounds of her conductors, looked up at the speaker, and beheld, with astonishment, an exceedingly beautiful face bending over her, such as she had heard, were sometimes found among the native tribes, but which she had never before seen, and perhaps, had scarcely believed to exist, where every thing seemed, to her gentle mind, associated with barbarism and deformity. But the clear, pale face before her, was as lovely as ever visited a poet's dreams. Clarence read at once, in its soft lineaments, as in a brook, a world of tenderness, and the dark melancholy eyes seemed to look down upon her with pity and kindness, as though their owner yearned, with the warm feelings of her sex, towards the beautiful and helpless stranger. A sweet smile played like a beam of light, about the small delicate mouth for one brief instant, then as quickly vanished, as Waswetchcul, for she only it could have been, having loosed the withes that fastened the arms of the captive, departed; having instilled more comfort into the heart of Clarence—less by the act than the expressive look of sympathy that accompanied it, than the most laboured protestations could have effected.

What a wild, strange sight was presented to the maiden as the night deepened, and the Indians gathered around a fire of blazing logs, the light of which was reflected on their scowling visages and ornamental dresses; glistening on weapons of various kinds suspended from the trees, and gilding the motionless branches of the pines that hung over them, until the band seemed canopied by an arch of foliage, though they were unroofed, save by the pale sky and its thousand stars. Inspired by the effects of the "fire-water," of which they had a copious supply, they danced, sang, and howled, in a perfect ecstacy of mirth, which a single word would have converted to the fury of revenge, only to be pacified by the immediate sacrifice of the prisoners. But their passions were restrained by the superior cunning of the chief, so that they contented themselves with the performance of all manner of antics and boisterous ebullitions of merriment, until they were tired. And throughout all the noise and confusion, the calm, plump countenance of an Indian babe, appeared at the top of its wooden case, which was hung up against the upright bole of a huge pine, and with unmoved expression looked upon the wild gymnastics of its elders; while the coal-black eyes of the papoose rolled about from one side to the other as if scorning to evince the slightest interest or emotion on the occasion. And there it stuck, hour after hour, swathed like a

Mummy in its little prison—an emblem of patience to all more civilized babies—without uttering a sound or a cry. At length the Indians threw themselves upon the fir branches, and with the exception of one who remained to watch, each wrapping his blanket or mantle of skin closely around him, was soon buried in sleep.

When all was silent, save an occasional groan which proceeded from one of the prisoners, the young squaw stole noiselessly to the nook, where Clarence lay awake, and without a word or sign, threw a robe of fur over her, while she folded another around herself and laid down quietly to repose by the lady's side.

The delicate kindness evinced by this act, gave a feeling of comfort and security to Clarence; yet she in vain endeavoured to follow the example of her companion. Anxiety and restlessness kept her from sleeping through the long night, and it was only when the usual prognostics of the dawn appeared in the heaven, that she sank into a fitful, lethargic slumber, from which she was roused by Waswetchcul, and she found that the band was already in motion, preparing for their departure. With a sinking heart Clarence was again mounted on her horse, and led by an armed warrior; while in advance the huge chief moved rapidly forward, distinguished from his followers by an eagle plume fastened to the solitary tuft of hair on the top of his shaved head; and in succession came the individuals composing the party, threading the forest in a long, serpentine line.

Passing to the northward of the mountains, they made a course directly towards the west, never pausing a moment to satisfy themselves of the correctness of their route—never applying to each other for information in a matter that appeared to admit of neither the smallest doubt, nor requiring any uncommon sagacity to determine. Thus they travelled on through the wilds which seemed never to have known before the footstep of man, by the aid of those mysterious signs known only to the native.—The upward glance of the leader at the moss on the trees, the peculiar inclination of certain plants, were as sure guides to those wanderers of the wild as the star and compass are to the voyager on the pathless ocean; the very language of Nature appeared intelligible to her dependant children.

It would be tedious to follow Clarence in her long painful journey, during which she derived great support from the presence and attentions of the Indian maiden; who, whenever she thought herself less likely to attract observation, would steal to her side, and reassure the captive with a kind look or a sunny smile.—And each night, like a guardian angel, she soothed the fears of Clarence with her silent but gentle companionship. Suffice it, that, after traversing a wilderness country, for the most part hilly, and interspersed with extensive lakes and water-courses, on the afternoon of the fourth day they approached the banks of a noble river, whose broad expanse was glistening in the sun. The bold outline of the shores, elevated in abrupt ridges of graceful curves, looked dark but majestic with the foliage of the thick woods, covering every point and eminence in primitive profusion; while, far as the eye could reach, the dim hills blended with the water, that appeared to expand into a capacious bay.

With a shout of delight the Indians hailed the beautiful stream, as emerging from a dense wood they caught the first glimpse of the extensive prospect, and their pace was accelerated—each seeming eager to reach his final resting place. Following the course of the river, an hour's march brought them opposite a few rocky islands covered with pointed pines. As they approached the shore by a well worn path the whole band sent forth a joyful cry, to give notice of their arrival in the neighbourhood, which was succeeded by the utterance of distinct notes, some of which were intended to denote the number of prisoners in their company, while others again, from their deep lamentation, were expressive of the friends that had fallen in battle since their departure. 'Ere long an answering exclamation, as if a multitude arose from an adjacent point; and a sudden turn of the track they were pursuing, disclosed the thickly studded wigwams of an Indian village, the inhabitants of which were already in commotion; and from the gates of the palisades with which the encampment was enclosed an indiscriminate swarm was pouring out to welcome the returning warriors. With loud yells and howlings of joy or sorrow, as some individual was recognised or missed from the war-party, they gathered around in a confused mass, asking hurried questions, and making the woods ring with vociferous exultation as they caught sight of the prisoners. These were immediately dragged within the palisades exposed to the execrations and violence of a furious mob, among which the women and half naked children bore a conspicuous part. Several rude hands were in the act of tearing the apparel from the shoulders of the terrified Clarence, when the chief sternly commanded them to desist, and leading her to a cabin of logs of superior appearance to the bark habitations around, delivered her into the keeping of an old haggard squaw, of malignant aspect.—The apprehensions of the half-fainting girl were somewhat alleviated by observing as she entered that her Indian friend, the beautiful Waswetchcul, also followed, and appeared to view the place as her customary abode.

Meanwhile a fearful scene was enacting in the centre of the village, which exhibited one of the darkest traits of the savage character.—Yet, strange to say, at that time, or even in a later period, a parallel might be found among those who professed christianity, and affected to emulate and spread abroad among the heathen the charity and humble virtues of a pitying Saviour. How could *they* accept mercy from those to whom no mercy was ever given? Verily, example is far better than precept! It has been stated that there were two prisoners accompanying Clarence into captivity;—but they were very dissimilar in appearance. One was a Milicete Indian who had been detected in giving information to the English of an intended attack of his party, for the sake of a bribe; which had, consequently resulted in discomfiture, and the loss of several valuable warriors. Aware of the stern ordinances of his tribe, and their retributive denunciation of a traitor, he knew well that no earthly

70

power could save his life. It was justly forfeited to the insulted laws of the nation, and with dogged sullenness he awaited his fate; but it was otherwise with his companion. He was a poor settler, from the British possessions in Acadia ragged and emaciated with toil and severe suffering; yet still, to the last, a faint ray of hope burned at his heart and would not let him yield altogether to despair; but alas! he was quickly undeceived. For the women commenced piling a heap of dry stumps and brushwood round a green sapling, which had been deprived of its branches and driven upright into the ground.

When the pyre was ready, the white man was forcibly seized, and in spite of his desperate struggles and wild prayers for mercy, he was stripped, and after his naked body had been covered with a black pigment, they bound him with wet withes to the stake—and then he knew that his doom was sealed. An old, withered beldame, with a bear skin half covering her body, and a flaming brand in her skinny paw, now began a mystic dance in front of the victim. As she approached or receded from the pile, her voice sent forth a shrill discant, which could be likened to nothing but a witch's incantation; and she herself seemed a very incarnation of sorcery and sin. As the rite proceeded, and she waxed more furious and unearthly in her screams and distorted movements—calling upon the names of the dead to cease their anger and rejoice at the sacrifice offered as a propitiation, by their forsaken friends, men similarly clothed, and with blackened faces, joined the powa dance, until, to the half crazed senses of the victim, a legion of demons seemed to be leaping and yelling around him. When the powowing was completed, the pyre was fired in many places, and the cries of the sufferer drowned in the mingled shouts and revilings of a savage multitude. Then as the hungry flames, like gliding snakes, were seem amid the thick smoke to crawl and lick with fiery tongues his naked limbs, they affected to spit on him, calling him a woman and a dog, and lavishing every epithet of scorn and detestation upon him, that their imaginations could devise, which seemed at last to rouse the

71

fleeting faculties of the white man, and caused a momentary triumph over the most acute corporeal agony. Every feeling but intense abhorrence of his cruel tormenters was forgotten for one brief instant: with a voice distinct and clear, which penetrated to the further limits of that pitiless crowd, he screamed a bitter curse to them and theirs, and as if the spirit had passed with the utterance of that dread legacy, his head drooped—his body fell. What did they there? It was dust that the fire consumed!

The mode of the traitor's death was different. He was fastened to a rock on the shore and stoned; but not until sufficient time had been allowed for the warrior to sing his death-song, which he did with a bold, haughty air, as though his death were a triumph instead of being a lasting disgrace to his kindred—for his name was henceforth to be a forgotten word among his people, and his deeds unremembered;—who would call his child after a traitor, or make songs in his praise? Yet the pride and self-possession instilled by habitual practice from his earliest years, and perhaps in some degree natural to the character of his race, effectually concealed any outward consciousness of shame; for not a single exclamation, save of exultation, escaped the guarded lips of the warrior; and though lacerated and bruised in a thousand places by the showers of missiles hurled at him in anger, he expired without a groan. When life was extinct, the mutilated body was tossed into the current of the river, as unworthy a place beside the sacred bones of his fathers. And here was seen a beautiful instance of the constancy of woman's love.—Along the beach and over the rocks, in the dim twilight, hurried a poor squaw; her hair floating dishevelled over her shoulders, and with a face pallid and contracted with an expression of torture and wild anxiety, watching intently a dark object floating down the stream. Now it approaches some point, and she strives to touch it with a long spear, then again, the deceitful eddy sweeps it away beyond her reach, and with distracted gesture she wrings her hands, and speeds on after the watery burthen. At last she has succeeded; the jutting rocks of yonder promontory impedes its progress.—Joyfully the woman draws the treasure to land, and the faithful wife beholds the mutilated, half-recognised remains of her partner. Then with great labour she scooped with her hands a shallow grave in the loose soil, and laying the body therein, covered it up hastily, and after smoothing the earth over the place, rolled a large stone at the head of him who lay buried, for a memorial, and went her way alone—but without a tear.

The day after the return of the war-party, the chief entered the hut where Clarence was, dressed with peculiar care, and decorated with ornaments of various kinds, among which shone several large brooches of polished silver. After having ordered the other inmates to leave the cabin, he seated himself in front of the maiden, in the Indian fashion, and with an air of grave importance and unusual condescension, addressed her in a strange jumble of English, French, and Milicete words, the purport of which was nearly as follows—

"Daughter of the pale faces, listen!—that you may be wise. Madokawando is a great chief; he says to his young men, do this and it is done. He has taken many scalps; he is a brave warrior. Go! ask the Anglasheou—they will say, Madokawando is very strong, he has drunk our blood—we can't touch him whom the Great Spirit loves. Ugh! the pale faces are fools and dogs that won't be content, but want the whole country. They run howling into the woods—all save one mad, very mad carriboo, when he run around—cos him head crazy. Open your ears, child! Madokawando could get much dollars for the blue eye's scalp.— Wennooch very good man—broder to Ingin.—But the chief say—no? Blue-eye will stay—be chief's wife—make fire—cook vittals, never leave him summer or winter, but always be like his own heart—that is very good. You see old squaw?" and here the suitor of Clarence pointed, with a disparaging look, at the door where his ancient spouse had disappeared. "You see that thing what go out? Him nobody. Me kick him away, all same like old mocassin when him worn out—don't be afeart. When next moon comes, Madokawando's wigwam will be ready for the

73

blue eye. Now he go down Ouangondy, see Wennooch—him very good man—more better than Anglasheou.—Ugh! they would eat up every thing from Ingin, so he would starve; but a Milicete warrior laughs at the greedy-bellied wolves, and gives them to the crows for food. The chief has spoken!"

Here the savage rose with an aspect of grandeur and self complacency, like one who has finished to his satisfaction, a troublesome but necessary business, and stalked out of the chamber, leaving his listener in no very comfortable state of mind, for although but half a dozen words in the whole of his speech was intelligible, still enough was understood to render her wretched beyond measure; and harassed as the poor girl had been already, by the fearful occurrences that so suddenly clouded the sun shine of her young life; the dreadful uncertainty of her fate caused an almost utter prostration of mind and body. Had it not been for the unceasing kindness of the beautiful Milicete girl, she could scarcely have survived the severe trials through which she had passed, and the vicissitudes which she was still fated to undergo.

Chapter IX

The morning was cold and dreary upon which three persons left the works of Fort Cumberland, and took the path leading down into the meadows without attracting observation, as there were few, if any, loiterers at that early hour, and every object was enveloped in a cheerless fog, which soon covered the garments of the travellers in a frost-like condensation. As they brushed the branches of the low firs in passing, a thousand drops were rained upon their heads; which, with the moisture imparted by the long grass through which they wended their way, rendered the situation of the trio any thing but comfortable. Crossing the Au Lac by the dyke, they pushed boldly out into the broad marsh—the visual extent of which was at present confined to a very limited circle—and, to increase the discouraging nature of the prospect, a cold, raw wind rushed past from the bay, whistling through the bending grass and driving the thick mist against the face and clothes with much violence, half freezing the one, and wholly saturating the other.

These persons, who might have been taken for Indian hunters from their garb and equipment, were Argimou, Edward, and his servant, Dennis. The chief led the way with his gun thrown into the hollow of his arm to keep the lock dry, and bow suspended at his back, which bore the additional burthen of a pack—with which indeed the others were also furnished—and at his girdle hung the long knife and keen edged tomahawk.

After him came Edward and his man, similarly clothed and armed, except that they wore skull caps of seal skin upon their heads, such as the Acadians sometimes used, and substituted as a covering for the feet, the stout-soled shoes of the Europeans for the light, flexile mocassins of the forester. Edward followed the rapid footsteps of the guide in silence and deep thought, which tended to sadden the joyful alacrity with which he had left his couch to commence his important journey. The picture of the poor old father of whom he had taken leave before his departure was continually before his eyes, and his mind was tinged with gloomy shadows and mournful forebodings, which the spectacle of the bereaved parent had awakened. How touching was the picture of that venerable soldier; broken down by suffering and anguish, when with countenance furrowed by grief and tremulous with emotion, he solemnly asked God to grant his assistance and blessing to those about to undertake the restoration of his beloved child.

Dennis Sherron brought up the rear in a very cranky humour, which was occasioned, no doubt, by the ungenial state of the elements; sufficient to make, as he said, "a philosopher, or even holy St. Patrick himself swear."—Thinking that a sufficient excuse for venting the strength of his feelings in sundry wrathful ebullitions, which, being addressed to himself, were incapable of giving offence to any body else, he commenced first by cursing his material and immaterial composition, from which not deriving altogether that satisfaction which was desired, he changed the recipient, and cursed the country, which was found much more palatable.

"Mother o' Moses! aint here a country? faiks, it's a con-tra-ry, more likes; be the same token that hits a meltin and a frazin yees, be turns—wan day a bilin an a roastin the sinses of a man with the hate, an the next a drivin intil him, like a sieve, lashins o' shiverins an could water. Sure, it's a blissin it was wan has the dhrap to warm the insides

76

whiles—praise be to God for that, anny way. Thunder! what a draft is tearing like mad over the bog, it 'ill be th' death o' me, it will.'"

Here Dennis' soliloquy was cut short, as an unusually fierce blast swept along a drizzling cloud, from whose penetrating properties he strove to shelter his face and neck by turning sideways, and burying his head under the lea of his burly shoulders, hugging, at the same time, the stock of his carbine closer under his arm.

Avoiding the swamps and stagnant pools, which were spread thickly over this portion of the great morass, by paths familiar to their Indian guide, they crossed the half-dismantled bridge of the Tantemar, and finally, after a weary distressing march of six miles, reached the termination of the low marshy district. As they advanced into the uplands, the fog gradually became less dense, and when the first hill top was gained, the sun suddenly burst upon the landscape.

Below them, heaving and rolling in snowy wreaths like a sea of billowy clouds, the travellers beheld the spectral mist clinging to the prairie they had left behind, which looked dim and dismal by the contrast of the scene around, lighted as it was by the clear, warm beams of the morning sun. Here a short halt was made to wring the water from their soaked garments and prepare for their journey through the woods.

With enlivened feelings the party pushed forward over an elevated country, shaded by extensive forests, which the choral songs of birds filled with enchanting melody. The active squirrel's shrill, quick chirp, gave its companions notice of the unwelcome intrusion of strangers into its secluded territory. The blue jay uttered its discordant cry, while the locust sang incessantly among the pines, and the brilliant butterfly flitted among the leaves like a gorgeous dream. But above all the cheerful sunlight touched and sprinkled the dancing spray, and poured in long beams of richest sheen through the leafy arcades, waving fantastic webs, dew-spangled, on the dewy moss and feathery fern; and forcing warm smiles from old, leafless, storm-worn trunks, and giving a bright glow to grim, hoary-looking rocks, until all things owned the spell of Nature's mighty Alchymist, the great *Eye* of Heaven, whose look transmutes every object into gold, making them leap out of the gloom in masks of laughing beauty.

Whether it was the transition that had taken place in the disposition of the weather, or the spiritual commune with a capacious black bottle which he had concealed in some secret pocket of his vestment, that imparted an impetus to the spirits of Dennis, our readers can best determine; but certain it is, that he followed his master with increased alacrity, and even ventured some pleasant remarks upon "the luck of having a good day for the beginnin;" and divers questions regarding the length of their excursion, and the "whereabouts would they find Miss Clarence, the blissid angils presarve her,"—to all of which his master, who found it necessary to humor him at times, returned a good natured, if not very satisfactory reply.

In this manner they proceeded for some miles, when Argimou suddenly made a signal to stop, which was scarcely complied with when a stentorian voice roughly demanded *"que vive?"* while at the same time the warning click of a lock was heard, and a peasant showed himself with a presented piece amongst the foliage of a thicket, a short distance to the right of the party. "Micmac," was the immediate reply of the chief, as, whispering the others not to move a step for their lives, he advanced directly to the questioner, with whom he remained for some time. When he returned to his companions Edward noted a change in his countenance, for it seemed darkened with a gloomy, anxious expression. Desiring them to follow, he led the way towards the left for a little space, when, stopping in a deep, shady nook that afforded a secure hiding place, he said, "My brother, Argimou cannot go yet; his people are here with their father, and the Sagamou is wanted. Rest here in peace till he returns."

Edward, who did not fully comprehend the cause of this sudden change in the intentions of his Indian friend, suffered a shade of distrust to cross his mind; however, he quickly dispelled the unworthy thought, and sought an explanation of the other's views, which being satisfactorily given, he acquiesced with the best grace that his impatience at any delay in their progress would allow, with the consciousness, however, that the disguise adopted at the instance of the guide had undoubtedly been the means of insuring their safety upon the expected rencontre that had occurred just before.

Argimou having provided for the security of his fellow travellers, rejoined the French scout, who conducted him beyond the thicket and through a small wood from which they emerged upon an open glade among the trees, where a piteous spectacle was beheld, furnishing a striking commentary upon the horrors of war. There must have been, at least, seven hundred persons gathered within the area, of each sex, and every age, exhibiting every grade of wretchedness; from forlorn sorrow to the depth of extreme misery and want. Here, were mothers striving to afford their babes that nourishment and comfort which they wanted far more themselves. There were elder children, clamouring for food, which no one had to offer, yet still they cried on, the tyrant cravings of hunger disregarding utter impossibilities; and, nigh at hand old helpless men, stricken to a second childhood by the event that had befallen, lay moaning and wishing for death to release them from their woes, and mumbling that the grave was their only home now—the peaceful, quiet grave! While some again, disturbed the sanctity of grief with wild, hysterical laughter, more allied to madness than mirth. It was fearful to hear them mocking happiness with shouts of glee and merry words, soundful but hollow, such as men, reckless with despair, put forth, the precursors of a failing brain or a breaking heart. These went about among the rest, calling on their fellows to be mirthful, for they had no cares, no dwelling places now but the woods—the brave old woods! Though there were others, strange to say, the very converse of the last, for they were full of hope, although half naked and nearly starved; these would whisper cheering words to less trustful sufferers, telling them not to weep or be cast down, for "*le bon temps viendra*,"

79

and they would be happy then. But there were some, and these alone carried arms, who sat stern and silent with their straw hats drawn down to cover their hollow eyes, and their heads resting on their clenched hands.—These men never spoke nor answered a word, but sat hour after hour, still and motionless, as if in a lethargic trance, or as though they had been petrified into stone; yet in *their* souls the shaft that wounded all, pierced deepest and rankled with the greatest bitterness; with the withering ice of their despair, was mingled the feverish thirst, the insatiable longing for revenge.

The Indian threw a troubled look over the multitude, and his eye kindled with quick passion, and his chest swelled with gathering emotion, but he lingered not, as he passed on to the farther end of the open space, where the blue smoke of several fires were visible among the limbs of the dark trees. Here were seated several hundreds of his own nation, men, women and children, but a strange silence was observed by the assemblage, and as their chief Sagamou stepped rapidly on towards a temporary wigwam, which had been made beneath a beautiful sugar-maple in the rear, no sound of recognition escaped the group, though many sad faces were turned upon him at his approach. Gliding noiselessly by, Argimou entered the bough-thatched canopy, and seated himself, without saying a word, by the side of a recumbent figure, enveloped in skins, and stretched out upon a bed of fir in the centre, around which were gathered the principal warriors of the tribe. The chief asked no questions, waited for no explanation—all was told by the melancholy spectacle before and around him. The Anglasheou had triumphed; the pleasant hamlets of their Acadian brethren and his own beloved village by the shores of Baye Verte, were destroyed, and their inhabitants driven out, like wild beasts into the forest, in company with his tribe, who had come here with their Great Father—the old Tonea, that he might die in peace. This was the same ancient warrior who had officiated at the inauguration of the Bashaba. When he saw the face of that ancient man, rigid, as if set in death; the eyes closed as in slumber—the long white hair, wreathed like a glory round the sunken cheeks; he almost repented having given his hand in friendship to one of the nation that had wrought this great evil. It seemed at that moment, a crime even deeper than ingratitude.

Shortly, old Tonea, whose senses were wrapped in a dull stupor, such as sometimes is seen to precede the dissolution of the aged, appeared to revive a little, for he began to murmur indistinctly, like a sleeping child. The chief bent down his ear to listen, but he could not distinguish the words uttered so feebly, therefore he said softly—"does my father speak?" At the unusual sound, the old Indian opened his eyes, but they were glazed, and incapable of vision, for he immediately closed them again, while he asked faintly—

"What voice troubles the dreams of Tonea, as the breeze of summer among the dead autumn leaves?"

"Argimou!" was the reply.

"There were many warriors of that name," continued the old man, whose memory was wandering amid the confused recollections of former years. "I have heard my fathers tell of one who led his warriors towards the frost where they fought the Esquimeaux, till the snow was red as the berry which the pigeons love; but that was long before the Wennooch came over the salt lake from the sun-rising, yea, many moons. Then there was Argimou, the son of Sebatis; we were boys together, and went out first with the Etchemins against the Nehanticks, where we learned to draw the bow and shout the war-whoop like warriors. But the Black-Eagle died long ago, before my foot was heavy or my hair grey. Who art thou, with a name of strength and a voice of other days?"

"Argimou, the son of Pansaway," answered the Sachem.

"Does the grave speak?" rejoined Tonea, "they said the young Bashaba perished in battle, when the Wennooch were overcome by the unjust Anglasheou, yet was he valiant, and strong as a young moose, and pleasant to an old man's eye, but he too is gone."

"A bird sang a false song in the ears of my father; he was a prisoner among his enemies, but they never saw his back, and so their hearts softened—he is here."

"Then draw near unto me, my son, that I may bless the arm of the nation ere I depart, for the Great Spirit calls, and I must go."

Argimou immediately complied, by bending reverently down, and placing the old man's hand upon his smooth head; there it remained for some time, while Tonea gradually sunk into his former trance-like state, when it dropped quietly down again at his side. Another long, unbroken pause occurred, and the watchers were doubtful if the spirit still lingered in its time-worn tenement, when the dying man, after a few struggling gasps—again spoke, but his voice was changed, and his features had assumed a more unearthly hue and expression.

"My children, have the snows fallen? for Tonea is very cold, and it is dark—dark! But that cannot be, for I remember, when we came here the earth was green, and the sun brighter and more piercing than the eyes of many eagles—is it not so?"

"My father is right," replied a warrior.—"The sugar-tree is covered with fresh leaves and they are glancing in the sunbeam."

"Then where am I, and who are these near me? my eye-lids are heavy with sleep."

"My father is in the country of the Micmac, and their warriors are around him;" was the reply.

"*Country!*" exclaimed the patriarch, with wild vehemence, starting up with sudden strength, and raising his bare, skinny arm to give full emphasis to the prophetic tenour of his words. "Children of the Micmac, listen to the voice of one who sees the dim cloud rolled away from the secrets of the days that come. He tells you that you have *no* country!—*no* hunting grounds!—*no* home! The strangers are as hungry as caterpillars, and numerous as the salt-water sands. I see the Wennooch hunted down like the deer; the hills are red with the flames of many villages; the big canoes carry them away to grow sick

82

and die in a strange land. The Micmac are very brave, I have seen their warriors drive the Mohawk before them like a strong wind, making the bears growl; but the thunder of the stranger is like the Great Spirit's voice when the storm lightning kills. The red man must depart! the game vanishes—the trees fall; there are foot-prints on the graves of our fathers. Children of the Micmac—break the bow—bury the hatchet, for I tell you that you have *no* country! *The White Gull* has *flown over all!*"

Awe-struck by the warning conveyed in the voice, whose solemn tones seemed still to thrill to their souls depths; the wild warriors gazed upon the inspired speaker, as though a spirit from the grave had come amongst them.—The eyes staring wildly at what they fully believed, some unearthly vision not permitted to their unexperienced view; the gaunt arm stretched out in prophetic fervour, the ghastly face with the long hair like moonlight, streaming behind; these still chained them with the spell his words had woven, though those lips were forever closed. But see! the arm slowly sinks—the rigid muscles relax— the body drops supinely back upon the evergreen couch.—Though the eyes still glared, as if their latest faculty sufficed to paralyze their great nerves, and caused the lids to shrink spasmodically from their dilated orbs, yet when the mourners looked down upon the old man, they knew that he was dead; and each felt in his heart, that a good spirit had taken its departure from the dwellings of the Micmac.

---

* This epithet is applied to the whites, by the Micmacs, from their not confining themselves to any particular locality.

Chapter X

The chief, with a hand that trembled slightly with the excess of his emotion, closed the eyes of the dead, and then—but not until that office had been performed, exchanged a glance of intelligence with his father, who sat directly opposite, any stronger exhibition of natural feeling being strictly prohibited by the mournful occasion of their meeting. And now a loud wailing and wild burst of lamentation was heard from without, as the news of their patriarch's decease spread rapidly among the thronged assemblage, manifested a universal grief for the loss they had sustained; for these simple people regarded old Tonea as the father of the nation, nor could the discernment of the nearest ties of kindred have been attended with stronger evidence of affection, than an event which they conceived to be the greatest calamity that could have befallen the tribe. No, never more in the council hall will that venerable white-haired warrior stir them with his eloquence, or instruct them with his wisdom. Never more in the "warm summer time," will he sit, as of yore, under the shadow of the broad oak, and bless his children, dancing in the calm twilight, or by the light of the silvery moon; nor will they see him smile with the joy of peace, as when the maidens would gather around decking him with sweet flowers and lifting up their voices in a song of praise.—Never more, when the snows fell, and the cold air drove the hunters to the shelter of their wigwams and the blazing fire, would they listen to Tonea as he rehearsed the legendary tales of ancient times—the warlike deeds of their ancestors until each youth, roused at the relation, longed to be a man that he might prove himself a warrior's child; and the maidens were taught to choose husbands among the just and brave, that they might be the mothers of heroes.

These reflections forced the big tears from many an iron-hearted warrior, who turned aside that men might not see how weak grief would make an Indian brave; but the women less regardful of appearances, let their tears flow on without concealment or shame. Who says that an Indian does not weep? The white man, if he feigns not sorrow, is conscious of a feeling which tells him there is a sacredness in woe that shuns observation as profanity, which seeks to hide itself from the eyes of strangers with a show of dissembling, a hollow garniture, often lacerating the torn heart it covers—such is an Indian's. Think you that cold studied look—that stern indifference of manner is an evidence of apathy and indocility? Ah! have we not often observed the native turn silently away from the unfeeling jest of the stranger, with a curl of quiet scorn upon his lip? Have we not heard the contemptuous comment, the sarcastic laugh which followed some intrusion of white men into their unpretending abodes, treating the inmates as children, forsooth! with their arrogant condescension—their unsolicited patronage; and we have blushed involuntarily for human nature and our countrymen. Go, spoiled child of fortune or artificial habit, snap for a time the heavy chains that bind you, with giant strength, to those dens where men smile and cheat by rule, growing infamous in multitude. Go and look upon the pure unhacknied face of nature; visit the wigwam of the red-man, *if you can find one*, and study, in their frugality and contentment, a lesson of wisdom, more serviceable than a volume of thread-bare precepts. There will ye find an only practical illustration of that beautiful and true moral of the poet—

"Man wants but little here below,
Nor wants that little long."

When the first violence of their sorrow had somewhat subsided,
the chief drew his father aside and acquainted him with the circumstances attending his capture; to all of which Pansaway listened
with deep attention, until his son came to mention the ambush at
the bridge, its success, the grief of the *Open-Heart*—meaning his
preserver—with his offer to assist in obtaining the release of the
Sun-Beam; when the warrior uttered the usual expression of surprise—"Ugh!" but said nothing. However, when Argimou concluded
by informing him that two of his enemies, the ruthless destroyers of
his people, were within a short distance, he started up, half drawing
the long knife at his side, while a gleam of furious wrath darted from
his swarthy face. But his kindling passion was restrained by the arm
and gesture of his son, who stood with fearless but reverential dignity
before him, while he spoke thus:

"Hear me, my father! Argimou has not the wisdom of his parent,
nor is his heart as strong; but the same rain that waters the oak makes
the small plant glad. So does the Great Spirit shed the knowledge of
good equally upon the grown man and the little child. The pale-faces
would, long ago, have dug the grave of Argimou had not one man with
a generous word saved his life, that the son might look upon his father's
face again, and be happy. That man is brave and without deceit. For
his kindness, I call him Brother; for his virtues—*The open-heart!* My
father knows that there are good men among all the red tribes, and why
may there not be a few also among the Anglasheou? True, they are our
enemies and have done us much evil; but if he saw the Open Heart
my father would say, this man is no enemy. Therefore have I sworn, by
the spirits of the air, to be just and grateful towards my brother; and
perhaps my father will also come, for we travel in an unknown path;
but his memory never sleeps, nor are his eyes dim—he can see his way

through the Milicetejik country to the banks of the Ouangondy, as well as he can follow the broad road that leads to the graves of the nation. I know my father will come."

Pansaway, while he listened to the artless appeal of his son, was affected with various emotions, altogether different from those which had excited him at the avowal of Argimou's intercourse with his foes. The feelings of the parent were awakened within, and as a flood of tenderness poured its softening influence into the Indian's heart, all his deep-grounded prejudices and antipathies were wearing imperceptibly away, as ice before a fervid stream.—Furthermore, he was aware of a personal object in the ready concurrence of his son, in a project to penetrate into the territory of the hostile Milicete, though the latter had not alluded to it in any way; so that after pondering upon the subject for some time, during which, Argimou awaited anxiously for his answer, he at length lifted up his head and said,

"My son is young, but he has the wisdom of the cobeet*; his words are very good. His father will go and show him a flower that grows by the river of many waters."

Pansaway smiled slightly, as he saw the confusion of his son at the hint conveyed in the latter portion of his reply, but Argimou merely remarked—"it is good," when both rejoined their brethren, who were now preparing the body of the deceased for its removal to the place of sepulture, in a distant part of the country, being appropriated from time immemorial as the cemetery of the tribe. After making the necessary arrangements, and deputing a subordinate chief to officiate in his stead, in the ceremonies to be observed on the inhumation of the lamented Tonea's remains, Argimou departed with his father, without exciting either the questions or curiosity of his people; his own reasons being considered sufficient to authorize any apparent inconsistency in his conduct. He tarried awhile among the poor helpless Acadians, telling them that the Micmacs would assist in erecting huts for their

---

* Beaver.

shelter, and bring them game for food; mingling words of encouragement with their *"adieus,"* the two warriors left the melancholy spot and came almost immediately, upon the advancing strangers; Edward, whose patience had been completely exhausted, having at the repeated suggestion of Dennis, at last been prevailed upon to leave their hiding place, being determined to seek out their guide, at all hazards. It was very fortunate that the rash attempt met with almost instantaneous success, for had it been otherwise, it is very doubtful if even the influence of the chief could have prevented their lives from falling a sacrifice to the exasperated feelings of the peasantry, or the fury of his own revengeful nation.

Hurrying away from the dangerous vicinity, Argimou explained to Edward enough of the foregoing scene to account for his prolonged absence, pointing out the valuable acquisition which the addition of his father would be to their party, as he was familiar with every foot of the region through which they would be obliged to pass. Edward, upon this, turned towards the strange warrior, and acquired an increase of confidence and satisfaction when he viewed his powerful frame, and bold, but melancholy countenance; though Pansaway returned not his scrutiny, but preserved a moody reserve, and seemed to regard the white men with involuntary distrust. The movements of the travellers were now directed with a greater degree of circumspection than at first, as they were in the track of the war-parties from the neighbouring tribes, all of whom not having as yet returned, there was a possibility of meeting with some of the stragglers on their journeying to the west.

However, they relaxed not their pace through the entangled forests; Edward and his servant finding it rather difficult to keep up with the rapid progress of the Indians, who, moving without noise, and with the agility of wild animals, over the trunks of dead trees, the half-hidden water courses and yielding swamps, afforded a striking contrast to the heavy tramp and uncertain, and even painful footing of their less practised companions. It was with a sensation of relief, which, though mingled with shame, Edward could not help admitting to himself, that after a tedious march they arrived at the bank of a river, near its mouth, appearing to have forced its way through a lofty hill, which rose steep and bold on either side, leaving an island in the middle of the passage, and he observed the Micmacs to throw off their burthens, as if to rest from further toil. Dennis quickly followed their example, for he was no less wearied than his master, which was surmised by the latter, from the numerous execrations that escaped him, whenever any impediment occurred to obstruct their progress, which impulsive ejaculations had become more frequent latterly, accompanied by a fearful crashing of branches, as if a buffalo were forcing its difficult way through the thick underwood, making so much noise that the careful foresters turned their heads several times with an expressive "*Ugh!*" to enjoin a greater degree of caution on the part of their unwieldy companion. But while Edward was in the act of divesting himself of his pack, Argimou, after a hurried conversation with his father, in their own language, silently left the place, and disappeared among the willow bushes that grew to the edge of the river. Some time elapsed, and still there were no signs of his return, Edward was about to question the stern-looking Pansaway, who seated with folded arms upon the bank in front, seemed totally unconscious of the presence of any human being but himself, so little did he regard the strangers; when the young chief re-appeared paddling a canoe with rapid sweeps towards them, from a point of the stream above the place where they were. Backing water gracefully, to check his swift career, the arrowy bark floated motionless beside the bank, and the Indian stepped lightly on shore; another colloquy then took place between the father and son, during which the long drawn respiration and heaving breast of the latter evinced the violence of his previous exertions. In a few minutes they commenced depositing their guns and packs within the canoe, into which Pansaway stepped carelessly and poising himself with much ease, walked along to the further end, where he seated himself upon his knees; while the chief holding the other with one hand, beckoned the rest to follow, which, with sundry misgivings and great difficulty, Edward accomplished—but here a new impediment arose. The moment that a just perception of the Indians' intention had impressed itself upon the understanding of Dennis, you would have imagined some horrible object had suddenly transfixed his vision. An expression of blank amazement and terror overspread his features, which were blanched to an unaccustomed tallow hue, the ruby tints apparently chased away from his cheeks by the intensity of his alarm, taking refuge at the end of a fungus-like nose, where they burned with a condensed radiance, perfectly fearful to witness—while in imploring accents he muttered forth,

"O mother of heaven! is it then yer honor? I can't—sure I can't; didn't I thry wasn't? an a drowned man I was, afore ye cud say by yer lave, or God save us. Didn't they rowl an rowl the could weather an th' life out o' me, a'most, afore they cud bring the sinsis back agin? And, by the same token, I tuck a great oath, says I—'may the devil fire me, and may I niver inter the gates o' glory, if iver the likes of Dennis Sherron put a fut intil wan o' that same, any more.' An sure it's a hagravation of blissed providence—it is, for a christian man to be meddlin with what's only fit for wild hathens an salvages, for doesn't yer honor know the ould jintleman helps them, and its glad we might be ourselves, if we was out of this, entirely, God presarve us!" and here the speaker crossed himself devoutly.

But there was no time to waste in argument, so that the objections of Dennis were overruled in rather a summary manner, which might be termed an application of the "*argumentum ad hominem*," for, at a sign of his master, the Indians laid violent hands upon him, and, in a twinkling, he was laid like a log, at the bottom of the canoe, where fear of being upset, kept him perfectly still, though he gave vent to his feelings by muttering occasionally in an unknown language; while Argimou placing one foot within the tottering fabric, with the other gave a strong push from the bank, that sent them out into the middle of the stream, then each seizing a paddle, applied himself to his task, causing the canoe to shoot swiftly along, while the broad blades dipped clean into the calm water, leaving only a string of hissing bubbles in their rear. Argimou then informed Edward, that, being desirous of shortening the route as much as possible, they had determined to search for the means at a well known landing place near at hand, where the Milicete war-parties generally left their canoes previous to entering the territory of the Micmacs, and he had been successful, for though further up the river than they usually landed, after some search he had discovered twenty canoes—describing the number by displaying his open hands twice, from which he had abstracted one of the best for his brother's service, and if he wished, he would teach him to use a paddle like a red warrior, to which Edward willingly consented, though his first attempts were rather awkward, occasioning several ominous lurches in the frail shallop, which forced divers groans from poor Dennis, and scraping the withe-bound gunwale with the shaft of his paddle producing a dull grating sound. But by imitating the method of the Indians he soon improved, and could not avoid admiring their steady, harmonious movements. Erect but supple, their fine figures were seen to great advantage by the free play of their arms and shoulders, as they cut into the clear water with powerful strokes, sending them forward at an exhilarating speed, while ever and anon, the oval paddle blades glanced for an instant in the sunlight, and then disappeared in the limpid element.

Chapter XI

Rounding the island at the river's mouth, they opened upon an extensive prospect of water, which was broken into sharp waves by the influence of a strong breeze, over which their little bark danced and bounded merrily, "like a thing of life," every wavelet giving a *thud*, as it struck against its thin sides. But while each leap of the canoe gave the others a glow of pleasure and excitement, poor Dennis was only conscious of the latter feeling, and what amounted to a pitch of agony; for there he lay, groaning and perspiring like a squeezed sponge, though he was sufficiently moistened by the salt spray that occasionally greeted him from the paddle of his master, or the crest of an unruly billow.

Coasting along the eastward shores of the bay at its termination, the "*voyageurs*" entered a spacious estuary, called the Indians Petito Condac; but since then, better known by the name of the Petico-diac; the expanse of which was shadowed by the bold elevation of its western banks, and beyond, the lofty ridge of the Shepody mountain obscured the rays of the now declining sun. Crossing over to the left shore they glided into still water again, and paddled on under the cool shade without a moment's relaxation. The Micmacs threw a searching glance up the river, but nothing appeared to create suspicion—all was still around. No living thing was seen upon the unbroken surface, save, occasionally, a fish leaping out of its depths, leaving a rippling circle behind; and now and then a loon would appear, like a dark spot in the distance, but it dived instantaneously upon their approach, and reappeared far behind the canoe; while sometimes a solitary duck would skim like an arrow along the river, almost touching the water with its pointed rapid wing. Edward was gazing with sadness upon the peaceful beauty of the scene around, when a sudden exclamation of surprise from Pansaway drew his attention to a clayey spot on the shore they were then passing, to which the warrior pointed with his finger, as he rested on his dripping paddle. A backward sweep of Argimou's arm whirled the canoe immediately toward the place; he also emitting the guttural "Ugh!" when he recognised the object that had attracted the notice of his father. Quickly leaping on the strand, they bent themselves down in close examination of several footprints plainly distinguishable in the tenacious soil among which were to be seen the marks of a horse's hoof. A brief survey sufficed to satisfy the sagacious natives, for Argimou, leading Edward to the place, and pointing beneath, said quietly:

"The *Sun-beam* has passed here."

"Ha! is it so?" replied Edward with emotion, but adding in a tone of doubt—"How know ye this? I see no marks by which these traces can be distinguished from those of an ordinary party."

"Can a red-man forget, or is a warrior blind?" replied the chief haughtily, roused at the want of confidence in his skill, implied in the question of the other; than which nothing could more easily pique the pride of an Indian brave.

"Look, the Open-Heart has eyes, and he can feel. You see this mocassin tread? Well, is it not very long; but that's no matter. See the big toe how it sticks out beyond all the rest, making the foot sharp, all one same like the beak of a Milicetejik canoe, that's only fit for torching in calm rivers, while you see all the other marks be

93

round like a Micmac *quetan** so he can hunt porpoise within the salt water, when the big waves boil, and he will be always dry. The first is Madokawando, the rest are his warriors. Does my brother see the prints of iron mocassins? What animal is it that leaves *them*? yea, surely the daughter of the pale-faces has been here."

If the lover was not thoroughly convinced by evidence, which to the acute perceptions of the hunters was clear as daylight—he was shortly undeceived, for a low call from Argimou's father, who had followed the trail a short distance through the trees, brought them quickly to his side, where the indubitable traces of a recent bivouac were discovered, and the very scanty shelter of branches, under which Clarence was rightly supposed to have slept—presented to the eyes of the agitated lover by the triumphant Argimou.

With uncontrollable emotion Edward threw himself upon the ground, watering with his tears the spot which was rendered sacred to him from having once sustained the pressure of his beloved; loud sobs shook his prostrate frame, and seemed as if almost rending his disordered breast.

The stoical Indians beheld with unfeigned surprise these demonstrations of grief in the soldier. Taught as they were from their earliest years to conceal all signs and expressions of suffering, as unworthy of a warrior, a feeling of contempt, for what they deemed a reprehensible weakness in the Englishman, rose in the minds of both; which, however, in Argimou at least, was soon softened by a touch of compassion.

The reader can surmise the source from whence, as from a clear fountain, a sudden stream of pity gushed within the heart of the chief. Had not that one common sentiment unconsciously created, from the first, a bond of sympathy between this rude forest child, and the polished, but pure minded stranger?

When the poignant sensibilities of the lover had somewhat subsided, he noticed the many indications of a temporary sojourn of those

* Canoe.

94

holding captive the dear object of his thoughts and aims, and marked the direction of the route the party had taken, running, as it did, along the bank of the river, expressing, at the same time an earnest wish that they would push on in pursuit without an instant's delay.

Upon their return to the canoe they found Dennis seated upon its edge, comfortably curling a cloud of white smoke from the corner of his mouth, for he had made shift, with flint and steel, to light his pipe—as great a curiosity as its owner, by the way—and seemed more reconciled to his fate. At that moment he had finished trying to settle with his conscience—whether he was responsible, considering the circumstances, for the infraction of his oath; but being unable to arrive at any definite conclusion in his mind, he did as others do on similar occasions, dismissed the subject: being inwardly resolved to consult the priest upon the first occasion that offered, as, doubtless, his reverence would settle the matter to his satisfaction.

Following the course of the river, they propelled their bark onward until they emerged from the deep shadow of the hills; then crossing over to the eastern side, the adventurers landed at a convenient spot near the junction of a tributary stream; for the sun had long set, and a strong current began to impede their progress, as the tide was on its ebb. Lifting the canoe bodily from the water, the guides made choice of a secluded spot among the trees; and kindling a fire, made preparations for passing the night—the underwood being cleared away, the arms and other articles deposited in divers places near at hand, and blankets spread upon the mossy ground. The light of the fire diffused a cheerful glow upon the little circle, tinging the foliage around, which formed a natural bower above their heads; and so calm and quiet was the evening air that not a leaf was in motion, save, only, where the heat and smoke, rushing upward, made them quiver as they escaped into the pure atmosphere beyond. After partaking of a simple meal of dried venison, prepared by the Indians, Edward stretched his fatigued limbs upon the soft moss, and wrapping his cloak around him was soon buried in sleep; nor was Dennis backward in following his example. But the forresters trimmed the fire and disposed themselves gravely by its side. Pansaway, filling a tobacco bowl in the back of his war-hatchet, lighted it and drew several long whiffs from its hallow stem without speaking, he then handed it to Argimou, who also puffed awhile, after which he returned it again to his father. In this manner the two-fold implement—emblematic of peace or war, according to its uses—was handed from one to the other three distinct times, when the elder warrior, replenishing it from his pouch, broke the silence by alluding to the object of their present journey; and proposing two different routes by which their purpose could be effected. One by pursuing the trail of Madokawando, which was the shortest and would lead them directly to the banks of the great river, where he knew the chief's village to be situated. The other was to follow the Peticodiac to its head waters, and from thence cross over to the St. John; a more circuitous journey, but presenting less difficulties than the first, as they would thus in some measure avoid the danger of meeting with war-parties of the Milicete, and lessen the distance they would have to travel on foot; which, though hardly an object to them, would nevertheless be a great relief to the pale-faces, who, as was evident, were unused to the woods, and unable to encounter its toils with impunity. The speaker avowed himself in favour of the latter course, but desired his son to offer his opinion on the subject, which he did with much deference, suggesting that the delay necessarily attendant on their deviation from a direct path to the sunset, more than counterbalanced the objections to an overland passage, therefore, though he fully admitted the truth of what his father had said, and he was much wiser than himself; still he was inclined towards their adoption of the roads first proposed.

When the young warrior had finished his remarks, Pansaway quietly laid his tomahawk down, and taking a burnt stick from the fire, traced upon a piece of white birch bark, the several courses of the Peticodiac and the St. John, with the lakes and tributary streams lying intermediate. Then, with a slight emphasising gesture and utterance, he pointed out with his finger the several lines upon his rude, but intelligible map; showing his son that the deflection was not so great as he imagined.—That the former river, though it appeared to come from the frost, would soon turn in the required direction, and so continue until near its head, when it bent backward and terminated in two small branches. That at its upper curve, a small portage would carry them, if requisite, at once into a broad-water that ran into Ouangondy; but he proposed to take a well known path which would lead them sooner to the latter. And finally, he dwelt upon the unpromising nature of the wide hilly tract of country, covered with dense forests, through which it was his son's desire they should journey to the sunset. Argimou, impressed with the force of the arguments adduced against his proposition, saw its inutility, and immediately yielded to the superior experience of his parent. Confiding most implicitly in his knowledge and sagacity, he entrusted their further progress entirely to the management and guidance of the latter, whereupon Pansaway, apparently satisfied, drew his blanket over his shoulders and laid down to repose, leaving the young chief to watch over the security of the bivouac.

Edward woke in the night rather suddenly, for he dreamed that he was struggling with a number of fierce savages who held him down with superhuman strength, while others were dragging off Clarence into the thick woods, that seemed to swallow her up forever from his eyes; and, O God! that dread shriek again pierced through his brain, yet he could not free himself from the hands that held him in their grasp. Disturbed by the terrible intensity of the vision, and that wild cry for help, Edward for a moment, thought the fearful sound still lingered in his ear, though his eyes were open, and his senses perfectly collected. But all was as silent as the grave, save the seething of a

half-rotten log, on the fire, over which a few distracted ants were running with wild agitation, as the heat drove them from their retreat in its
interior, and gradually encroached upon their only remaining place of
refuge, until they fell, one by one into the smoky flames; or, occasionally, a long heavy breath from the sleepers beside him. Beyond the
fire, and scarcely recognisable in the dim light, he observed the dark
figure of Argimou, upright, still and motionless as the trees around.
He was about to speak to the Indian, when again the sound which had
started him from sleep, rang through the forest, arresting the faculty of
speech, and causing his flesh to quiver, so wild, thrilling and unnatural
it seemed. It was unlike anything he had ever heard, yet it approached
nearer to the cry of a human being in torture, partaking the character
both of a scream and a holloa than aught that at the time, he could
attribute it to; and it appeared to issue from the very heart of the forest,
echoing among the groves, and reverberating from the hills and projecting shores of the river.

In the meantime, Argimou observing a movement among the
sleepers, turned his head towards the fire, and seeing the astonishment
depicted in the face of Edward, his own composed features relaxed in a
smile as he said playfully—

"Does my brother know that voice?"

"It is some one in distress," replied the other, hurriedly, "let us haste
to his deliverance;" and the soldier was in the act of springing upon his
feet, when the chief approaching, put his hand upon his shoulder, and
said—

"Stop! I will bring him to my brother;" and placing his hands to his
mouth, he gave a long, clear cry, so perfectly resembling that which
he had heard, that Edward at first fancied it to proceed from the
same throat. The effect was instantaneous, for both Pansaway and
Dennis bounded from the ground as if they had been shot through
the heart, though the former quickly recovered his composure, after a

few explanatory words in the Indian language had been addressed to him by his son, who motioned the half awakened Irishman to make no noise, with which request he found it exceedingly difficult to comply; being strangely puzzled to account for the unseasonable uproar. Hark! another repetition of the same discordant scream, with variations, penetrates, painfully, their ears; not, as at first, softened and indistinct from distance, but apparently uttered from the very tree under which they were gathered. Edward's eye instinctively sought among its dark branches for the cause—but in vain. At that moment, the twang of a bow-string was heard, and a light streak glanced upward among the leaves from the place where the chief sat; a faint shriek followed by a bundle of feathers fell heavily at the feet of Edward. The mystery was explained; for, gazing at him with closed eyes he beheld the quaint, venerable-looking face of a dying *owl*.

"An troth, a clever man he wor, that gave it that name," remarked Dennis, "for devil a bird ever *owled* the likes of it afore, anny way, an that's the truth."

After this incident, Pansaway took his son's place as sentinel, in spite of Edward's entreaty that he himself should fulfil that duty, while his companions reposed. But they would not admit of any such thing, well knowing the fatigue of the Englishman, and the difficulty one unused to their habits, would have in overcoming the natural tendency of sleep. Edward therefore resumed his attitude of rest, but busy thought chased away slumber from his eyelids. How dissimilar were the relative positions of his native companions and himself.—Here in the great wilds, where the knowledge and resources of civilised life were worthless as chaff, and he felt himself as a child endeavouring to read a book, of the characters of which he is entirely ignorant; here were beings apparently as familiar with the mysterious secrets, the subtile indications of nature's working in the wilderness, as the European with the principles of an art he practises, drawing forth wisdom from its original source, rendering every material subservient to some useful purpose, and supplying those natural wants which are essential to the comfort and happiness of man, simply and effectually.—While to the creatures of civilization, the very perfection of means creates a multiplicity of necessities, and in thought, as in habit, they become artificial and depraved—in fact—mere rickety machines. The sated tastes crave for the indulgence of unnatural luxuries to stimulate their exhausted powers, until the hydra disease, multiplied and nourished by the festering, vitiated system, coils its serpent folds securely within their vitals; and surely, a sophisticated morality must ever accompany physical abasement. So thought Edward, and we leave it to the unprejudiced philosopher to determine, not the justice of his arguments, but the actual degree of their general application. Then he *listened*, long and intently, to the awful silliness of the surrounding woods, broken only at times, by those indefinable sounds produced by the creaking of one tree against another—which so often startles one in the forest; though there was not a breath of air stirring. The wind seemed dead, and night to sorrow for its departed moan. His reflections naturally wandered from the deep repose to the myriads of living things, hidden beneath the leaves, or in the secret lairs, now hushed and powerless by the spell of slumber; their natural fierceness rendered innocuous by that best physician of the weary earth—sleep. Subdued by its potency, the grim bear forgot his strength and his hunger—the fox his craft—the rabbit his timidity. No struggle for life, no care for food; there was a brief truce between the robber and his prey; and Peace, taking advantage of the temporary suspension, of that universal law, which, for some wise, though mysterious purpose, has bequeathed eternal strife and carnage to the world—stole softly down and pressed her lips upon the aching brow and the wayward heart.

Chapter XII

With the dawn they were up and moving, for the boar of the tide was already rushing upward from the sea with great noise and impetuosity. Taking advantage of the rapid current, they launched the canoe and darted along with swift speed up the river; the shelving mud banks of which were quickly disappearing, as the encroaching fluid poured in from its mouth, and filled its half empty bed. Ere long, the correctness of Pansaway's observation was fully proved, for the stream made a gradual bend toward the west, or, as he would have significantly termed it, to the sunset; and so they went on, hour after hour, uninterrupted by sign or sound of any human being. Once Edward ceased paddling, and directed the attention of the foresters to a low, dark object moving slowly along the water, from a distant point above. But he was told, that what he fancied a canoe, was only the trunk of some tree, uptorn by the tempest, or decayed with age and washed from its place by the freshet floods when the snows thaw. Sometime afterwards they came up with it, and as the canoe shot past, it looked like the blackened corpse of some dead dryad of the woods. Its scraggy arms protruding bare and leafless from the gigantic trunk, were deformed with shreds and gouts of slimy swamp grass and interlaced brambles, uprooted in its struggles to cling to its more congenial element. It appeared to have been floating about for a lengthy period, having altogether, a most dreary, woe-worn aspect. Argimou related that sometimes, by such a tree grounding in shallow parts, or becoming entangled with rocks or projecting branches from the shore, multitudes of other wind-falls were intercepted in their passage to the salt water, until the channel is altogether closed with organic remains, and in this way many rivers become completely choked in their upper courses, and thus continue impervious to the "*voyageur*" for many years, oftentimes causing an inundation of the surrounding country, until they are destroyed by means of fire, or some great storm or freshet bursts the barricade with tremendous force, leaving the pent-up waters again free.

The river became narrower as they advanced, until it was altogether shaded by the foliage of the beautiful birch and maple trees, growing to the water's edge, and they glided beneath a continuous bower, while the sunlight glanced like silver on the breeze-ruffled leaves, though they were themselves sheltered from the heat of its midday beam. The wild grape hung in graceful festoons from the supporting branches, intermingling and lost in the profuse verdure around; and, here and there, some half-hidden flower would woo the passing eye with its contrasting tint, or peculiar formation. And, oft times, the brief mournful call of a bird would echo an instant, among the leafy arcades; and then the silence of the solitude seemed never to have been broken by so clear and musical a sound.

At length, as the ebbing tide prevented them from making any progress without considerable difficulty, they landed, and shouldering the canoe, the travellers followed the bank of the river for many miles. With much ease the Indians carried their burthen, which was at last deposited in a small gully, overgrown with willows, and carefully concealed, in case they should require its services thereafter.

Here a rest was made, and the party refreshed themselves with a hearty meal of moose meat, after which, a short consultation was held by Edward and his guides; the latter explaining the course they deemed it most prudent to follow, in their passage through the Milicete country, on the borders of which they now were. Edward, as may be supposed, was only too willing to concur in their views, being well aware of his incapability of judging in a matter so foreign to his usual sphere of intelligence. He merely urged them to make no unnecessary delay—for a feeling of restlessness had taken possession of his mind, and even the arrow-like speed with which they had travelled, hitherto, appeared slow and tortuous to the swiftness he deemed compatible with his wishes. Something seemed to gnaw incessantly within, and would not give him a moment's rest or ease, unless he were constantly in motion. Strapping on their packs, they proceeded on with increased caution, as it was thought probable there might be some of the Milicete encamped thereabouts, for the purpose of fishing, the river being a favourite resort at that season. However, though they passed several fresh traces of their fires and wigwams, they met with no hindrance to their progress. Deviating from the bank of the river, near its upper bend, they plunged directly westward through the forest, and arrived in the evening at a small spring; from which, when Pansaway had cleared away a thick coat of dead leaves that concealed it, a clear, cool stream welled out of the rocky ground and lost itself in the moss that fringed its border, like a carpet of richest green. The Indian bent down and took a long draught, smiling as he beheld his stern features reflected, mirror-like, in its dark depth. But the expression soon changed to sadness, when he remembered the long years that had passed since he last saw his face in that spring; and he traced the changes time had made upon its lineaments, but felt them to be far less than the scars vicissitude had graven upon his heart.

They spent that night under the beech trees which grew plentifully around the natural fountain, and Edward bore his portion of watching, being relieved towards morning by Dennis, on trial. But, alas! for the competency of human resolve, when arrayed against the strong fortress of disposition or confirmed habit; he kept awake bravely for a certain period, equivalent to the time generally allotted a sentry, by the rules of military service, for quiet meditation, or to give him an appetite for sleep, ere a relief enables him to test the virtue of the experiment— after which, feeling rather drowsy and uncomfortable, a sound might have been heard similar to that produced by the sudden extraction of a cork, followed immediately by a backward inclination of his head and shoulders towards the stars, at which he appeared to be gazing through a short telescope, until, apparently satisfied with his astronomical observation, he recovered his former position, and lighting his pipe, rubbed his eyes with the back of his hand, looking quite brisk and wakeful, muttering, at the same time, something about the impossibility of catching a weazel asleep, or Dennis Sherron. How long an impartial observer would have considered, as just, a comparison between the two animals, we cannot say, but the fact is incontestable, that when Argimou awoke, it was broad day-break, and Dennis was fast asleep; emitting, through his nose and mouth, sounds similar to a saw and axe working for a wager, and his pipe was still clutched between his teeth, though it had long expired; yet, nevertheless, he gave it a hard suck now and then, in his sleep, as if he were smoking in a dream—and when the chief shook him by the shoulder, he mumbled indistinctly, "guard turn out!" and "weasels be d——d!"

There would be little to interest the reader, in dwelling upon the several incidents that rendered the day's journey less irksome than it would otherwise have been. Edward beheld with astonishment, the extraordinary growth which vegetation acquired in those solitudes; the great girth of some trees, the wire-drawn height of others, as if in the constant effort to reach the air and light, above the gloomy and crowded space. Their lower branches were sear and brittle, snapping at a touch; but their leaf-crowned tops waved, like feathery plumes in the breeze that played over the forest, though no breath disturbed the indefinable stillness beneath, nor was there aught to indicate its existence, but a constant sound, like a roar of agitated waters. He noticed also many strange freaks of nature, such as trees and branches twisted and bent in every variety of unusual posture, and bulged out in enormous tumefactions, as if endeavouring to get rid of the excess of nutrition; while, projecting horizontally from the huge boles, broad funguses were seen, spreading their lobes and lobules, one over the other, of various and brilliant colours.

Now and then on reaching some lofty ridge, the eye could range over miles of hill and valley, all covered with the thick, interminable forest. It was magnificent to see the different shades produced by the peculiar nature of the trees, or the intervention of a cloud, as it sailed overhead, obscuring the sun's rays which shone with increased brilliancy upon other parts of the prospect; and all was in motion. The trees waved and bowed gracefully to the warm breeze, as it swept along the hill sides, tossing the foliage like green waves; and over this majestic scene the vision wandered in an ecstacy of delight, while the soul felt awed by its intense solitude—for there were no traces of man or any living thing in its beautiful retreats and no sounds were heard to break the eternal stillness, but the occasional note of a bird, or the moan of the homeless wind.

At one time they were entangled among the mouldering remains of an ancient grove, prostrated by some devastating storm, and piled in indescribable confusion around. Over these wind-falls, at the expense of several bruises, the white men toiled painfully, but the agile Indians leaped in their mocassins from trunk to trunk, with the lightness of squirrels, poising themselves gracefully as they stepped along the slippery bridges; sometimes high above the heads of their companions. By the time this impediment was overcome, Edward and his servant were completely tired out, so that they were obliged to halt. Meanwhile, some wild pidgeons, which were very numerous thereabouts, almost darkening the sky as they flew over in large flocks, had been struck by the never-failing arrow of Argimou—who forebore to use his gun, as he was fearful of alarming some straggling party of Milicete that might be in the vicinity. These being soon denuded of their feathers, were split open and roasted, affording a delightful repast to the wearied travellers. Indeed, the sight even made an old, hungry wood-pecker's mouth water, who was clawing up the side of a hollow tree, hard by; and, forthwith, he commenced tapping away furiously with his bill, in search of live ants, which were bolted raw—he holding in thorough contempt all culinary processes whatsoever. Refreshed by the savoury food, Edward fell into a contemplative mood, to which, in fact, he was rather prone, as the reader may have discovered ere this. As the Micmacs were finishing their frugal meal, he thought how little, after all, the luxury, the advantages of a civilised state of society, were capable of ameliorating the moral or physical condition of man. What benefit had art and intellectual culture, after the lapse of thousands of years, conferred upon his nation that these simple children of Nature did not receive from their mother's hand, unsolicited? His belief in the progressive improvement of the human race was shaken, as the lamentable truth forced itself upon his understanding, that mankind seemed to have journeyed further from the right, as they deviated from the plain habits and principles of the primitive ages. Was there want and woe and crippling disease among the haunts of luxury and wealth? Here in the rude forests he beheld plenty, cheerfulness, and frames untainted by the enervating maladies of the Old World. Here, among men unrestrained by penal codes, or chains, or strong dungeons, were to be found the most unflinching virtue; the elements of a beautiful philosophy; a mortality that would put to shame that thing of cir- cumstance, which in cities takes shelter under the name, as though hypocrisy could deceive heaven with the same facility that it mocketh man! Did the bigoted followers of a gloomy creed pay their blind vows at the altar of an earthly idol, in mistake for the divinity? here, in these deep, solemn shades was a temple "not made with hands;" where "even the green leaves seemed stirred with prayer," the soul turned irresistibly to the worship of the true and only God. And here the poor Indian lifts up his voice in earnest gratitude to the Great Spirit—the author of all blessings—to him who sends the summer to melt the snows, to fill the desert places with the song of birds, the track of wild game;—whose voice is heard in the thunder—whose power is made manifest in the storm. And why should his prayer be rejected and the white man's heard? Here were no fawning sycophants, no slanderers of their neighbours, no smiling faces with false hearts, no robbers in the garb of honesty, no niggards that would grasp the accursed gold and see their brethren starve. When men met in the wilderness it was as sincere friends, or open, determined foes.

"O! worse than a bloody hand is a hard heart!"

Reflecting somewhat thus, upon the character of those nations, denominated savage—thereby, as with a sweeping censure, excluding them from the pale of human sympathy or association, he reverted to those ancient tribes that have become bywords for virtue, bravery, and all those qualities which make one people greater than another, by rules drawn from those subtle truths taught them through deep observation of the natural and moral world; subduing by the force of the indomitable will, the weakness attendant upon humanity, until their very children became heroes. And he discovered a great resemblance between those remarkable people and the hunters of the new world.

With recruited strength the party pushed on, crossing a river, near its source, which appeared to flow northward, but Pansaway—whose reserve had gradually worn off, as he became more accustomed to the presence of the strangers, and imparted much information to Edward, relating to the country through which they were travelling, though he spoke the French "patois" much less fluently than his son—informed him that after one day's journey, it turned to the sunset, and grew very broad before it joined Ouangondy, near its junction with the salt water, and its name was Kennebeckasis; furthermore, at its mouth was situated the Milicete village, where, doubtless, they would find the one they sought. Stimulated by this intelligence, Edward forgot his fatigue, and, increasing his exertions, they arrived at nightfall on the banks of a second river near a lake, from which it seemed to take its origin.

Here they made their bivouac, and the soldiers, completely worn out by their day's tramp, were glad to cast themselves on the soft ground, deeming it the most luxuriant couch they ever rested upon, nor was it long ere they were both immersed in the oblivion of sleep. But as for the Indians, their tough sinews and hardened, compact frames appeared incapable of weariness. Lighting their pipes they extinguished the fire, and conversing together beneath the light of the rising moon, now nearly full, sailing in the misty sea of light clouds, subduing without rendering altogether obscure, its rays. The wippoorwill uttered incessantly, its triple call to the night; not in sorrow, but rather as if, like some great king rejoicing in his solitude, it strove to fill the whole voiceless forest with its unaccompanied song.

The old warrior was occupied in a manner which above all things an Indian loves, namely, recalling the traditions handed down by his fathers, from the earliest times, which are perpetuated with wonderful fidelity, by oral transmission alone. Then is it, that these singular people are enabled to indulge largely, in those talents for oratory and metaphor, which are so peculiarly the gifts of the red man.

Pansaway, as they proceeded on a journey, every step of which reminded him of some past scene, had become more absorbed as it were, in the recollections of a former period of his life. At the present moment, however, his reflections were deep in the perusal of an old legend that had been lying carefully preserved like a scroll, in his memory, since he was a child, and only required a moment's abstraction of thought to render its characters as distinct and legible as when they were first impressed upon its tenacious page. At length he laid his *to-ma-gan* down, and raising his right arm impressively, said to the attentive chief as follows,

"The *wick-quill-yetch** tells his tale in the beam of the round moon, but Pansaway will read a *belt* by the light of times that are gone. Listen, my son! to thy father's words, that when he goes hence they may not be forgotten like a coward's deeds. They are the words thy sires have spoken—the deeds they have done! I am the son of Natanis, whose father was Sabatis, a just man and a famous warrior that lived when the great Mambertou was bashaba of the Micmacs; about the time that the *pale-faces* first came from the great waters beyond the sunrise, to the red man's country, and asked a little ground to build their huts and plant corn; for they said they were sick with their long journey on the salt water, and very hungry. So the Sagamou's heart grew soft to the strangers, and he gave them land, and when they would have all perished—for the snows were deep and very cold, the Micmac brought them food from the forest, and preserved them from death. When the thaw came, many more war canoes with great eagle-wings whiter than the gull's, and filled with warriors, flew over with the wind, from that unknown country; and the Sagamou wondered that they should wander so far to see a strange land, and what they wanted of the poor Indian—for he had only the skins of wild animals—his stone arrow—his strong heart—his fathers' graves; but these strangers were rich and powerful with precious ornaments and clothes that the squaws love, and they used the Great Spirit's thunder in battle. Yet they said they only came to see their brothers, the Micmacs, and smoke peace with them, and the Sagamou wondered, for he had never heard his fathers tell of this nation, nor was there any belt that preserved their name or their friendship. But they were very peaceful and generous, and built a fort and armed it with the great thunder. But the Micmacs were not afraid, for they were brave and numerous, having

---

* Wippoorwill.

just returned from the frost, after fighting the Esquimeaux for many moons. But the hatchet was still unburied; the marriage song unsung.

"Listen, O my son! to the words thy fathers have spoken—to the deeds they have done!

"Who can count the green, salt waves? The hairs of the head who has numbered? Such were the tribes of the sunrise—such were the great Adenaci! Thick as the quills of the mat-tu-wess,* were their arrows; their arms, as the whirlwind, strong. When the fierce eagle screamed, they laughed; they jeered when the storm howled! Yea, louder than many eagles or the north wind's voice, was the sound of their war-cry;—when they whooped the black bears trembled!

"But why are the tribes gathering? Why is the bow strung? Because the war-path is open, and it leads to the country of the Armouche-quois.† Over the broad sky there are clouds. On the salt lake there are waves; and red as the blood we must shed, are the streaks that the sun-set leaves.

"The white foam dashes in the roaring wind. The keen lightning quivers. The rocks and the hills are shaken! Yet in the storm, and the thunder, and the darkness, went Mambertou and his warriors, from the Micmac country to the tribe of the Ouangondy. Their course was known by the stars. By the great northern bear were they guided; they were lighted by the pale fires of the north.

"Peol Atteou came with the Mareachite warriors, and Toquelmut, the fierce eyed, with his Terratines—wild as the carriboo, and as swift: light as the birds of the air. Like the fins of the sea-dog—like the roll of the black porpoise, was the dip of countless paddles in the wave of the great-water. Green as the leaves on the tree, or the grass of summer, was the path in which they travelled.

"The rivers came down with the red men in swarms. From the Passamaquoddy, the Penobscot, the Kennebis, and their thousand isles

---

* Porcupine.

† A numerous and powerful people, inhabiting the country near Cape Malabarre—(Cape Cod.)

came war-parties. Their faces were terrible with war-paint, and when they shouted their battle-song the strong winds grew still! Listen, O, my son! to the words thy fathers have spoken—to the deeds they have done!

"There remained not one wigwam in the country of the Armouchequois! The tribes of the sunrise came, like a fire in the forest, and consumed them, root and branch. Their villages were made desolate by the storm. The owl screeched in the lone council-hall! In the grove lay their dead, unburied. The snows made them a pale grave, and their spirits were glad; but when the thaw came, their ghosts lamented over their uncovered bones! The wolf picked them clean; in the wind and rain were they whitened. What will their children say, when they are asked for their fathers' graves? They are a dishonoured people! Like a red man's hair are the long black weeds, where the salt waters come and go. The white foam licks the rocks and plays with their floating scalps, like the locks of a drowning man; while the white-gull shrieks, and the cold waves moan.

"In the sun, in the moonlight, in the storm, by the rocks, by the isles, by the great mountain, the tribes returned to the mourning. In joy, and in grief they came. Over the foe they had triumphed: over their dead warriors they mourned. In skins of the dark otter were they wrapped, in skins of the precious beaver. They must rest in a cedar grave, by the bones of their fathers. Can they sleep in a strange land? Their spirits glide in the evening track—in the trail of the red sun they follow. They go to the hunting grounds of the just, with the foeman's scalp and the brave man's spear!

"By the Kennebis, the Penobscot, the tribes returned to their homes, by the branching Piscataqua. From the isles of the Passama-quod to the rushing Ouangondy, there was a sound of joy, there were songs of rejoicing warriors.

"But Mambertou went on to the mourning, over the blue waves. Between the Etchemins and the Sourquois the salt-water rolls. He comes to drink the fresh rivers, like a thirsty man. He comes and goes with a sun, and swells very large in the light of the bright, round moon. Beyond the big-drink was the Micmac country; it looked the same like a bank of grey smoke—bodiless and dim. Why should a Micmac fear the thick mist, or the howling storm? Is he not the hunter of the salt-water? Is he not born within its roar?

"In the mountain, where the ice never melts, where the salt mist curls. In the great vallies, by the rivers of the moose and bear, there do our warriors dance—there is the pipe lighted! The wampum is woven—the scalps are dried—the hatched is buried? The braves rest in the shade and tell their deeds. The children listen and burn—the maidens turn pale with fear.—The father's place is empty no longer in his wigwam, or by the council fire of the nation.

"And Mambertou made a strong friendship with the *Wennooch*; its chain shall never grow rusty! The old bashaba and the pale-faced chief were like brothers in their love. In his arms Mambertou died. A warrior may be brave, but he cannot live for ever. Who, like the white-haired Mambertou, has seen twelve hundred moons rise? You might count their number in the scars upon his breast! His name could never die!

"Such is the story of Mambertou, when he went with the tribes of the sunrise to fight the Armouchequois, in ancient times. Such, my son, are the words they fathers have spoken—the deeds they have done!"

Pansaway ceased, but his chest still swelled with proud emotion which the relation of this tradition had awakened; and his dark eye gleamed, bright and piercing in the moonlight. While the attitude of the chief resembled that of a wild cat, ere it makes its deadly spring; so much was his fierceness roused by the wild legend of his father. Grasping, with iron clutch, the long knife at his side, he appeared upon the point of pealing forth the dread whoop from his parted lips. When he had recovered sufficient composure to speak, he said with emphasis—

"Ugh! Mambertou was a great warrior!"

"Ay," replied Pansaway—"many times has the axe been sharp-ened, the war-song sung.—Many times has the Micmac bent his bow against the light-haired stranger, who is greedy as the blue eyed *pedge-a-way**. Many times has the earth drunk blood. Yet never since that time has such a warrior been seen among the hunters of the Micmac. But why should I—a humble man, try to brighten the name of the great Mambertou? Who has not heard of his deeds. Who has not seen his grave?"

The old Indian having concluded his story, laid himself down qui-etly to sleep, while Argimou kept watch until midnight.

At that time, Edward—as had previously desired, was awakened by the chief who relinquished his duty to the soldier, and sought his own scanty portion of rest, though not until, with habitual caution, he had placed his carbine at his side ready for instant use, in case of sudden alarm, for between the place where he lay and the sloping bank of the river, were only a few thin bushes, through the stems of which glistened the broken, shallow water.

Hour after hour, the soldier sat at his post, thinking of *her* and his distant home, without a whisper to break the current of his reveries, except the murmur of the adjacent river, as it laved the bank, or was parted by the rocky impediments in its course; even the lonely wippoorwill had long since ceased its song. Then he imagined that many persons were near him, and that they were speaking—he could even hear distinctly the words they uttered; but strange to say, although they resembled in garb and features, the Indians with whom he journeyed, yet he knew them to be his friends, for they spoke of old events that had happened, and called him by name. Starting up, all at once, he could scarcely believe at first that he had been dreaming; but all was still and quiet as usual. Angry with himself, that he should have allowed sleep to overtake him, he determined to be more watch-ful, and to cure a disagreeable heaviness in his eyelids—treacherous

* Codfish.

113

experiment—he commenced counting the stars, that were becoming more visible in the north-east as the moon declined. This, at first, seemed very easy, but their scintillation soon confused his sight, and finally, they appeared countless, and then—but he thought it quite natural—they performed a dance, in imitation of the gnats he had noticed that afternoon, gambolling in a shady nook, by the river side.— That was the last thing he remembered.

Chapter XIII

The day was about breaking when Argimou awoke, suddenly—for something was snuffing and snorting violently above him as he lay. Turning his head softly, he looked up and beheld what, at that moment, made his strong nerves tremble with superstitious fear. He thought, as he afterwards said, that *Mun-doo** was looking at him; but recollection soon came to his aid, and with it returned the wild courage of the warrior.

Directly over him, with starting eyes and nostrils expanded, was the head of a large moose, protruding from the willow branches in which its body was hidden, and apparently under the influence of extreme terror; for its long upper lip was retracted from the glistening teeth, and upon its stretched neck the stiff hairs rose like the bristles of a wild boar. When, to complete this apparition, we add, that the forehead of the animal was furnished with a pair of broad, branching antlers, the first sensation that predominated in the mind of the half-awakened Indian, may well be excused. When Argimou had regained his self possession, he sought immediately the gun at his side, which

---

* The evil-spirit, Satan. This curious rencounter, with the ludicrous incident to which it gave rise, actually occurred, though at a different period; and it is related as told the author by the Indian hunter to which it happened, some years since.

was drawn forward slowly and without noise, though his arm shook with intense excitement. Laying a finger on the trigger, and pointing the barrel among the leaves—as nearly as possible in the direction he imagined the body of the animal to be concealed; for one second not a fibre of his frame quivered—then a loud explosion rattled sharply over the woods, which was instantaneously followed by a shrill cry. The moose gave a spring forward over the body of his destroyer, and across the startled sleepers, striking Dennis smartly with his hoof, as he fell with a heavy crash among the branches of the thicket beyond.

Now the individual thus unceremoniously treated, was a bit of a practical philosopher, and an "ould champaigner," and being strongly impressed with the necessity of that primal law, denominated self-preservation, he had, with a praiseworthy solicitude for the promotion of science, and its being made applicable to the amelioration of man's condition here, with, also, great thought and self-mortification, as a step in the grand scheme—discovered what he conceived to be the great "*helewent*" which interfered most with the comfort of the human system. Nor was he the only wiseacre that regarded Nature as the inveterate enemy of mankind. Plodding, like his betters, in the quagmire of metaphysics, he traced effects to their maternal origin, and, at last, concluded that *cold*, or, in scientific language the negation of caloric, was the adversary he had to overcome; for he observed that all life came from heat, which axiom he deduced from many familiar examples, such as the germination of "praties," the hatching of chickens, etc.; and it followed, as a plain inference, that any deprivation of that essential quality, would cause an approximation to the opposite extreme. And was it not the case? was not cold the blighter of vegetation, the terror of the animal kingdom, the nipper of noses; and did not all bodies become cold as soon as the life was out of them? But what occasioned him most immediate alarm was this. In the course of his philanthropic investigations he ascertained that there was inherent in the human body a continual tendency to cool, and he strove to overcome this propensity, as the main cause of man's want of longevity, in later ages; for it was clear that when a certain quantity of heat was deficient in the system, the person must die. So that, it might be said, he firmly believed that within the two principles, heat and cold, were "clasped the limits of mortality."

He had another idea, equally original. He thought that the blood of man rose and subsided twice in twenty-four hours, simultaneously with the tides, with a circulation somewhat similar to that of the sap in trees; flowing upwards from the feet to the head, and "*viceversa*." Now, to correct the injurious defect in his own constitution, he had early taken to the use of strong drinks, to create an artificial stimulus, and keep up the desirable "*quantum*" of warmth in his inner man. Deriving astonishing comfort thereby, and following up his experiment, he devised a plan to fortify his outer man, during the unavoidable exposure to which he was subject when on a campaign. This was simply a blanket, the two sides of which were sewn together, like a bottomless bag.—This gave great relief when lying out at night, as it was slipped over his body, to which it closely fitted, confining the motions of his arms, and rendering its divesture a matter of some difficulty,—closely resembling that peculiar article of attire which is kindly forced upon the acceptance of demented persons by the generosity of their guardians and friends;—and it may be, that many a saner man than Dennis Sherron has slept in a coat of the same pattern.

Now, whether it was the stroke of the moose's hoof, or the noise of Argimou's gun, that awoke him, we cannot say; but the fact is incontrovertible, that Dennis gave a great leap, somewhat in the manner of a fish, immediately after the extraordinary intrusion of the four-footed beast upon his slumbers, as before related. With a celerity which he never afterwards could account for, he wriggled himself upon his legs, and the first things that struck his comprehension, were a strong sulphurous smell, and a thick suffocating smoke that enveloped every thing around. Accordingly, the foremost idea that suggested itself to his confused brain, was a visitation from the lower regions. He thought he saw distinctly, through the stygian cloud, the figure of a native of that blessed country approaching to claim relationship and honor which he was by no means desirous of obtaining—not being an advocate of the "actual cautery," as a promoter of the living principles; he even caught a glimpse of a decided tail, whisking in the smoke, and knowing that to be an unquestionable proof of satanic origin, he hung his brief decision thereon.

What could he do? He was not a coward naturally, but there are modes and circumstances of bravery; there are limitations, beyond which, that inestimable quality ceases to obtain any influence over human actions, and here was a case in point. Who could face so unexpectedly, a denizen of the tartarean world? Besides, his arms were firmly pinioned to his side by his straight jacket, rendering him as helpless as an infant; and worse than all, he could not even make the sign of the cross, the only infallible means of protection prescribed in similar emergencies. As for moral courage, he had never heard of such a thing. But the tail—*alias*, Argimou's gun—decided the motions of Dennis. Following the instinctive suggestions of his great primal law—self preservation—he turned his back instantly and fled into the woods, crashing, stumbling, and howling, in his precipitate course, for he imagined a troop of the unhallowed brood were rushing after him in full cry. Some time he held on in his mad career, until further flight was stopped by the intervention of a perpendicular rock, against which he suddenly dashed. Here he was found by the rest, who had heard his retreat and followed quickly, shouting for him to return. Edward could not avoid laughing at the figure which his servant presented, as he stood revealed by the grey light of morning with his back to the bare rock. His hair was disordered and standing out like diverging rays, from fright; his eyes protruded from his head with an insane expression, strictly in keeping with the singular apparel in which his body was encased, giving him the appearance of a madman broke loose from his keepers; while he mumbled a number of inarticulate sounds, like one in sleep, indeed the poor fellow's senses were so thoroughly confused, that it was not until his master had spoken several times and endeavoured to conduct him back, that he was undeceived with regard to the diabolical character of those near him. At last he was prevailed upon to return to the bivouac, and his astonishment may be imagined when he beheld the huge carcass lying close to the place where he had slept. Having received a satisfactory explanation of the phenomenon, he said not a word, but with a series of violent distortions worked himself clear of his blanket—somewhat in the same manner that a caterpillar casts its skin—when, seizing a knife, he deliberately severed the threads that connected the sides together, thereby rendering a second addition of the foregoing predicament, as far as human foresight could discern, utterly impossible.

Edward experienced a sensation very like shame, when he thought of his careless neglect of duty; but Argimou laughed when he mentioned the subject, and merely said,

"My brother was weary. He knows not the woods; nor can he say unto the spirit of drowsiness, like a red-man—'I will bind thee, thou thief, with chains, and not until I call thee shalt thou come, for thou art a warrior's slave!'"

The chief rekindled the fire and commenced skinning the dead moose. Upon examination, it was found that the ball had penetrated the heart of the animal, which Edward—having learned the uncertain manner in which the aim had been directed—thought an excellent shot. Argimou, however, did not appear to regard it as evincing any great skill in woodcraft, but expressed his wonder at their finding a moose so far in the Milicete country; telling his companion that that species of deer generally confined itself to the hunting grounds of the Micmac, and seldom was known to stray so far to the westward. A cloud of anxiety settled upon the Sachem's face, as he added—

"Our wise men say, it is a bad thing for any wild animal to follow

119

the hunters; it is an evil sign. Wherefore has this thing travelled in our track? Because he must obey his master what sent him; and, as sure as the Great-Spirit's word, ill luck will follow."

Not understanding the mysterious allusion that seemed to fill his ally with serious alarm, Edward turned from his dismembered carcass and was immediately struck with the grave demeanour of his other guide. Pansaway had seated himself before the dissevered head of the animal, and from his impressive action and low earnest tone, appeared to be addressing it in an expostulatory manner. Of course the soldier could not understand what was said, as the other spoke in his native language, but he drew foreboding conclusions from the sudden change so evident in the bearing of the two forresters.

Let us translate, for the reader's benefit, the strange harangue of Pansaway to the spirit of the slain deer.

"It grieves me, my cousin, to see you so low. Where is the fine mist gone? Where is the breath of thy nostrils? The morning will not hear thee call. Thy sister will listen for thy voice, in the autumn time; she will be very sorry when you come to her no more. Poor fellow! he cannot hide away from the hunters, in the deep lake waters, any time again. The snow will not see his tracks, nor will he feed on the pine-tree bark when he is hungry. His legs were swift, his scent was keen; but death, O! Death is strong! Do not be angry, my cousin. What have we done? we did not know his face in a strange land. He does not stop here. Who has coaxed him away from the sun-rise? He must, O! he must be strong! But my cousin won't do us any hurt. We were born in the same country—we go to the same home. What is his master's name? that we may speak to him. He must be a wise Micmac. The moose would not do things for a stranger; what does he want of his friends, that he sent a messenger so far? He must be a very cunning man. Do not be angry, my cousin. The cat-bird is very deceitful, but the moose could not listen to his song; what would his own bird say? O, no! he would not do that thing. I am sure that my cousin's master is a wise and an honest man. *A-di-eu-tue!*[*] I am sorry—I am sad. Thy face looks mournful: dull is thy once bright eye. I would say to your free spirit—come back! and roam in the land of the morn! but it may, O! it may not be."

In an exceeding short time they were regaled with broiled moose steak, which, though not in proper season, was much relished by the travellers. Indeed Dennis, soothed and refreshed by his breakfast, forgot altogether the adventure of the morning; and while the Indians were preparing for their departure, he filled his doodeen and, with the luxury of a confirmed smoker, commenced twisting and curling white wreaths from the corner of his mouth, in all kinds of fantastic flourishes and spirals. He had taken off his cap to be more at his ease, and his blushing head contrasted pleasantly with the green foliage behind where he sat.—His master was wiping the night dew from his gun at a little distance. Pansaway sat directly opposite, beyond the fire, with his carbine lying across his knees, also smoking his hatchet-pipe, with seeming composure; but a close observer would have seen that his keen eyes were turned suspiciously from time to time upon the thicket at the right of Dennis. While the chief, partly hidden from the view of the latter by an intervening branch, was occupied in cutting up venison for more convenient carriage, and making up the packs of the party.

Suddenly, the Indian expression of surprise escaped the lips of Pansaway, and his pipe was immediately dropped, while his ear was turned in an attitude of intense listening towards some sound that had caught his attention, in the copse on his left. Nor was he at fault, for that instant the well-known twang of a bow string was faintly heard in that direction, followed by a whirring sound, as an arrow, cutting its swift passage through the smoke of the fire, dashed the doodeen from the mouth of Dennis, and buried its flint head deep in the stem of an ash tree hard by where it quivered "like a reed shaken by the wind!"

---

[*] Farewell to thee.

"Holy Mother! wat's thon!" exclaimed Dennis, clenching the inch of clay that remained between his teeth with terrible energy, while he felt his nose carefully, for the missile had actually tickled its extremity as it passed. But the old warrior motioned him to be still, making at the same time a sign with his finger to Argimou, who stole noiselessly away among the willows, in a line parallel with the flight of the arrow from their unseen assailant. Not a muscle moved in the face or limbs of Pansaway, during the momentous silence that succeeded, though a second arrow, urged with truer aim, passed through the hair of Dennis; who, with his master, had sprung upon his feet in a state of uncontrollable excitement. They were about to fire at random among the bushes, when a deep groan was heard; whereupon the stern, imperturbable old Micmac, perfectly assured of the result, calmly relit his *to-ma-gan* and puffed away as if nothing unusual had occurred.

Rushing to the place whence the sound proceeded, they found the chief bending down over the body of a dead Indian, whose bloody head and breast told a sufficiently expressive tale. The soldiers shuddered as they beheld the mode in which so many of their comrades had been destroyed, and Edward could not avoid a momentary sensation of repugnance toward the author of such unnecessary mutilation. But he soon overcame the prejudice common to his race against the usages of savage warfare, when he reflected that, after all, it arose from a false fastidiousness; the result, rather of difference in habit and idea, than indicative of a superior national morality, for he remembered, with a sense of degradation that both the French and English governments sanctioned the custom of offering large rewards for the perpetration of the very act he deprecated, not—as with the Indians—for the sake of preserving a trophy of their prowess, but for the express purpose of diminishing, as much as possible, the numbers of their opponents. Each scalp was the warrant of a liberal premium—somewhat as, at the present day, a bear-killer receives a bounty, upon the production of the animal's paw—thereby giving encouragement to a wanton destruction of human life. As for the barbarity of the thing, many of the English settlers were well known to practise the same performance upon the Indians they slew, and even ministers of the gospel, with fanatical zeal, had stooped to gather, with their own hands, the bloody spoil. But the refined French of the Canadas, not to be out done in anything, with a genius for inventive cookery, in which they are allowed to excel all other nations, after torturing to death some prisoners that were captured at the massacre of Shenectaday,* perhaps with the same view that bulls are baited, viz., to enhance their quality and flavour— *boiled them into soup*, graciously serving out the infernal decoction to their less barbarous allies. But this is digression.

The three were standing beside the lifeless foe, upon whom they each gazed in silence.—Edward, at length, picked up from the ground, the bow that had so nearly caused the death of one of their party at least, and as he examined its construction, asked "what warrior is this that you have slain, Argimou?"

The chief wiped his red blade on the bearskin robe of his dead enemy, and replied, exultingly—

"One who is stronger than many warriors, and wiser than the serpent what charms."

"I do not understand you," rejoined the other, "dost thou think he is alone? may it not be, that even now, we are periled where we stand?"

"The *Boo-wo-win* is alone," was the brief reply.

Edward asked the meaning of the expression just used, but the Indian taking a roll of fresh roots from beneath the garment that partly covered the bosom of the dead man, said to his questioner,

"Come, let us go to my father, that he may know of this thing. They are destroyed—master and slave. The sky is bright again, my brother. Uh! Who can say like Argimou?—I have killed a *Boo-wo-win!*"

Returning to his father, the chief, without speaking, laid at his feet the fresh scalp, to the solitary lock of which was bound the dried skin

---

* See Colden—page 78.

of a snake, and the coil of roots he had discovered; whereupon the old warrior manifested considerable surprise as he remarked—"it is good."

Then followed a rapid colloquy in their own language, during which, many references were had to the above mentioned articles, and, by their expressive gestures, they seemed to connect them, in some way or other, with the moose they had killed, for Pansaway pointed several times to the horned head, the only part of the animal that retained its original appearance. After the earnest conference had terminated, Argimou turned towards Edward, and addressed him as follows—

"My brother asked what a *Boo-wo-win* was? I will tell him. What does he call that man, among the *pale-faces*, who is greater than those which fight their battles? He who vanquishes the bad spirits of the pestilence, with roots, and charms, and wise words?"

Edward thought for a moment, ere he replied—

"You mean one who dealeth in medicines."

"Ay!" quickly interrupted the other, raising his arm emphatically: "the *medicine-man*.—Such is a *Boo-wo-win*. The white medicine-man is strong, and knows many things. But Indian medicine-man is much wiser and more powerful; for he can speak to the wild animals and scare away the evil spirits from the body, to their homes in the earth and the air. Over every thing has he power, except *The Great Spirit*, who is above all things. But though the *Boo-wo-win* cannot make the thunder and the storm, the green leaf or the winter ice, yet above other men he is very strong.

"He can say to this animal—no matter what kind, may be otter, beaver, snake, wild-cat, bear, carriboo, moose, any kind of live thing at all—'do this! Go, and search hard for that man; he must not live any more!' Then that man may sing his death song; for he will surely die!

"But you see, my brother, as there are some nations more wise and powerful than others, so are their *medicine-men*. You have seen that a Milicetejik *Boo-wo-win* cannot be very mighty, for I, a plain Micmac warrior, have taken his scalp. Then comes the *Boo-wo-win* of our nation. He is a *walking-fear* among animals and among men! But, above all nations, the Mohawks are the most terrible.—They are brothers to the bears.* They are a nation of *medicine-men*. Who has killed a Boo-wo-win of the Mohawks? Who says he has taken *his* scalp? I would laugh him to scorn!—it is a thing that cannot be! These great men send animals into the hunting grounds of their enemies, and find out their secret thoughts. They even can go themselves into the wigwams of strange tribes, and be like air to their eyes. Ay, the Mohawk *Boo-wo-win* can throw his arrow up in the sky as straight as the stem of a pine tree, and yet will it go on till it strikes the heart of him he hateth—'tis certain brother. Who can turn away the white-man's ball and the Indian's knife?—Who but the Mohawk *Boo-wo-win*! Then, you see, these men work with roots that grow in the woods, which scare birds and snakes; and so they stop away many days—sometimes many moons—in search of these things, and they always go by themselves: for if any other eye looked upon their actions they would be weak, all the same like one little child. Now," concluded the Indian, "does my brother believe that the *Boo-wo-win* is alone, or that the moose followed in our track?"

Edward, whatever his own opinion might have been, was careful to avoid all dissent from the argument of his simple companion. He knew that it would be useless to attempt combating the deep-grounded prejudices of the natives, and felt too thankful for their escape from the serious danger with which they had been threatened, to venture any imprudent remarks upon so unimportant a subject. Covering the body of the Milicete and the remains of the moose with boughs and heavy stones, the travellers resumed their packs and departed from the eventful bivouac. Dennis lingered in the rear, with slow, disconsolate pace, making a mental oration over the fragments of his broken

---

* The words *Mohawk, Mohog, Maqua,* and *Moowin,* mean *bear* in several Indian languages; therefore, the Mohaws were sometimes styled *"the tribe of the bear."*

pipe—shivered emblem of mortality—which he held in his open palm, and regarded wistfully for some moments. At last, he picked out the piece of the stem that had remained in his mouth after the catastrophe, and casting the rest upon its original earth, "ashes to ashes, dust to dust," he put it carefully in his pocket, as a "parable of his ould clay." Then, reverting to his great first law, he commenced an abstruse calculation of the loss of caloric he would sustain by the unfortunate accident; which, with the prospect of his main supply being shortly exhausted—for the black bottle gave indications of being very low in spirits—was becoming a source of much uneasiness to the feelings of the philosophical Irishman.

Chapter XIV

The Indians impressed upon their companions the necessity of preserving the utmost silence and caution, as they moved on, for they were now approaching the haunts of the Milicete, and knew not at what moment they should be called upon to act, as it was thought very possible that they might fall in with detached stragglers or hunting parties. The clouds that had prognosticated, for some time, a change in the weather, now condensed the moisture with which they were surcharged, and watered the woods with a heavy shower of rain, rendering the plight of the party any thing but agreeable, as they journeyed on under the forest trees, which afforded little protection from the watery deluge, for every leaf multiplied the torrent, by gathering the drops, spout-like, and transmitting them in huge globules to the thirsty ground. Every bough which was shaken slightly in passing, sent a shower-bath upon the heads of the travellers, and in short time they were completely drenched, their heavy packs gaining additional weight by the fluid which they absorbed; so that, though the weather soon became more favourable, and the bright sun shone upon the woods, still they felt fagged and uncomfortable. At length they emerged at a cleared spot upon a bend of the same river, at a higher part of which they had bivouacked the night before, and the rapid, shallow waters sparkled and danced along cheerfully in the fresh morning beam.

Here they halted among the ancient ruins of what, as Pansaway said, was once a village of the Acadians, though it appeared to have been deserted for many years, the only traces remaining of man's having once abode there, being a few grass-covered heaps of stones, a number of crumbling logs, and an old, shrivelled, worn out moccasin.

After a reconnoitre of the place, to assure themselves of its security, a fire was lighted, and blankets and outer garments, being rung out, were suspended upon stakes before the flame. Edward and Dennis employed themselves in drying their soaking hose, but the restless natives were wandering among the mouldering fragments of the French settlement, which they seemed to regard with deep interest and curiosity. Old Pansaway had seated himself upon a stone, beneath the shade of a large cedar tree, situated upon the verge of the surrounding forest, and he seemed absorbed in thought, for his head rested upon his hand, and his features had assumed an expression unusually grave and mournful. Making a sign to his son, who stood with folded arms at a little distance, the young warrior was soon at his parent's side, when, motioning him to be seated, Pansaway addressed him in these words:

"Would you ask, O my son! of a people whose hearths are deserted, whose foot-prints are washed away?—Listen, and be wise.—Thy father's heart is a grave where the deeds of the past lay buried; their dim ghosts, travelling to and fro, have worn a pathway down into its depths. Where are the *years* that have gone—where are *their* grassy graves?

"Whither has the smoke vanished—like a dead man's breath? Why are the ashes cold? Roll back, O moons of my youth! for the night is dark and mine eyes are growing dim.

"Thy father was like a green twig of the forest that delight-eth in the fulness of its living joy, and he had heard of battles and of men, but his arm was tender, and his knife red only with the game he had vanquished; for the grass grew in the war-path of the Micmac, and though the hatchet was not buried, yet had it become edgeless and rusty. So he said to himself, I will go away from my people, and tarry among the tribes of the sunset, and learn to be a warrior, that I may have honor when I return. Therefore, when the snows melted, thy father left the hunting grounds of his brethren, and wandered by strange paths among tribes that were friendly to his own. And he found that the earth was very big, and that the country of the Micmac became as a little wart, upon its side, with a shape like a *wallum-quetch** claw; and, likewise, that there was no end to the nations and the languages; and that the sun never set, but was only hidden by the hills and the trees.

"These are the red tribes of the sunset, and they are numerous,— yea, very strong!

"First are the Mohaws, or tribe of the bear; these are nearest the sale water, and the Souriquois; the Oneidas, the Onondagoes, the Cayugas, the Senekas are next, on this side the great river that runs from the big lakes, near the evening; and they are called the Iroquoi, or the five nations. Then came the Algonquins on the other side of that great river, by the frost; they were once glorious hunters, they were the masters of the earth! Beyond them stopped the tribe of the Huron, about the lake that bears their name. They were no hunters, but tillers of the ground, and their hearts were weak as water—yea, they had a woman for their Sagamou! Further on, were the Foxes, the Otters, the Canzas; warlike people whose war-cries filled the woods by the rivers that flowed to the sunset; whose hatchet was never buried. They eat the flesh of their enemies, they hunted the buffalo on wide plains of many day's journey, they were fierce—they were without hearts!

"But of all the nations thy father saw, the Iroquoi were the bravest and most wise. With them he first learned to fling a tomahawk, and how a warrior should die.

---

* Lobster.

"He has seen the *black-caldron* hiss like an angry snake, he has seen the war-dance of the linked tribes: he has shouted their battle-cry. The club is red—the eagles are drunken with blood—the bright knife is stained—the wolves howl with joy.

"Come back, O, days of my youth! for my limbs are heavy and my heart very sad.

"Listen, my son, to the strange things thy father beheld, in the times that are gone. He has seen the worm from which the shells are got to weave the wampum belts, so precious amongst nations. He has seen them clinging to the body of a drowned man, in the rivers of that land.

"The bird what mocks he has seen, and listened to his song in the night, by the waters of the Wabash. By the dim Ohio—by the salt-licks he has seen the great bones of that animal whom no man has beheld alive or hunted—whom the Great Spirit slew.

"He has looked upon the strong Niagara, in the country of the Iroquoi; where Erie, like an overfull gourd, pours its waters into Ontario—where the rocks are like a wall, and the lake rolls over like the hollow of your hand, so that you can walk underneath, and be alive; though its voice is louder than the thunder, and it makes a man's heart leap, and moves the hair upon his head with fear.

"There the winds skim the foam from their war-caldron, by the beat of the torrent's drum, and the *Storm-slayer* hangs in the wave clouds his many-coloured bow. Ugh! The wonder of the Iroquoi is a great warrior. He is stronger than the north wind—*he* cannot take his scalp. He shakes his grey locks at him and laughs; *he* cannot bind him with his ice-chain. His lick burneth the frost's cold hand, and melts his sharp knife away. Ay, more mighty is he than the winter or the whirlwind, for he never grows weary. It is *Kesoulk's** plaything! It is the Water-spirit's home!

---

* Great Spirit—God.

130

"But after many moons word came that the nations by the summer had taken up the hatchet with the Wennooch, against the blue-eyed Anglasheou. So I joined a war-party of the Abenaci, and crossed the hills and the forests till we reached the shore of the salt water; and I felt glad when I tasted its green waves, and saw them rushing on, with a leap and a song, to the country of my childhood's home. We met many of my own people there, and I laughed! for they looked all the same like the children of the pale-faces. The Micmacs are smaller and less red than the tribes of the sunset. The salt mist has washed their faces white—the cold water winds have stunted their growth like the pine on their rocky shores.

"Roll back, O moons of my youth! for the night is dark, and mine eyes are growing dim.

"There was a gathering of many tribes from the Pascataqua and its streams—the Penobscot and the rivers by the setting sun. They were like the branches of a tree, they sprang from one trunk, one root—they were the tribes of the Abenaci.

"Numerous as the fire-flies in spring, were the fires of their wigwams, and more bright than many stars, they shone in the calm Kennebis. On its banks were they encamped, under Castine their Bashaba—the son of the Wennooch sachem, whom the red man loved. In peace were they come to hear the *Great Voice* speak—the wisest among men.

"O! it was a pleasant place—the Norridgewoack—where they built a fort, and sat under the trees, or in the big chapel, and listened to the good word.

"There the Great Voice of the Wennooch dwelt among the hunters, and talked in the languages of the tribes. He told them how the world first was, and called the Great spirit GOD. He said that men were very wicked and unjust, and that a great flood came—higher than the highest mountains—and swept away the animals and the nations from the whole earth, all but one man and his family—for *Kesoulk* saw that he was good, and told him to make a big canoe, and put into it an animal, male and female of every sort, of the earth and air; so, when the waters rose up, he and his people were carried on the top, it might be, for one moon.

"Then *Kesoulk* looked down, and when he saw that all were dead he was very sorry; and raising his finger, he said to the storm—'be still!' and it was so. For the waters went away, and the man and his children and the live things walked upon dry land, and the earth was again covered with people and wild animals.

"But they became bad a second time, so *Kesoulk* sent his son (*Which-wil-le-nix-cum,*)[*] in the body of a man, that he might teach them how to be good. But wicked persons took him prisoner, and nailed him to a cross, and so he died. Yet his spirit was very mighty, for it went up to the sky in a great storm, and the dead rose from the ground, and the hills were rent and shaken. My son," here Pansaway drew near Argimou, and spoke low,—"I have heard it said that the Anglasheou was that bad people, and so, for a punishment, the Great Spirit set his curse on them evermore, and they became wanderers upon earth.

"Such is the word that the Great Voice spoke to the tribes at the Norridgewoack.

"But the black Powa is dancing—the war-axe is bright! By the starless night, by the clouded moon, the red fire is burning—the war-song is sung! Bring the paint, O ye that can arm a warrior! Make him look terrible in battle; let him be a death-howl to his enemies.

"I see many light-haired scalps, I see many spoils. By the shores— by the rivers of the morning, I have drunk the Anglasheou's blood: I have heard him screech his death-song by the salt water's roar. Let them come to the Kennebis; the arm of the red man is strong.

* Jesus Christ.

He will count their scalps: he will tread upon his bones! There is Mogg—the bloody knife—and his tribe, and Assacombuit, the greatest sachem; there are ninety-eight notches on his war-club—you will find so many pale scalps in his wigwam. He has seen the sun rise beyond the salt water; he has seen Oranthio—the white-gull drops dead at his name.

"The warriors are hungry. The black crow waits, for he scenteth the strangers from afar. Is the Anglasheou a woman? or a singing-bird in a red man's ear?

"Such was the song of the tribes, when they made ready for battle at the Norridgewoack.—The braves of the Abenaci came down from the hills and strung their bows, but not to chase the deer; and while they danced by the smoking pile, the keen flashing of their knives was as the blue lightning in the cloud. Such, O my son, was the gathering of the sunrise tribes, when they sharpened the axe, and stood still for the coming of the Anglasheou.

"The stranger came, and the earth and the river water were the colour of a red bird. Cold Death stalked through the village and rested in every wigwam, and brave warriors looked upon him, and sang their song without fear. What could the Indian do against the long spears and the thunder that kills?—he could only die.

"The Great Voice went out to talk to the wicked stranger in the words of peace, but they answered him with a whoop and a shower of death-hail; and though many warriors rushed out before his path to save their father, it would not do, for he fell down—he and the warriors that were with him—at the foot of the cross he had set up to *Which-wil-le-nix-cum*'s memory. And so the Great Voice departed from among the forest tribes: and Mogg, the Bashaba, died like a man, with his wet knife in his hand, and his eyes open. Go to the wigwam of Assacombuit, and you will see many more light-haired scalps: you will feel many more notches in his war-club.

"But the tribes were scattered and stricken by the thunder, and their homes were made desolate.

"When the storm ceased and the sky was clear again, miserable men went back to seek for the Great Voice that was still; and when they had found him, they wept. Ay, stone-hearted warriors—wild hunters of the Abenaci, shed tears over their father, and were not ashamed.

"Woe to the Anglasheou! They had taken his white-haired scalp, they had torn his flesh, they had filled his mouth with dust of the ground, and his bones had they broken. But his spirit could not curse his enemies; for he said always that it was not a good thing to give evil for evil.

"Then they buried him where the chapel had once been, and Norridgewoack was his memory. And the tribes departed in sorrow, and their father remained alone in his bloody grave.

"Where is his spirit—O where? His word was like the summer, like rock-water to a thirsty man—like the calm glory of the morn.—But the green leaf turns red, and the forest time doth come; and the spring—the sugar tree runs, the blue rivers roll on, yet the Great Voice he never returns. Where is his spirit, O where? Listen, my son, and be wise.

"The Wennooch and his brethren came to the sunrise seeking for a home, and here they built them huts and planted corn. But always were they sad and lonely, saying that they must live near the Great Voice's grave. So after many moons those red men who had been signed with a sign and a word of power—among whom was thy father—returned to the evening and dug up the bones of the Great Voice, and brought them back with them unto this place. Then, a second time, we buried them, and set up a cross by the head, and planted a cedar to his memory; and the Wennooch was glad and lamented no more.

"Look down, O my son!"—here Pansaway pointed to a slight inequality in the soil at his feet—"Dost thou see a grave? canst thou read a name?" And putting aside the spreading branches of the cedar tree with his hands, he showed his son an ancient, moss-covered cross, the broad top of which he scraped clean with his knife.

Had a white-man been there, he might have discovered, perchance, the half-obliterated words, "PERE RALLE." But the chief, not being able to understand the letters of the old world, was contented with the perusal of a curious hieroglyphic, which was deeply inscribed over the unknown characters; for he knew that in the written language of his nation, the same symbol was used to signify, "*the Word of God*."

As the father bent with reverential awe before the hoary relic, that sacred emblem of christianity seemed reflected in the moonlight on his swarthy breast; for escaping from the loose folds of the tunic that had concealed it heretofore, a silver crucifix hung from the old Indian's neck, glittering by its suspending chain.

What psalm is it that saith—

> "The sad remembrance of the just
> Shall flourish when he sleeps in dust?"

Truly, the small stream that had flowed quietly on through the wilderness, making the desert places green, poured not out its pure offerings in vain; nor was it altogether swallowed up and lost in the great ocean of time. The red man's friend might be forgotten in his own land and among his own people, but with the children of his adoption his memory would never grow mouldy: the Indian never forgets. Here was one of that race, after a period of thirty years, bearing witness to his successful ministry, and speaking volumes in his praise.

Pansaway, after a few moments' pause, resumed his tradition—

"But whither has the smoke vanished?—Why are the ashes cold? Because, after many years, the pestilence came and licked the blood of the Wennooch, so that their children died and their corn was blighted. Therefore, thinking that an evil spirit haunted the place, they quenched their fires, and took their goods and cattle, and travelled further to the sunrise, till they saw the morning come over the great water, and there they lived peacefully, evermore until now.

"But these things were before Pansaway looked upon the face of his son's mother. How strange is the life of a man! How joyful is his morning—his evening, how sad. Where are ye—O remembered voices. Hopes of the daybreak, where have ye your home?"

Chapter XV

Pursuing their route, after some delay at the deserted hamlet, the travellers advanced with great circumspection, while they began to observe indications of their approach to the sea coast; among which, was the sterile, rocky nature of the country they were passing through, and the more diminished growth of the trees. The soft, light foliage of the hard wood became more rare and scattered, giving place to the less graceful but more sturdy evergreens of the different species of pine, which clung to the scanty soil of the hill sides, and were grouped upon the granite rocks, like grim warriors guarding the land from hostile intrusion. The dark and broken summits of the ridges were bristled with their spire-like stems; and, here and there, alone, forlorn and tottering on some precipice's verge, a grey-haired old sentinel fir, would wave its scraggy arms solemnly in the wind, as if to warn the strangers away; while the crow flew over head, flapping lazily, his ragged wing, and croaked hoarsely as he flitted past—like an evil thought; indeed, the character of the whole scene was stern and forbidding as the savage people who were known to make their homes within its forest lairs.

About midday, they reached a long strip of marshy interval, situate between two ranges of hills. Its level plain, being covered with long, rank grass, contrasted richly with the deep foliage of the picturesque high grounds on its verge, which, like the banks of a bold river, advanced and receded in every variety of point and indent, whose effect was enhanced by the endless shifting of light and shade, as the cloud and sunshine ran races over them. This secluded valley stretched away southward, as far almost as the eye could discover, terminating in an open sheet of water that rolled in long, white billows at its foot, with a booming roar.

The guides pointing in that direction, shouted, "*La Baie Francoise!*" but that portion of the sea was better known to Edward by the more modern appellation of the Bay of Fundy; and had he doubted the correctness of his companions, the sudden change in the temperature, and the grey cloud of mist that shut out the line of horizon from view, were of themselves, sufficient to prove its identity.

Yes, there was the eternal fog—that curse which hangs forever about the coasts—haunting them like a remorseless ghost in the summer season, sifting each particle of warmth from the prevailing south wind, and collapsing the vital impulse of every living thing doomed to struggle on within its blighting influence.

Edward, who had been journeying for some days through the thick luxurious forest, where the heat was sometimes overpowering from its intensity, beheld with surprise, the pigmy growth of vegetation upon the borders of the sea; and his blood felt chilled by the cold, raw air which rushed with a strong draught up the marsh. Descending to the alluvial tract—which presented further appearance of having at one time, been the bed of a great river, the guides, instead of crossing to the opposite side abruptly changed their course and followed the valley down; keeping close at the foot of the hills bordering on their left. Argimou and his father now began to examine, carefully, every foot of ground over which they passed, conferring at times earnestly in their own language. After proceeding some distance in this manner, they appeared evidently at fault, and the chief, turning toward Edward, with a somewhat anxious look, said,

"My brother remembers when on the evening of our first day's journey, we looked upon the tracks of Madokawando and the *Sunbeam*, and how the trail, after rising the river, turned straight away to the sunset; well, that was good. Then, you see, my father said, we will follow the river to the evening, and get between the frost and the Milicetejik trail—and we did so. Now, many days have we journied on a long path, but we have seen no marks crossing to the frost, therefore we know if the *Sunbeam* was brought to Ouangondy, at this place—between us and the salt water—we would surely find foot-prints of the war-party; but it is not so. Our eyes are croocked and we are like bats in the daylight—the way is dark before us."

While this disheartening information was being afforded the lover, Pansaway had gone on somewhat in advance of the rest, and as his son ceased speaking, they saw him stop, as if waiting for them to come up. When they reached the place, he was leaning musingly upon his carbine, and gazing upon some object of interest on the moist, black soil at his feet. Ay, there they were. The same footmarks they had witnessed before on the bank of the Peticodiac. There was the same remarkable moccasin-print among the numerous impressions on either side, and, above all, there were the deep indentations of a horse's hoofs, whose could it have been but Clarence's?—and away they ran, directly to the westward.

Argimou gave a leap of delight, in which, however, he was completely eclipsed by the enthusiastic Dennis, who afterwards went on his knees and kissed the impress of his enemies, swearing that they were "the rale sort—the darlints, and he'd hould them agin any white man or Ingen that 'ud gainsay his say, for a half-pint, or a fig o' backey; so he would!"—As no one seemed inclined to accept the challenge, Dennis was obliged to cut another gymnastic flourish in the air, which was accompanied by something very like an Indian whoop, ere he could relieve the effervescence of his feelings. Edward spoke not, but he could with difficulty restrain his emotions. Shading his eyes with his hand, he gazed at the tracks of Clarence's horse for some time, and then suddenly stepped onward in the direction they indicated, waving his arm, as a sign for the others to follow. Fording several swamps and pools of water, which appeared to be supplied by the influx of the tide, and a deep creek that ran through the centre of the marsh; the party lost sight of the trail as they ascended the rocky uplands beyond. But after passing by the borders of a small lake, they again discovered traces in the swampy ground, and, taking the precaution of making Dennis—who was more largely gifted than the rest, in the development of his lower extremities—lead the van, they followed in Indian file, each threading in the footsteps of his predecessor; preventing thereby any suspicion to their character or numbers, in case they should attract the casual notice of an enemy.

After this fashion, they advanced in silence and without making any noise for some time through deep woods and thickets of spruce and cedar intermixed, guided by the tracks which were very distinct in the moss and wet loam, until, having reached a half stagnant pool at the extremity of a morass, the trail turned abruptly to the north-west, over the high ground. Here it was again lost, but Pansaway needed not further assistance, for he kept on without hesitation, as a man confident in the knowledge of his way. They were still on the confines of the morass, and about crossing the summit of a precipitous fir-covered rock, when Dennis, who had deviated slightly from the path of the guides, approaching too near its verge, his clumsy foot slipped on the green mould, causing him to lose his balance, and the heavy pack, with which he was encumbered, preventing him from recovering his perpendicular again, he missed his hold and tumbled over the side of the rock with a tremendous crash, among the bushes; while his gun, cast violently from his hand, exploded as it struck the ground below.

With expressions of impatience and strong displeasure, the Micmacs hurried to the spot, but they were anticipated, for when they stood upon the edge of the steep whence their luckless companion had been precipitated, the terrible war-cry of the Milicete rang in their ears, and they beheld seven Indians rushing, with uplifted tomahawks, towards the extraordinary apparition which the fallen Dennis must have presented to their eyes, from a canoe by the side of the shallow pool. The advanced foeman had reached the half insensible Irishman, and was on the point of burying his axe in the other's brains, when a ball from Argimou's carbine laid him dead at the soldier's side. The Milicete, astounded by this proof of a new enemy being in their vicinity, having probably imagined that Dennis was some prisoner who had escaped from a returning war-party,—stopped abruptly, and before they had recovered their momentary surprise, Pansaway and Edward poured in a deadly discharge, which made two more of their opponents bite the ground, one being shot dead, the other struggling in the agony of a mortal wound.—Then, with a shout of defiance, the Micmacs drew their knives and bounded down the steep face of the rock, followed by Edward, brandishing his tomahawk, gaining swiftly the level of the ground below, they rushed with great impetuosity upon their remaining foes.

The Milicete uttered in wonder the dread name of Argimou, as they recognized the far-famed warrior of the Micmac; yet they wavered not, but awaited with dogged determination the collision of their enemies. It came. For one brief moment there was a swift play of steel in the sunlight, a tossing of limbs wildly, a yell of fury, it might be pain; then the Milicete gave round and retreated, closely pursued by their opponents. But a fourth body was left stretched upon the green-sward behind, and Pansaway's robe was dripping with blood from a flesh wound in his breast.

Here now remained an equal number of combatants, and the conflict was continued with unflinching stubbornness, though the Milicete retired before the desperate onset of the others. As each became separately engaged with his adversary, the distance between the parties gradually increased, until all chance of assistance from either side, in case of need, was rendered doubtful; therefore, as each knew that upon his own resources he has alone to depend, a deeper character was given to the combat; fighting as they did, purely for life or death.

Edward was engaged with a powerful savage who aimed several blows with a knife at his body, which were parried with much difficulty by means of the hatchet with which he was armed. So rapid were the thrusts of his opponent, that the Englishman was obliged to act altogether on the defensive; not having time enough to hazard a blow in return. At length he was forced to fall back before the savage, who seeing his advantage, suddenly caught the uplifted axe in his left hand and wrenched it from the other's grasp, but before he could strike his keen weapon into the unguarded breast of his adversary, Edward had darted upon him, and they fell together, to the ground. Fast locked in the embrace of hate; they rolled and twisted with dreadful distortion of body and limb, one seeking to sever the vice-like clasp of the other, for the purpose of using his knife to advantage; the other, with the strength of despair, endeavouring to prevent that object, as he well knew, that his life would be forfeited if he relaxed in the smallest degree, his exertions to hinder the Milicete's arms from bursting the bonds that confined them tightly to his side.

The superior strength, however, or the power of physical endurance which the savage possessed, was gradually overcoming the almost exhausted grasp of Edward whom he had forced underneath, and a few moments would have sufficed to determine his fate, had not Pansaway, who had vanquished his foe, perceiving the critical situation of his ally, hastened speedily to his deliverance. Finding that he could not arrive until it would, probably, be too late to save him from the deadly stab of the Milicete—the old Indian, at a great risk, but which was warranted by the urgency of the occasion, threw his tomahawk before him toward the prostrate pair, and his well practised skill did not fail him in the extremity.

True to its aim, the weapon cut clean and crushing into the spine of the enemy, who sank back, with a baffled cry, into the arms of Edward, from whom he had partly raised himself. A wild shudder—an agonized spasm—and Edward felt the limbs of his foe stiffen above him in death, while a torrent of hot blood welled from the open mouth, which was lying close by his left ear. Removing the dead Indian from off the soldier, Pansaway helped him to arise, but he staggered with debility, and was obliged to rest himself on a small hillock, while his preserver went in search of his son, who was not in sight, as the trees were scattered in clumps over the place where they fought, and prevented them from seeing each other during the struggling conflict that had taken place.

Pansaway, advancing a few paces, discovered that Argimou was still engaged with his adversary, who wielded an enormous club, the powerful sweeps of which were avoided by the active Micmac, while at the same time he managed to plant several blows with his knife upon his opponent's body, though he was unable to close with him, in consequence of the rapidity of the other's motions—now to one side, now to the other; while the chief kept advancing, and both were approaching the shallow pool before mentioned.

But when the Milicete saw the father of his enemy approaching, his heart failed him, and throwing down his war-club with a shrill yell, he sprang toward the canoe, and jumping in, pushed out into the stream and plied his paddle with amazing swiftness—causing the light fabric to shoot like a dart towards a wooded point, which, if placed between it and his pursuers, would enable him to escape, as the morass was impassable at that place, being interspersed with sunken pools and quagmires.

Again Pansaway raised his glittering axe dripping with gore—if one man escapes they are undone—whirling round like a revolving wheel, the missile flew from his hand, cutting the scalp-lock from the bowing head of Milicete, who screamed in derision as it dropped with a splash into the dark water. One more canoe's length and he is safe—vain hope!

The chief unslung his deadly bow from his shoulder, where it ever hung, and with the speed of thought fitted an arrow to the string. For one instant that eye is stone—that arm is iron, so devoid are they of motion—the thumb is at the ear, the string at its utmost tension: away the shaft speeds on its fearful message! One wild shriek told that it had taken effect, though the object was immediately hidden by the shrubbery of the point, beyond which the canoe had glided. On gaining a position which overlooked the place, it was seen filled with water and floating level with the surface, but its occupant had disappeared beneath the turbid stream which was coloured with black mud, oozing from its disturbed bed, mingled with a bright ruddy tinge—imparted by the bleeding body below.

Drawing the canoe to land, they turned it uppermost upon the bank, and then hurried back to the place where Edward was. By that time he had somewhat recovered his strength, and proceeded with the others in quest of Dennis, who had not been seen since the commencement of the fray, they having left him where he had fallen—the unconscious origin of a circumstance that had well nigh put a sudden termination to their scheme, upon the very eve of its accomplishment.

Passing the bodies of the Indians, they found that they were all quite dead, but an expression of stern ferocity, which even death could not eradicate or tame, still lived upon their bronzed visages, the latest they would ever wear. 'Twas the last seal of the unconquerable spirit ere it left its perishable tenement forever.

Dennis was discovered seated by the rock with a woeful air, somewhat in keeping with the appearance of a bloody rag which was fastened round his brow, for he had received a severe bruising in that quarter by his unfortunate sommerset over the precipice; and in the absence of other appliances, had made shift to manufacture a bandage from the capacious skirt of his under garment. But all this was a trifle when compared to a far greater misfortune that had befallen him; for, alas, there at his side lay the shapeless fragments of a black bottle, the lumpy bottom of which alone remained entire; and from that and the mossy ground there emanated an odour very much like rum. Poor Dennis! With the inveterate faith of an Empric, in the infallibility of some all-curing panacea, he had applied the last remaining drops of his *"elixir vitae,"* to the lumps upon his forehead, and afterwards began talking to himself in a very disconsolate mood.

Pansaway, at the urgent entreaty of Edward, allowed him to examine his blood stained breast, but the warrior laughed as he displayed the superficial wound in his pectoral muscles—deeming the matter not worthy of an attention at such a moment. In fact, no time could be more precious, for the evening was advancing and an attempt to effect the liberation of Clarence, from whose supposed place of durance they were then not far distant, if not made that night, might be attended with obstacles which it would be impossible to surmount—surrounded, as they now were, with numerous and watchful enemies.

With hasty purpose the dead bodies were dragged to the side of the swamp and thrown into the pool, as the most effectual means of concealing them that suggested itself in the hurry of the moment. But there were crimson stains upon the green sward they could not hide; a record of their fate, traced in characters of dreadful import, over their grave, which they could not obliterate.

Secreting the canoe with care, near a small rivulet that ran from the morass, and drained its half-stagnant waters into a creek below, they resumed their march; yet not before Argimou, turning again to be assured of its security and concealment, saw with deep concern that the rapid watercourse was already tinged with the blood of the slain. It might divulge a secret to the Milicete he had much rather should remain forever buried in oblivion.

The sun was setting as the travellers stood upon an elevated knoll, and gazed with excited feelings at the prospect before them. Beneath, at a little distance from the position they occupied, was spread out the calm surface of the Kennebecasis, not, as they had first seen it, racing through the over shadowing forest in youth-like career; but, having acquired its matured growth, rolling a broad, majestic river, near its confluence with the St. John. At that time the flood appeared enclosed, as it were, by the projecting points which pierced far into its expanse on either side; though to the right the eye could descry the more distant headlands and coves which the river swept past, on its passage to pour itself as a tribute into the bosom of its mightier neighbour.

Directly in front, several islands, crowned with dark pines and birchen spray, rose from the sheet of clear water, like emeralds in a lake of molten rubies, for the deep flush of evening tinged with few clouds that hung in the western sky with the richest hues, from the mellow orange to the most brilliant carmine and purple with every variety of intermediate tint which, like the colours of a dying dolphin, changed incessantly as the orb of day sank lower beneath the hills westward of the St. John; or the light strips of cloud, like crimson banners, sailed imperceptibly onward. While from the firmament above a roseate blush was transmitted to the mirror below—so pure, so transparent, that the limner would have despaired at any attempt to imitate its exquisite, though fleeting delicacy, by the poor resources of his art. The wooded shores, on either hand, were overflowing with exuberant vegetation, and the feathery foliage on their crests and projecting limbs, reflecting the direct rays of the level sun ere it sank, shone like glowing gold above the dark evergreens and the crimson tide; then as the radiance vanished from the leaves, and the twilight approached, all individual character was lost in one indiscriminate mass of shade. Beyond the opposite shores, which rose bold and majestic, long sweeping lines of hills could be distinguished, receding in beautiful perspective, one above the other, and thrown out in relief by dissimilarity of shadowing, until the prospect terminated in an undulating, mountainous ridge, blue and indistinct in the waning light and the hazy horizon.

The whole scene blended the elements of the beautiful and grand in a degree that Edward was fain to confess he had seldom, or never, witnessed before. The pellucid, spacious river, with its wooded amphitheatre of hills, infinite in form and shade; the fairy isles, studding its expanse with their rich green coronals—the gorgeous sky, the deep harmony of repose which pervaded all, were sufficient to arouse the admiration of the coldest observer. But an object of more engrossing interest, at the moment, withdrew the eyes of the lover from that which at any other time would have called forth sensations of most passionate delight, so replete with graceful profusion and majestic dignity were the romantic features of the landscape.

Upon a sloping bank of the river, directly beneath the place where the travellers stood, and close to a long narrow strip of land—which appeared to connect the nearest islet with the shore, were to be seen the enclosing fence, and white wigwams of an Indian village, among the rude cones of which was contrasted the dingy walls of a log cabin, nor was Edward wrong in the surmise that within its roof was contained the precious being ever uppermost in his thoughts.

The thin grey smoke, ascending from the clustered dwellings, mingled in a dim cloud which lingered among the adjacent trees, like a blue vapour, and in one place a fire was burning briskly in the open air, by the side of which several squaws and children were seated, variously employed, while, ever and anon, an old wrinkled woman would rise and stir a pot that hung, by a forked stick, over the flame, and the merry urchins set up a shout of glee, whenever their blunt arrows would strike against a deer's hide, which, being stretched on a frame of poles, offered a broad mark for their juvenile archery. So distinct and close appeared every object about the hamlet, that Edward almost doubted the prudence of venturing so near, in the full light of evening;

but all seemed uncommonly quiet, and devoid of any thing to evince suspicion or alarm at the propinquity of a hostile party.

Keeping within cover of a thicket, the adventurers awaited till the deepening shades might enable them to put in effect their plan for the deliverance of the captive. It was proposed that Argimou, by his own suggestion, should endeavour to open a communication with the niece of the Milicete chief; the latter being supposed to retain the maiden as his own perquisite. If, through her assistance, the escape of Clarence was effected, Edward determined to follow the advice of Pansaway, which was, to return to the place where the late struggle had occurred, and transport the Milicete canoe by a short portage to the seacoast, through the means of which they could arrive, in a short time, at the British post from whence they had set out; or, perhaps, fall in with the naval force, under Captain Rouse, which was known to mediate an attack of the French fort at the mouth of the St. John, about that time. Edward well knew the impossibility of subjecting Clarence to the vicissitudes attendant upon a journey on foot through the wilderness region they had themselves traversed, and no other mode of performing the project presented itself to his mind. Trusting every thing, therefore, to the providential sagacity of the Indian allies, he yearned impatiently for the moment of action to arrive. His thoughts, meanwhile, were wrought almost unto madness, by the wild suggestions of fancy, as he imagined, with dreadful distinctness, the fearful scenes which the tender Clarence must have gone through; indeed, what surety had he of her being still in existence? might not their merciless foes have long since put an end to her sufferings by harsh treatment, or well-known usages, too horrible to conceive? He saw his beloved exposed to the gaze of heartless savages, and bound to the torturing stake; he saw the blood gushing from numerous wounds inflicted with malicious vengeance by her persecutors; her fair arms are extended in supplication, her face is phrenzied with agony and horror! such was the vision which his vivid imagination conjured up to distract his brain,—racking every nerve with the throes of mental anguish as the lover indulged, not unnaturally, in ideas of anticipated evil, when the period drew near which would enable him to determine fully the justice of his fears.

Old Pansaway, as usual with him, when he rested, was seated, with his carbine on his lap, in a musing attitude, his hands supporting his head, and his eyes directed towards the group of islands; now blending their various shades of green, as the cold grey of advancing evening began to usurp the gorgeous colouring of the sky and river. His curiosity was attracted by a long, low object, moving parallel with the shore of the most extensive one among the cluster which was most remote from the village beneath.

Had a spirit of prophesy whispered into the Indian's ear, as he watched, half instinctively, the motions of the distant canoe, that 'ere another century had flown, those small islets he saw before him, would be the sole remaining possessions of the powerful tribe, an insignificant portion only, of whose noble hermitage was then visible, would he have given credence to the tale? Why, there was scarcely soil sufficient, on their foundations of rock, to afford *graves* to the bold hunters of the Milicete!—*Yet is it even so!*

Chapter XVI

L et us now, with the facility of the prince in the eastern tale, transport the reader on the winged steed of imagination to the interior of the dwelling that contained the imprisoned maiden.

She was seated on a low block of wood, with an air of torpid dejection, as though misery had at length worn down the edge of her acute sensibilities, and left her a prey to that direst of all evils, the apathy which springs from despair. The soiled apparel hung loose over her wasted figure; having lost that round, elastic fulness which seemed moulded by the fair and joyous spirit that graced its every motion in happier times. The rich bloom had departed from her cheek, and the brightness from her mild blue eye, while the once beautiful hair hung in dishevelled mazes—significant token of grief—on either side of the pale care-pinched brow, without the tinge of gold, which, like sunlight, erst slept among its luxuriant curls. Dry sorrow was drinking her young life slowly, but not less surely, away; and, as hope gradually expired in the heart of the poor girl, the fiend wormed its way closer to the core, until it obtained full possession of the deserted tenement, and like the miner of the fruit, fed upon its juices until it faded and withered.

Near her sat Waswetchcul, who was feeding with green leaves two young moose that had been brought in by some hunters, as a present from the borders of the Micmac country, and were fastened by thongs of their mother's hide, to a ring in the floor of the cabin. It was curious to see the docile manner in which they cropped the foliage off a small branch that the Indian girl held in her hand, and appeared gratified and soothed by the soft musical tones in which she addressed them, from time to time, as if they were capable of comprehending the mysteries of human language; yet are the accents of kindness universal in signification and suited to the capacity of every sentient being. The unequivocal expression of sounds needs no interpreter but nature, to render its meaning intelligible to the brute creation.

Still was it strange to observe the distinction which they made between the two maidens, for when Clarence, impelled by a feeling of pity towards the motherless pair—they, too, were captives—passed her soft hand caressingly over their backs, they whined piteously and turned their heads away from the proffered food like frightened children; yet a gentler or more harmless being than Clarence Forbes, never yearned with overflowing sympathy towards the needy or the distressed.

After a while, Waswetchcul resumed her work which was lying beside her, and commenced covering a bark box with the beautiful coloured quills of the porcupine, to form a peculiar pattern which was marked out in lines, with some sharp instrument, on the yielding material. Holding a bunch of quills at the corner of her mouth, whence they were severally abstracted as she proceeded in her embroidery, she accompanied her labours with a low plaintive song. So sad and melodious were the strains, that Clarence—though she knew not their import, overcome by the magical power of association which music is so well known to possess—could not restrain her tears; for every note, wild and mournful in its swell or cadence, as the singer breathed her every feeling in accordance with the mutations of the song, awoke some sweet remembrance of past days. Gushing forth, as from an unsealed fount, the large drops coursed swiftly down her fair but attenuated cheeks. Oh! what a joy it was to weep! The captive felt that it would be a blessing if it were permitted that the dark stream of her life might be poured out with that soul-welling flood.

'Twas a simple legend that Waswetchcul half carelessly sung, in the expressive language of her people, and the air was wildly irregular, but sorrowful as the subject it was intended to convey. Those only who have listened to the untutored, but dulcet voices of the Indian maidens, caroling their hymns or national discants in the recesses of the forest, can well conceive the extraordinary effect—the pathos which was imparted to the following by the Wild Fowler of the Milicete.

SONG:

Always by the blue waters;—aye, always,
Poor Naten sits weeping so mournfully,
She has gathered the grapes and the white lily;
    But the fruit is untasted,
    And the lilies are dying.

Oh! fair is her face as the moon's soft beam—
Like a bird her voice—as the honey bee
Her breath—as the star of eve her eye;
    But where is her memory?
    Oh! where is her memory?

By the break of morn went a hunter forth,
His snow-shoes tracks o'er the hills, they say,
Followed the deer until close of day;
    But the frost-wind's breath was cold,
    And it blighted that hunter bold.

The berries and the vein'd water cups
She has plucked, and the tears in her eye,
Like their fountains, are never found dry;
    She is crying bitterly,
    Under the butternut tree.

Ever by the river side;—aye, ever,
The poor maiden wanders, wanting to die
Like the flowers, though she cannot tell why;
    It is sad, very sad to see
    She has lost her memory.

As Waswetchcul ceased her strain, the faint cry of the night hawk was indistinctly heard in the evening air, and through the open door the low hum of insects fell drowsily upon the ear, broken, at times, by the mellowed shouts of the children, calling to each other among the wigwams of the village, while the shades were deepening around as evening melted imperceptibly into night. It was one of those twilights—so pure, so unutterably calm—by whose influence we are ofttimes whiled away from the distracting cares and engrossing objects of life; for the deep hush of nature awes the troubled heart into stillness and rebukes the vain disquietude of man. Why are our fondest and purest emotions ever linked with sadness?—Why in such an hour—when stirring within us, the immortal spirit spreads its wing and soars nearer to its home, enticed away by the spell and hallows all things—do we muse on sorrow, nursing it even unto tears? And yet doth that causeless grief sooth and elevate the soul it fills, loosing the shackles of mortality, and lightening the load of earth upon our breasts, until we wonder at our love for the dreary world, for the base things that perish, and deem ourselves as exiles from some fairer and more genial clime. Come hither, O mournful Twilight! and tell us why ye are so powerful;—wherefore so sad? Lulled to rest by the deep repose of nature, the two maidens sat, silently indulging in a reverie of interwoven thoughts in the pleasant stillness of the summer eve, nor dreamed how soon and wildly its enchantment would be broken.

Why does Waswetchcul start and throw back the dark hair from her ear with sudden impulse? Listen! The clear hoot of an owl is borne upon the calm air with a plaintive cadence;—it is repeated—whereupon all doubt as to the cause quickly vanished, for the girl's eye kindled with a bright flash of joy, and her cheek burned, as springing up from her listless attitude, she hurried away at the beck of that well remembered call.

Clarence, surprised at the unwonted excitement of her companion, knew not to what could be imputed the sudden change she had witnessed, neither had she been conscious of the sounds that had interrupted the reflections of the other. Unnerved, as she was, by suffering and constant dread, her heart beat violently in her bosom, and she trembled with excessive agitation.

The previous day there had been an unusual bustle in the village, warriors hurrying to and fro, and signs of hostile preparation. But the commotion had altogether ceased after a short time, and a large party, including their most effective men, had departed from the place; so Clarence concluded, from the few loiterers she observed about, and the unaccustomed quiet that succeeded. The chief she had not beheld since the occasion of his memorable speech, and she felt a great relief from his absence, which had been infinitely increased by that of his wife, the malignant old squaw, before alluded to, who had gone that morning, on a visit to her kindred on the other side of the river, leaving the captive in the gentle custody of Waswetchcul, who did the utmost that lay in her power to diminish the grief and hardship which she saw, clearly, was breaking the fair stranger's heart. Often in the night, the only time that she could do so without observation, would she go over to where the captive lay sobbing, with convulsive vehemence, and passing her arms round Clarence, kiss her forehead, while she strove, with the most endearing arguments which her language was capable of affording, to chase away the sorrow from her friend, and when she found her efforts of no avail—for Clarence knew not a word of what she said,—then would she also weep, and strive to bear a portion of that anguish she could neither dissipate nor assuage.

After a brief absence the Indian girl re-entered the hut, and gliding to the hearth, she drew a brand from the smoking embers and blew it into flame, then approaching Clarence, the latter saw that her face was flushed with excitement, and that her eyes were sparkling with unusual light, as she put a small strip of bark into her hand. Was it a dream? or did she in truth behold what entranced every faculty with amazement and delight? On its smooth white surface were traced, in familiar characters, these life-restoring words—

"Courage, dearest—there is help at hand.—Follow the messenger without delay, to him who will offer protection with his life."

Clarence read the scroll, and then uttering a cry of joy, sunk into a deep swoon.

By the aid of a little water sprinkled over her face, Waswetchcul succeeded in soon restoring her to sense, when, enveloping her fragile person in a blanket, and concealing her brown hair beneath the low lappets of a squaw's cap, the girl put her finger to her lips, significantly, to enjoin silence, and beckoning the willing Clarence to follow, passed quickly out of the cabin.

Pressing her hands tightly over her heart, to controul its violent throbbing, and folding the mantle closely around her, the timid captive trod swiftly in the footsteps of her conductor, secure from observation by the completeness of her disguise. But her courage almost failed her and she trembled with agitation, as they passed through a lane of wigwams, at the doors of which, several elderly Indians sat listlessly smoking their long stone pipes; and she was scarce able to avoid screaming with terror as a tiny arrow from one of the children struck her shoulder and bounded harmlessly from the thick envelope, against which it had been playfully aimed. The loud shout that hailed the successful marksman, only added to her apprehensions, but she was immediately screened from further view by some low cedar bushes that fringed the confines of the encampment.

Waswetchcul, removing one of the enclosing palisades, motioned for her companion to pass through, after whom she immediately followed, and having replaced the picket, led the way among the birch trees covering the ascent of the hill beyond.

Clarence, almost bewildered with the rapidity of her flight and the dangers she had just escaped, saw that her conductor was joined by an Indian whose figure she could barely distinguish in the gloom; but where was *he*? and who were those advancing towards her, in the garb of her foes; was she the victim of a vain delusion? O no! A voice that made her thrill with long unfelt rapture, whispered her name; the next instant she was clasped securely in her lover's arms, and weeping hysterically upon his faithful bosom.

Chapter XVII

A s the soldier held, in a fast locked embrace, the form of his rescued love, he felt himself amply repaid for his toils in her behalf, but there was but little time allowed for fond endearment then.

"*En avant! En avant!*" muttered the deep voice of Pansaway, and imprinting a wild kiss upon the lips of his betrothed, Edward lifted her in his arms and hurried speedily away from the dangerous vicinity.

Relinquishing the precious burthen, when she had sufficiently recovered not to need any further support, Edward breathed words of comfort and encouragement into the ear of Clarence as they traversed the woods with rapid haste, guided by the Indians in advance, after whom stalked Dennis, in high spirits, indeed all were much elated at the ease with which the most difficult part of their project had been effected, namely, the abduction of the captive from one of the strongest villages of the Milicete.

It was not without considerable difficulty that they pursued their course, for the night was setting in the forest, and the underwood grew thick and in many places impervious, rendering the passage tedious and painful in the imperfect light.

As they approached the morass where the canoe had been secreted, they were alarmed at a faint sound of lamentation that appeared to arise from that quarter, and making a detour, as a proper precaution, in case of some unforeseen danger awaiting them, the fugitives arrived at an elevated spot that overlooked the scene of the previous contest, where, with feelings of the deepest mortification, was beheld a sight which caused an immediate destruction of their fondest hopes.

Some distance on their left, and in the very spot where the deadly fray with the Milicete had occurred, was gathered a group of phrenzied savages, evincing by their gestures and vociferations, every token of sorrow and impotent rage.

They had discovered the bleeding bodies of their dead brethren, and had dragged them from their watery grave and laid the disfigured corses upon the verge of the morass, where a crowd was collected to lament over their mysterious fate. The dull flame of a new-lighted fire threw a ghastly glare over the whole scene, and played, like blue lightning, over the stagnant pool of the swamp; now shrouded in a thick, unwholesome vapour, and only revealed as the unsteady flicker of the flame flashed across their surface. The unearthly appearance of the assemblage was also heightened by the more vivid light of numerous torches which were tossing, in wild confusion on every side, and among the adjacent trees, as the bearers threw their limbs about, and leaped into the air, with extravagant grief, or rushed, now here now there, in search of something upon which to wreak their excited fury, for they seemed frantic with excess of passion; and with the yell of baffled vengeance, was mingled the howl of distracted men, and the low wail, or shrill, piercing accents of woman's grief, as they bent over the dead, with streaming hair and distorted faces, visible only by the red and searching torchlight.

Clarence clung with terror to her lover's side, when she beheld the dreadful vision, and turned tremblingly away, as some more violent shriek would burst from the maddened Indians, who, brandishing their weapons, were now scattering themselves through the adjoining woods, in search of the unknown foe.

Cut off from their intended retreat, hemmed in on every side but one, by infuriated enemies, there was but one course left to the fugitives—and that, after a moment's parleyance, they quickly availed themselves of.

Preparing for immediate action, the guides loosed the knives in their sheaths, and grasped their carbines with stern determination, as they struck into the wood upon their right, while Waswetchcul led them by the most secure route, being familiar with the ground over which they were constrained to proceed. Edward again lifted the helpless Clarence in his arms, and closely followed by Dennis, dashed onward with desperate speed through the thickets of cedar and spruce, which grew plentifully thereabouts.

As they skirted the deep ravine on their left, through which a gleam of water was observed, they were quickly informed of the manner in which the discovery had been made—for, on the further side of the hollow, at some distance below, were noted the fires of a large encampment, that seemed, from the confused noise heard in that direction, to be in great commotion, as it was most probably apprised by this time, of the extraordinary incident that had taken place. The wigwams were clustered among clumps of cedar, and along the edge of the precipitous rocks, at the base of which an ample stream that seemed to expand beyond into an extensive flood, reflected brightly the beams of the numerous campfires. When it is remembered that into this dell the blood-stained rivulet from the swamp tracked its way, it can easily be imagined how the natives had been enabled to trace to its origin the suspicious colour of the stream that ran past their very wigwams.

It was fortunate for the fugitives that there was one among them who was acquainted with the localities, for the sagacious Pansaway avowed himself, here, completely at fault, as the village in their vicinity had been established since his former visit, and having no definite knowledge of the path they were pursuing, it was a difficult matter to determine whether or not it might lead them into more serious difficulties than those from which they had as yet escaped. In this dilemma the Milicete girl was alone capable of acting with any degree of certainty, and she instantly settled the matter by conducting them toward the thickly wooded heights upon their right. Gradually ascending, they toiled onward over huge fragments of rocks and through dense thickets for some time, when, as Edward was on the point of falling with his burthen, from sheer exhaustion, the Indians halted, and looking down he saw that all further progress in that direction had terminated; for they were standing upon the verge of a steep precipice far beneath which the rays of the pale stars appeared, as if reflected upon a black void, or an opaque mirror whose surface was invisible, lying at an indefinite depth below; and from the southward, swelling on the warm breeze of night, came the angry roar of agitated waters.

Edward inquired what river that was, for he saw that they were standing on the brink of a mighty flood, overshadowed by the gloom of the hills through which it flowed.

Pansaway turned to the soldier, and stretching out his left arm impressively, replied—"Ouangondy."

Concealing themselves as much as possible, within a small gully, into which they had been led by Waswetchcul, where the cedars meeting thickly overhead, excluded all observation from without, and offering an additional pledge of security, in being situated on the very brow of the cliff, and more suitable for the nest of an eagle than the resting place of man. Here it was that our adventurers calmly awaited the pursuit which they well knew would inevitably follow upon the first intelligence of the captive's having disappeared.

Several times, considerable alarm was excited by shouts and cries that resounded through the forest, though at a great distance. Occasionally these sounds would approach nigher the retreat of the fugitives; and Argimou, who kept watch on the rock above, once or twice descried the blaze of a flambeau, twinkling like a star, now growing full and bright, then wandering, or suddenly obscured, as it moved at random through the woods. But at length all cause for immediate apprehension terminated, for the light vanished entirely from among the trees as the cries became fainter and more remote, and finally ceased altogether to trouble the solitude around.

Assured of no further molestation, for that night at least, the chief rejoined the group in the hidden lair, and seeking the spot where Waswetchcul awaited his return, a little apart from the rest, he seated himself by the girl's side, and folded exultingly to his heart the *wild flower* he had so secretly wooed and won. His promise was fulfilled; he had sought his love by the banks of her own river, and never more would the cripple of the Penobscot gaze upon the fair face whose cheek now rested upon his own, making the blood tingle with tumultuous pleasure as it rushed through its channels, warmed and quickened by the soft, smooth pressure. In the silence, in the solitude—beneath the thick cedar shade, through which the prying stars pierced not, the children of the wild poured out their whole soul in the fervour of delicious commune. What to them were the "pomp and circumstance" of that, which among those misnamed wise, is but a mockery of genuine impulse, a restriction of natural enjoyment? *There* were no cold formalities—no starched petrifactions of humanity—with eyes of envy and hearts of ice, freezing the gushing current of delight in young bosoms, with the callous frigidity of conventional rule: the languid pace of hacknied sensibility, deeming the reduction of mental and physical incitement to the low scale of vitality that actuates a polypus, to constitute the *ultima thule* of principle and philosophy.

Lighted by the pure ray of love, implanted by the good Creator as a source of inestimable blessings to mankind, in their wearisome pilgrimage on earth, these two simple beings forgot the perils that surrounded them, in the oblivion that enwraps joy's wildest dream— ay, whose reality is a dream!—In the deep, solemn night—dark as their eyes, voiceless as their sealed lips—the "*Flower of the Wilderness*" unfolded its leaves beneath the warm atmosphere of passion, whose mild dew descended, pouring a refreshing balm into its depths, enhancing its fragrance, deepening its fairest hues, nor were its grateful odours, its stores of unrifled sweets withheld sparingly in return. The pale moon rose up sorrowfully out of the sea, like a spectre, and the stars vanished away, while darkness drew its broad mantle from the sky; what heeded they? *Love* was their full moon, their living light; *Hope* their o'erarching sky, whose beacons never waned;—the *present*, their universe!

And where was Edward and his rescued Clarence? Soothed and revived by his empassioned tenderness; restored to happiness by the certainty of his existence, his presence, and her own emancipation from a lot of hopeless captivity, not even their present jeopardy, nor the dreary prospect the future presented, sufficed to check the sudden revulsion of feeling that accompanied their unlooked-for meeting. Like a ruffled, tempest-tossed bird that seeks the guardianship of its parent's wing, as a babe clings closely to its mother's bosom for protection; even so did poor Clarence nestle her fair head upon her lover's breast and give vent to a full flood of delicious tears. 'Twas *his* arm that enclasped her—*his* low, broken words that instilled comfort and gladness into her woe-worn heart; and feeling the surety of this, and the sense of safety and confidence which such knowledge bestowed, what sufficient cause had she for further sorrow or apprehension? After a full interchange of thoughts, and an unreserved relation of all that had happened to either, since their separation, the maiden prayed fervently awhile, and then sobbing like a child in its first grief, sunk with weariness in the arms that encircled her, so, pillowed upon a breast that swelled with overflowing love for her, Clarence enjoyed the first unbroken slumber that she had experienced since the fatal morning of her departure from Fort Lawrence.

With fondest care, Edward watched, hour after hour, the sleeping maid; wrapping a warm mantle that he usually reposed in, during their journey, closely around, to shield her from the damps of night, he folded the attenuated form of his beloved nearer to him, until he could count the quick pulsations of her heart, and drank the soft breathings from her half-parted lips, listening with strange delight, to the low murmurs which, like a fitful breeze, ever and anon, caught his ear as they escaped from the slumberer; the offspring of some evanescent dream.

Oh! who can imagine the depth of those thoughts which shook the soul of Edward, as gazing upon the sweet face beneath, upon which the placid moonlight fell, itself, as purely pale, he traced the ravages of sorrow and wretchedness upon its tender lineaments, deprived as they were, of the deceptive lustre which enthusiasm ever imparted, at other times, and the dazzling radiance of the then shrouded eye; his own were blinded with moisture, when he conceived the extent of those sufferings so touchingly delineated in the features of his beloved. A large drop glistened tremulously upon the white cheek below; 'twas pity's offering, moulded in the fond eye that bent over, wrung from the pained spirit's wildest emotion. There is something fearful in the intensity of human sympathy, when it urges to sorrow, in true affect on something very beautiful—'tis so pure—so steadfast, but in its profound, passionate tenderness there is much that is inexpressibly sad.

When the moon had climbed half way to the zenith, the gloom that shrouded every thing like a black pall, was entirely dissipated, or sought refuge under the lofty steeps and the o'ershading trees. A striking and comprehensive scene of flood and forest was revealed in the clear, mellow light, from the elevated spot where the party rested.

This was that bold commanding range of hill, or rather mountainous steep, which, terminating abruptly and in some places almost perpendicular, forms the northern shore of the St. John, where it makes a sudden turn eastward, ere its stormy exit, as though—like a condemned exile, tearing himself desperately away from the dear associations of his early years—loath to leave forever the gorgeous scenes—the majestic solitudes—the haunted dells—the laughing mountain sides through which, in calm and playful breeze, it lingered lovingly, erewhile.

The mighty stream glided far below, without sound or any perceptible motion, from the height they occupied; and beyond, full wooded banks rose high, dark and awful in their utter stillness, for not a leaf shook—not a bough waved. To the left the river swept for a little space, then expanding into a capacious basin, upon which the moonlight shone like frosted silver, flowed directly onward until it appeared to terminate, for the enclasping eminence and wooded points confined its level sheet on every side; but upon the very verge of the liquid expanse, where the eye in vain attempted to penetrate the dark zone of hills, and the groves cast a deeper shade, an incessant flash, as of waves in violent commotion, broke the general gloom of the surrounding shores, and the exceeding quiescence that reigned elsewhere around; while the bright streak was parted by black lofty masses that seemed distinct from the adjoining banks, but whether they were islands or jutting promontories, from that distance, and in the indefinite light, it was impossible to discover.

Edward knew that the rumbling noise which had for hours excited his notice by its continual din, must proceed from that place, and be concluded from what he beheld, it was the broken fall at the mouth of the St. John, where was situated the French fort we have alluded to before, and he was satisfied of the correctness of his surmise, when he discovered on bending back a projecting limb that obstructed the view, that on the hill to the left of the torrent, where its ridge was slightly depressed, the sea seemed to rest, for it glittered above it like a radiant belt, unobscured to its far horizon, and presenting a clearly defined outline against the pearl-grey sky.

The break of day found the party awake, and concerting measures for their further guidance. After a long deliberation, during which several measures were proposed and discussed, that suggested the means of escape from their present precarious situation, Edward, as usual, determined after some hesitation, to adopt the advice of his allies, which was, on many accounts, most preferable, and the only method by which there was a probable chance of their effecting a safe retreat from the neighbourhood of the Milicete, tho' their personal liberty would be compromised thereby. Completely hemmed in by revengeful enemies, from whose vigilance their present security appeared providential, the only course remaining open was the river, the rapids of which were said to be passable, when the tide was on the flood; and to afford the means of prosecuting this plan, the chief proposed abstracting a canoe from the Milicete village on the following evening. But this route, though less liable to a rencounter with their foes, was still extremely hazardous, as Waswetchcul informed them that a short time before, her uncle, with the fighting men of his village, had gone to the salt water to assist in the defence of the French fort, against the armament, whose destination seemed so well known to the enemy. Indeed it appeared to the soldier, quite impossible that they should reach that fortress without being intercepted by outlaying parties of the natives, as it had been decided that they should yield themselves up as prisoners of war, rather than endure the uncertainty, and perhaps ultimate captivity and death, in its most harrowing forms, which might result from an attempt to run the gauntlet through the very heart of the hostile tribe; and even were they fortunate enough to achieve that step, what progress could be made with so weak and delicate a charge as Clarence, debilitated as she was already, would surely become? At Fort Bourbon, as it was called, Edward could depend upon securing courteous treatment, and above all, suitable comforts for his betrothed, until, according to established usage, an exchange could be effected and their freedom regained. Amidst this cheerless prospect, one bright hope would intrude itself, and like a ray of sunlight in a Rembrandt picture, illuminate the else repulsive void.

As nearly as he could judge, the projected attack of this same fort was to be made at about that very time, and the intelligence of the

Milicete girl rendered it probable that an investment had not yet taken place, which—if the case, and provided they made the descent of the St. John, unmolested—would afford a ready means of relief and restoration to the British settlements, should they find Captain Rouse in the vicinity, on their arrival at the sea coast.

Having concluded upon adopting the *dernier resort* above mentioned, and leaving their ulterior movements to be biassed by the aspect circumstances thereafter might assume, Edward turned his attention to the more immediate perils by which they were encompassed. Nor were they of trifling consideration, for scarce had the cheek of Clarence, who was wonderfully refreshed by her slumbers, begun to glow with somewhat of its pristine bloom, as the lover spoke in low, earnest tones at their side, when it was blanched to a deadly hue, and she trembled with sudden agitation, gazing, meanwhile, with a look of dread, at an object beneath the cliff. Following the direction of her eye, Edward observed three canoes dart simultaneously into view from a point of the stream above, and sweep down the river with astonishing speed, directly under the eyrie-like cleft, where they were concealed.

"Ugh!" ejaculated Pansaway, "the wolves are on the trail of the stray deer; but their noses are full of dust. They cannot see the *Sunbeam*; for you see, their eyes are all the same like the owl's in the day-time. What say ye, brother?"

"Yes," replied Edward, with despondency, unconsciously adopting the style of the natives; "but well I know their errand—they go to give notice of the captive's escape, that the warriors may quicken their scent, and wash the film from their eyes, that they may seek for the unseen enemy; is it not so?"

"The *Open Hand* has said it;" rejoined Pansaway, "but the Micmac shall be as the wind;—you can feel him—you can hear his war-cry, but always with a powerful arm and a sound, he comes and goes—no man knoweth whence or whither; and even where the *wind* can pass, there may be *Sunbeam* follow!"

Still as Edward beheld the prospect thickening with danger, his heart sunk despairingly; for himself he had no care, but the thought of what might befall the cherished being, whose fate was so closely interwoven with his own, almost unmanned him. The feeling, however, was only momentary, for he rallied quickly, when Argimou, who had been reconnoitering, told that a party of the Milicete were ascending the brow of the hill on their left. Quickly drawing Clarence within the furthest recess of the fissure in the limestone rock, where she was soon joined by Waswetchcul—the soldier, with his companions, planted themselves, well armed, among the thick foliage of the cedars at the mouth of the gully, to await the ordeal which they were about to undergo.

Was it a shadow that moved from out the gloom, cast by yon tall pine, on the forest's verge? Ah, no! See how stealthily the phantom steals onward—would it were such!—the spirits of the dead are harmless! See the dark vision, how cunningly it creeps along; now pausing to listen, now rolling its gleaming eyes on either side, and clutching a long knife with a warmer grip than ever, perchance those bony digits deigned to proffer friendship. Awake, Edward! 'Tis the living thou hast to dread. Seest thou not his war paint, his shorn scalp, his haughty gait? Truly, it is time that thou shouldst know a Milicete warrior, though he may appear somewhat strange in his fantastic embellishment, yet every line, every shade of which is significant either of personal attribute, terrible incentive, or the stern and unchangeable purpose that actuates the wearer's heart.

Closely following the leading savage, the whole spectral band, like a string of shadows, one by one, passed the pine tree and came fully into view. It was a sight that might have made the flesh of a bolder person than Edward creep with terror; for each individual of the war-party was entirely naked to the waist, and painted in emblematic devices of a most startling and extraordinary character.

The leading warrior was clothed as with skeleton armour; for upon his dark skin was traced in ghastly white, bone after bone, a horrible portraiture of death; the eyes, like bright jewels, glowing, as it were, from deep hollow caverns, and the grinning mouth lengthened and distended, apparently lifeless and distorted by the deceptive potency of art; while with the resemblance of rib and arm bone, marked out in all their characteristic leanness, the fear-inspiring warrior strode before his followers—as some old tenant of the grave, who, aroused from sleep by the cry of disappointed vengeance, had come to conduct his countrymen to the lurking place of their undiscovered foe. The rest, if not presenting so hideous an exterior, were severally formidable, though after a different fashion. One was wound as with a huge, scaly serpent, portrayed in vivid colors, and usurping with its reptile head, that of the body around which it was curled; the basilisk eyes dilating in a series of fiery rings, and the jaws distended—as if to seize its prey; while the low crown was furnished with a bristling crest, formed from the black pinions of the crow. Another, again, was covered with a variety of figures traced in sombre tints, while his face was striped red and white, in alternate bars.

This painted crew—that seemed more like the perverted creations of a delirious brain than any thing human or real—was evidently occupied in making strict search for the enemies that had left a bloody token of their hostile intrusion on the previous evening. To an unconcerned spectator, it would have been curious to mark the subtle motions of the savages, as they scrutinized every bush and hollow within sight of those concealed; now moving parallel to each other— now encircling the ground, like baffled hounds—then crossing and recrossing in every imaginable direction, while all the time, not the smallest sound was uttered; but their eyes were in continual motion, and the morning ray shone occasionally upon their bright weapons as they flitted backwards and forwards, among the rocks and cedar groves. But to those most deeply interested in the issue, the spectacle was productive of gloomy apprehension of discovery, and the most intense excitement.

Edward was several times on the point of firing involuntarily, as one of the enemy would approach rather too near their place of conceal-ment; and Dennis was with difficulty restrained from enacting some extravagant ecstacy, which would, unquestionably, have led to their immediate disclosure. Fortunately, Clarence was spared the trial that operated on the rest, for being precluded from all observation, by the narrow limits of her place of refuge, she knew not, at that time, the little space that intervened between her friends and an exasperated foe. Yet, even when the danger seemed greatest, when the snake-coiled Milicete thrust his serpent head close to the dense screen of the cedar, behind which the party was ensconced, and their discovery appeared unavoidable, the Micmac warriors were calm and collected. Twice Argimou's bowstring was at his ear, and as many times gradu-ally relaxed again, retaining its arrow, as the eye of the searcher was observed to denote only the acuteness with which its faculty was brought into play as it roved, hither and thither, without evincing any change in expression, such as would have surely hailed the first assur-ance of its object being achieved.

At length the fugitives breathed more freely, for having searched minutely over every foot of ground to the very verge of the precipice where the secret gully was situated, the savages gradually moved on in pantomimic masquerade, and after a time, altogether disappeared in the gloom of the shadowy forest.

"The holy saints be glorified!" ejaculated Dennis, devoutly, as he laid down his firelock and filled a stone pipe that he had procured from the chief; "ivery shoul of 'em, St. Patrick especially ah-min! May I niver, if ever I seen the likes afore;—praise God all the same. Musha! Iv it didn't make the wather pour aff o' me like a mill sluice—so it did. The bloody hathens! May be I wouldn't been letting the hate out o' wan o' thim, only for ould sarious, who'd a been a christian man uv the black inimy hadn't spoilt his skin in the makin', and the Segimmes likewise.—Tare-an-ages! I've seen many a white man that couldn't luck at thim in the fashionin uv a pipe or the judgmatic lying uv an ambushment; by the crass—I say it."

"Ugh," exclaimed Pansaway, as the enemy departed, remarking to the chief;—"the Milicete *boo-woo-win* is pretty strong, he can arm a warrior with war paint, but he cannot sharpen his eyes with cunning words."

"Argimou laughs at the blind moles of the Milicetejik—he has vanquished their *boo-woo-win*;"—was the proud reply.

As Edward moved from his position, he felt as though a heavy load had suddenly been removed from his breast, and while he sought the nook where Clarence had been left, he could not withhold his belief in the assurance of his guides as to the probability of their being able to accomplish their ultimate escape.

"The *Open-Hand* sees," said Pansaway, "that the Milicetejik is a hog what buries its nose in the ground; he crawls on the earth like a blind worm, and cannot look at the sun—as a Micmac—without shedding tears. You understand?"

"I do;" replied the soldier, with a smile.

"Well," was the rejoinder—"very well; go to the *Sunbeam* and say, when comes moonlight may be we can go, make your heart strong. Certainly we will go down Ouangondy—certainly we must see Anglasheou, and *he* will go home and say—'*Sunbeam* has come back again, my father.'"

Chapter XVIII

Remaining close within their secret retreat, the party experienced no further molestation during the day, which was not altogether spent unprofitably, at least on the part of the chief, who made several excursions in the neighbourhood, to ascertain the exact position of the Milicete village, and the local circumstances which might be rendered available in his projected plan to obtain a canoe for the purpose before mentioned. Accordingly, having satisfied himself fully of the feasibility of his scheme, as soon as the twilight deepened into night, and the objects around became blended in one indefinite mass of shade, while the increased roar of the falls, which through the day had altogether ceased, as the salt water poured upward and lessened the inclination of the river current,—told that the tide was ebbing from the sea coast, Argimou departed, carrying with him the warm wishes and fervent hopes of the rest, for upon the success of his perilous adventure all their future prospects of deliverance mainly depended.

An hour having elapsed, and there being no evidence of the chief's approach, Edward began to entertain fears for his safety, when the notes of a wippoorwill were heard beneath the steep bank to the left, upon which Pansaway, who was near, rose and asked the soldier what he called that bird? Edward avowed his entire ignorance of the species that emitted the sounds, while the old Indian, as he tightened the lacing of his moccasins and took up his pack and gun as if to depart, quickly rejoined—

"The Micmac listens to him in the dark, talking to the white moon or the red stars; and some people do say, because he sings always when other birds are asleep, therefore *he* must be some poor squaw who broke his heart when bad husband left him alone.—Then you see, he didn't go to the good land when he died, and so the spirit of that poor squaw came back again to look after him; and that's the reason why he does always sing by night, sometimes cheerful, more often very sorry, saying, *'come to me! come to me!'* We call him *wick-quill-yetch*, or the night-hawk what sings. Will you come and look for this singing bird?" asked he, playfully—"may be we will find him pretty soon."

Directing them to proceed with caution, the guide moved from the covert and commenced descending the bank at a place where it sloped less vertically to the river side. Edward, leading Clarence, followed in his footsteps, with the Milicete maid and Dennis in their rear. They were much surprised to find, instead of the bird they sought, something far more welcome in their present circumstances, for the Europeans saw with joy, that, floating motionless and close to the sedgy shore, was the promised canoe, from which Argimou stepped lightly, and while the others disposed themselves severally in its interior, under the direction of his father, he returned to the secret hiding place and brought down the remaining packs and arms.

When all were embarked he took the seat reserved for him, and pushing the canoe clear of the bank, the whole party were fairly afloat and speeding rapidly on their hazardous passage to the sea. Sweeping to the right, when they reached the curve of the stream, they came in full view of the Indian village, the numerous lights of which were reflected on the placid river in long, dagger-like corruscations; no sound broke the deep repose of the hour, except the shrill bark of a dog which echoed and re-echoed among the headlands and coves with startling effect. Gliding past close within the shadow of the western shore, they shot noiselessly along the broad expanse, which was spread out before them, embayed, as it were, by a dark zone of hills, through which, directly in front, the river rushed with foaming impetuosity, slightly luminous by the rays of the low moon just rising in the east, while, as they approached the rapids, their booming reverberations increased and the bed of the river seemed shaken with the continual sound that rolled like thunder, majestically above its surface.

Entering a cove that indented the western shore, near the verge of the falls,—where it was their intention to remain until day-break, when the flood tide would allow them to proceed in safety to the coast,—Edward congratulated Clarence upon the ease with which they had accomplished the descent thus far; while as they paddled towards the shore, which was cast completely into shade, the moon breaking from a dark mantle of clouds, shod a sudden brightness upon the scene, with a power almost equal to the light of day;—that beam was their salvation! Close under the bank, and only a few yards in front, lay a canoe that they had not before observed, in consequence of the deep gloom in which it was concealed, and ere their way was stopped to effect a retreat before they were recognized, the opportunity was lost, for no sooner had the brilliant light glanced on the side of their bark vessel, then a loud yell proclaimed their discovery, and, like an arrow, the Milicete darted out after them in rapid chase.

It was futile to think of outstripping the enemy, o'erburthened as the canoe was, and even if that were possible, every moment would but bring them nearer to the encampment it had been their purpose to avoid, which was sure to be alarmed by the shouts of the pursuers, when their destruction was certain; for there was no course open to them but that by which they had just descended, and, when once beyond the noise of the rapids, a single war cry would suffice to conjure up, on every side, a legion of exasperated foes. It was an instant of great emergency, requiring the utmost judgment and self-possession to determine the most prudent mode of action, and it was promptly taken advantage of by the unmoved Pansaway.

With a calm clear eye he measured the distance between the two canoes, and then glanced towards the fall which was close at hand, before him, indistinctly glimmering, were barely discernible, the light of the hostile village, and his choice was decided; 'twas a desperate expedient, but it suggested the only hope of escape. Making a sign to Argimou, who was steering the canoe, its direction was speedily altered, as a half-turn brought the prow to bear upon the eastern shore, then with a whoop of bold defiance they dashed their paddles into the rapid current and struck immediately across the river, while the Milicete, with wild shouts and reckless determination, followed madly in pursuit.

Then occurred a scene of most thrilling excitement which it would be impossible to portray, with the force of its terrible truth, by the power of human language. Such periods sometimes make men suddenly old in mind and features, as though the former were prematurely blighted by the scathing fire that seared the latter like a parchment leaf. Such wild moments condense in one intense pang, the fears and agony of a life, turning the hair white; an enduring memorial of suffering long after it has passed away.

Without a word, the guides bent their sinewy frames to their herculean task, making the canoe and its living contents almost fly out of the water with the tremendous strokes of their paddles, and sending the troubled element boiling and hissing behind in a long luminous track, as they urged impetuously onward in desperate career; while each minute, they were drifting nearer the vortex of the fall which yawned beneath, as if waiting to engulf them in its remorseless waves. The calm stream over which they darted, looked like ink—so black, molten and still, but, nevertheless, it was bearing them swiftly and surely onward to the torrent's edge, which rolled with a gradual slope below, where, in startling contrast to the river above, as far as the eye could distinguish, was to be seen one perfect sea of foaming waves in endless commotion; while the ear was deafened by the eternal din rising up from the tumultuous war of waters.

When the dangerous passage had first been attempted they were considerably above three small islands covered with pines and situated close to the opposite shore, the last of which reached to the extremity of the fall, but as they advanced, the current swept them gradually down, until it became a matter of doubt whether they would be able to reach the lowest of the group, which if impracticable, inevitable death would follow. Therefore, to overcome the fatal influence of the current as much as possible, the canoe was propelled obliquely upward, being directed towards a point far above its intended destination, and the enemy, inspired by revenge rather than a desire of saving their lives, brought their canoe, likewise, stem on to the stream; so that the two were moving in parallel lines, their broadsides being presented, while each instant they were drawing nearer to each other and the wrathful whirlpools.

The bewildered Clarence, in an agony of terror, shrieked aloud, but the sound was lost in the overwhelming roar of the torrent, and then she hid her face beneath her lover's mantle to shut out the dreadful sight. Edward was assisting the propulsion of the canoe with main strength, and the Indians bowed their heads as they plunged their broad blades into the tide, and brought them up again with quick action, dripping and glistening in the moonlight.

Meanwhile several shots had been fired at them by the chasing canoe, which fact was known only by their effect, for the report could not be heard. One bullet dashed the paddle from the hands of Edward, and it was with some difficulty caught by the chief as it flew past. Another perforated the thin bark of the canoe near the gunwale, where Dennis lay quivering in an ecstacy of rage and apprehension. As soon, however, as he observed the shot hole, he was roused into a complete forgetfulness of his precarious situation.—With frantic energy he sat up in the canoe, and seizing his gun, rested it deliberately upon its side and fired at their pursuers. A shout of exultation escaped him as he beheld the steersman of the Milicete fall heavily over the side of the canoe, which was nearly upset in consequence, causing it to swerve from its course and drift sideways down upon the fall.

This event seemed to add new life to the Micmacs, for they appeared to employ an increase of strength as they neared the islets, and strove by vehement efforts to gain a landing which was offered by a ridge of low rocks which formed an imperfect communication between the two last, whose sides were almost perpendicular and incapable of yielding any means of escape from the torrent that rushed furiously by. A dozen strokes of the paddle would decide the matter; life or death depended upon the issue. The feelings of those not actually engaged in the employment of most violent muscular exertions, were wound up to a pitch of distraction; but though Clarence shrieked piteously, and Dennis, prompted by partial insanity, made as if about to spring at once into the dark tide, the Indian girl sat still, motionless, and pale as the sculptured marble. Her large, full eye was dilated, but it quailed not as she viewed, unshrinkingly, the foaming and whirling rapids; and turning to the chief who sat behind, guiding the frail bark with consummate skill, and eyes intently fixed upon the rocky ledge they were approaching, there centered her every thought and feeling.

A statue could not be more hushed and stone-like in its awful calm, than Waswetchcul upon that terrible occasion.

What is that giant power which steels the soul with fortitude in such momentous scenes, where the weak, the undistinguished at other times, stalk forth, like gods, superior to fear, while the strong, the arrogant, shrink away with prostrated energies of body and mind? Strange is it that the tender, sensitive woman should often meet reverses and death with a degree of courage and noble endurance, which the hardy and rough-hearted are incapable of exhibiting.

Urge on, brave men! A few more strokes and ye are safe. God, how the stream leaps and roars along the adamantine sides of the islands! Will the shallow fabric ever stem the torrent that rushes there? Alas!— in vain, in vain! Like a straw the canoe whirls away with the flood; the pines, the rocks appear to fly backward. They shoot by the landing with the speed of light, while everything reels before their eyes and their brains grow giddy; yet can they almost touch the ledge of rock with the foremost paddle. In vain, in vain! Down into the abyss of death, the whirlpool gapes beneath; its angry voice is in their ears shrinking for prey. O heaven! is there no hope, and must they die?

One look of despair—one short prayer for mercy, and the canoe was borne along by the rapid, and all chance of life seemed gone, but even then, when the horrors of the fate before them were half experienced in the intensity of anticipation, the eddy dashed them on the rocks midway between the islands, which they had tried their utmost to reach without avail, and before the canoe could be again influenced by the current, Pansaway had leaped upon the slippery sea-weed, with which the ledge was covered, and with superhuman strength lifted it bodily with its occupants half out of the stream.

What we have taken some time to describe were the events of a few brief moments, but whose history was burned in scorching characters, the traces of which would never wear away upon the memory of those that participated in their peril. The whole party were instantly rescued from their hazardous position without scarcely the consciousness of their providential escape. So sudden was the transition from absolute despair to a sense of relief,—vague, indeed, but O how boundless!— that the mind was unable to span at a single effort, the immeasurable space that separates the two extremes of good and evil; it seemed impossible that they could be saved, that they stood actually upon the firm rock, and were no longer the sport of the treacherous waters.

Edward had hardly borne Clarence to the strand when she swooned in his arms. Turning to seek the aid of some one, he saw that the

Indians were watching the motions of their pursuers, for they stood staring with painful intensity towards the fall, and their figures were rigid and seemed rooted to the rock. Following the direction of their gaze, the soldier's nerved heart grew cold, and his hair rose, as he witnessed the awful catastrophe from which they had so recently been preserved.

The Milicete canoe, at a short distance from where they stood, was hurrying with frightful rapidity towards the rapids, while its savage crew, desisting from their useless toil, with the exception of one warrior, stood upright and tossed their arms wildly about, and shook their paddles with unrelenting hate at the rescued party; but if they spoke, the feeble sounds were drowned in the voice of the mighty torrent. Like a lightning flash the canoe shone as it dashed down the dark declivity with its human freight, whose extravagant gestures were seen for an instant with hideous distinctness, strongly relieved against the ghastly foam into which they sank, then the watchers sought in vain, among the boiling billows, for further traces of their enemies; every earthly vestige had entirely disappeared. Yet they caught one more glimpse of the canoe, but at some distance below the first fall, for it shot up perpendicularly into air from out the whirlpools, as if poised by the weight of one clinging with expiring grasp to the lower end; then it gradually subsided again into the yeast of waves, and as it sank, a cry was faintly heard to penetrate the din—shrill and piercing—such as the last utterance of a strong man's agony and despair;—but the deep thunder of the torrent made reply, and the waters curled and danced over the Milicete's unhallowed grave.

"*Open Hand!*"—shouted Pansaway, placing his mouth close to Edward's ear, "did you hear an eagle scream? 'Twas louder than Ouangondy, and even the Great-Spirit can scarce hear himself speak when HE drives the salt water away. 'Twas the death-howl of Madokawando. Water is more stronger than the cunning Sagamou. I know him. His arm was big, his war-whoop very noisy—but he had a fox's heart!"

Lifting the senseless girl in his arms, Edward with some difficulty ascended the steep margin of the island, which, though covered with ragged pines and underwood, was formed of iron-like rock that terminated almost perpendicularly on every side, as if worn by the constant strife of waters which for ages had swept its bare brow. Having gained the mossy soil clothing its summit, he tried every means to restore the consciousness of Clarence, but it was long ere her senses recovered the violent shock they had sustained. At length she woke, as from slumber, and gazed wildly around. A fit of hysterical laughter and lamentation succeeded, which finally resulted in a flood of tears; then sobbing tremulously, she fell gradually into a tranquil sleep. Wrapping his cloak closely around, the lover left her in Waswetchcul's care, and assisted in raising the canoe from the seaweed below, which was considered an insecure position, and then crossed to the further end of the island, which was but a few paces in extent; here was witnessed one of the wildest sights it had ever been his fortune to behold.

From the elevated spot on which he stood, to the place where the view soon terminated, the river was walled in by towering precipices that frowned in savage grandeur, while on the eastern side they presented an impervious shield to the lambent glances of the moon. Sweeping round, with point and cove and disjointed fragment, the eternal barriers approached their clasping arms from either bank, until within a surprisingly short distance of each other, when they terminated abrupt and sheer, and through this narrow intersection, as through a giant's portal, the majestic St. John, with all its countless tributary streams, burst in wrathful impetuosity, when making a sudden turn to the left, the river disappeared from the sight, apparently bounded by a lofty hill covered to its base with dark evergreen woods; with which, indeed, every summit and beetling crag was crowned,

179

adding to their commanding altitude and heightening the peculiar character of the scenery.

From the point where the perspective vanished, to the insulated rock on which the adventurers had taken refuge, the stream widened with a gradual curve, and again slightly contracted its limits till it seemed, with its bold margin, not unlike a boiling cauldron, for its whole visual surface was wrought into a sheet of agitated foam, which assumed a ghastly lustre in the beam of the phantom moon. The vexed waves, torn and split by the ragged channel through which they coursed, tossed and shook their white waves like warring steeds, now springing on with leap and rear—now turning its dizzy vortex; here belching up, as if ejected from hollow caverns below, there eddying back with slow and solemn motion, along the chasms and echoing coves.

The group of islands were close to the left bank, from whence they appeared to have been wrenched by some stupendous earthquake which split the solid rocks, and tore a pathway through the hills to let the waters through. Between the shore and the two lower islands—on the last of which, the party were,—the rapid rushed with a considerable inclination, and the swiftness of a fierce mountain torrent, curling and dashing on its stormy passage, and in a line with the further shore, to which it extended, Edward observed, to great advantage, the unbroken fall of the river as it rolled with gentle hill-like swell, and without any appearance of motion, into the frothy whirlpools where the hostile Milicete had so horribly vanished. And over the snowy rapids and the cold blue river above, the pale light gleamed and flickered as the black clouds intercepted its rays, while the deep base of the cataract, resounding from the steeps and concavities, sang its tremendous anthem to the night, and with its powerful vibrations the islet trembled beneath their feet, as though it were about to sever from its hard foundation and resist the fickle river no longer with its tower-like parapet of stone.

How grim and stern in the uncertain moonlight the titanic heights looked down upon the fretful waters at their base, rebuking, as it were, their feverish career, with calm, though storm furrowed brows. The gaunt, spear-topped pines bristled like a ridge of hair, along the summits of the cliffs; their midnight shade—like the Almighty's hand—seemed to still the tempest where it rested upon the struggling wave; and dread and unsparing as the red-man's vengeance, the lonely spirit of the place seemed to sit upon his savage throne, and brood, with malign delight, over the smoking gulf and its sepulchral gloom.

Chapter XIX

Through the long hours they watched the falls with unwearied patience, but it was not until towards morning that the tide turned, and a change was observed in the area of labouring waters; for the commotion was gradually subsiding, and consequently the noise grew less overpowering to their ears as the flood swelled upward from the sea, tinging the river water with its brine. While they waited for the rapids to become sufficiently calm to admit of their venturing down without risk, to the French fort—which, as Pansaway said, was in their immediate vicinity, and only hidden by the abrupt bend of the river below the projecting precipices that so singularly confined its course—the warrior related to his son, who in turn interpreted its meaning to Edward—the following extraordinary legend that he had heard when he sojourned with the Milicete, many years ago—

"You see," said Argimou, when his father had ceased, "the great Ouangondy did not always go through this place to *La Baye Francoise*, but when the first time was—as many moons back as there are hairs upon brother's head—it ran by a broader path; the same where, he remembers, in the swampy vale we came a second time upon the trail of Madokawando that is dead, and drank joy with our eyes as we looked upon the *Sunbeam's* journey. Now listen, and my father will tell thee, by the voice of his son, the ancient speech which says how this thing was.

"Older than the oldest tree, or wampum belt, or grave, is the story of Ouangondy.—How many times has the ground turned white and green, with the frost and the summer; how many tribes have been born, battles fought and warriors died, since the *Great Unknown* were swept away with their villages and pride? Ay, how many?

"The Milicete sees their ghosts gliding over the mad waters where their bones lay crumbling, when the moon shines, or the lightnings quiver; and some do say that they have heard them shriek as the thunder of the storm rolled along the mountains, or shook the hollow rocks with its angry growl.

"Yet whether the spectres of that mighty nation do linger about the place where they perished—they and their name, nevertheless, it is certain that here they stopped, and here by the Great Spirit's arm were they overthrown.

"The memory of other times is always bright among the forest tribes, and our father's word is as an arrow—true, and goes straight into a child's heart, leaving its mark there evermore.

"No one knoweth whence the *Great Unknown* came. Some said from the inside of the ground; and some that they were thrown up in a wild storm out of the salt water waves. The *Man* above, if he would choose to speak, could only tell; for he knoweth the secrets of the dead, and the thoughts of live animals and men.

"Now, these people came and drove the tribe away from the salt water, and built villages, surrounding them with high walls of stone, and fished more than they hunted; yet though not numerous, still were they very powerful and of great stature;—even like the shadow of an Indian when he stands beside a clear lake, in the grey dawning of the morn. Such were the light haired strangers who drove the red men to the woods in the olden time.

"The hunters looked out from the shade, and saw them dancing in the night, by the light of the red torches. By the gleam of the crackling pines their pale eyes glared, while they drank their foaming horns and vexed the hills with their fierce songs of battle. And ever when they would raise high their deep cups of bone and shout as one man, in a strange tongue, they turned always to the pathway of the morn.

"The Indian's heart grew cold when he beheld these wild warriors resting by the cedars of his fatherland, and he prayed to the spirits for help, upon the high mountains and in the dark groves of fear, where the dead slept—where their ghosts tarried. Ay, by the sacred groves— by the haunted shades the red man coaxed the breathless manes—the viewless things that hover in the still air, in the leaves, by the torrent, by the caves of rock, on the black whirlwind, on the blue lightning that kills,—to come forth in their dreadful strength and drive them away like weak flies in the storm: but they were angry and would not come.

"Then it happened that the wild strangers fell to fighting with each other—brother against brother—and all because some had found stones that shone like a sunbeam, among the caves of the valley; and they that had little fought with those that had more, so when these were killed they possessed their treasure. Therefore, in this way, became they enemies to one another, and the yellow stones were a destroying curse; for friend died by the hand of friend, and the spear and axe were painted with the blood of kindred; and the pure earth was stained.

"Then once more the red men prayed to the strong powers of the woods and the air; and they rose up against the wicked race, and tried to scare them from the land. But though the forest moaned, and each spirit of its countless trees awoke in wrath; though the red stars burst and were hurled along the sky of midnight by the dread spirit of the air, and the armed watchers of the north rushed up and roofed them round on every side with ribs of fire, and shook their flaming swords at them in fury; yet the *Great Unknown* were not afraid, and would not go away; for they had hearts of stone.

184

"Then the Great Spirit that ruleth all things gathered the lightning in his waving hair, and with the tempest, like a hungry eagle, perched upon his shoulder, came down from the sky and rested upon the mountains. The earth trembled with fear, and silence fell over it like a shadow, what time *Kesoulk* looked below and frowned; and in that black night the hard hearts slept without a dream.

"He said to the wind—'*go!*' And to the lightning—'*speed!*' Then shrieked the tempest through the vales and the proud hills were broken. Then roared the mad thunder, and the crooked fires cut through the land like winged knives. The rocks were split and hurled about like pebbles among the bad strangers, and their hearts melted with horror, and they were crushed. The earth was rolled and tossed to and fro, like waves; the forests were struck down, like grass in the mighty whirlwind, and the Indian thought the end of the world was come. In that black night, strong warriors hid their faces and died, and the ancients appeared, for the ground shook so that they could not rest in their graves, therefore they came forth and stalked upon the hills, and talked to the thunder and the whirlwind.

"At length *Kesoulk* said to the storm—'*cease!*' And, like a weary bird, it folded its wings and returned again to sleep within the hollow of his hand.

"When every thing became still, and the sun rose once more in peace, the red tribe looked out of their hiding place and wondered. In the green valley where the *Great Unknown* had built their habitations, there was a sound of torrents—there was a gleam of waters!

"Their limbs quivered, and their strained eye-balls reeled with dread; for the hills of rock were shivered, and the mighty Ouangondy had been forced to wander by a strange path to the salt water; and even where the strangers had been there rolled and leaped its roaring wave!

"After a while the hunters came down and dwelt by the borders of the valley that was, and the unknown race troubled them not any more; for they slept beneath the river of many waters;—bright Ouan-gondy was their grave.

"Oft times, when the fisher takes his spear and torches by night on the still water, he starts and grows pale with fright, when he sees a white bone glistening among the long reeds that wave below. Then must he go home straightway, and ask the wise man for a charm of power, else will the spectre of the bone come to him in sleep, and he will sicken and die with the curse that clings to the spirits of the *Great Unknown*.

"Such, brother, is the awful word which shakes the brave that listens, more than the battle or the storm; such is the story of power, telling how the salt water race were struck down by the Great Spirit's wrath.

"Who can stand before *Kesoulk*? His arm must be most powerful—his heart very strong!"

By the time that Edward, disturbed by the call of Pansaway, started from the reverie into which the preceding extraordinary legend had plunged his thoughts, day was dawning in the east, while the rapids, having entirely subsided, the river glided with an upward current, every moment increasing in height and swiftness, past the shores and islands. Awaking Clarence from sleep, which had great effect in com-posing her excited feelings, the adventurers were again afloat over the spot where they had made their hurried escape from the falls, as the ledge was now submerged by the flood tide.

Paddling along under the black precipices, where the silence—only broken by the crackling note of a restless kingfisher, winging along the side of the cliffs, or perched briefly, on the branch of some gnarled tree, watching for its finny prey—was deeply contrasted with the reverberations that a few hours since had shaken them to their very centres—they emerged from the rocky gateway, where to the left, a huge fragment, torn from the steep, lay half buried in the flood that swept peacefully at its foot. The next instant the dark mounds of Fort

Bourbon were visible, as they turned the stream, and the eyes of the beleaguering force they wished, yet had scarcely hoped they might be fortunate enough to descry. Still an involuntary pang of regret wrung the breasts of the Europeans, as they beheld with bitterness, the utter solitude of all around, while they were quickly drawing near the strong hold of their national enemy. There remained now the only alternative of delivering themselves up as prisoners of war, and claiming protection from a foe it was no longer possible or prudent to avoid.

As the canoe approached the insulated point of land upon which the fortress was situated, near which was a second island of bleak and irregular appearance, it struck Edward that an indescribable air of neglect reigned about the place, and it certainly argued little for the watchfulness of the garrison, that they were enabled to gain within pistol shot of the walls unchallenged; for no warlike voice issued its stern summons from the ramparts, and neither sound or motion of life was observed about its defences; nor did the lofty flag-staff look as though it had lately borne a banner, for it was tottering over the bastion, and from its truck, drooped woefully, a remnant of the broken halliards.

With astonishment they passed along by the foot of the glacis, and gazed anxiously at the grassy ramparts, while still they were unquestioned, unwarned. Rounding the northern angle of the fort, a view was obtained of the open sea on either side of a beautiful green island that parted the broad expanse which was tinged with a faint crimson hue by the prophetic blush of day. They landed at the eastward front and entered, wondering, through the unclosed gateway, where the first sight of the interior suggested a ready explanation of the mystery.

The fort was tenantless and dismantled.—The works, partially blown up, or otherwise destroyed, presented a scene of wide confusion, among which were conspicuous the blackened heaps of half consumed buildings; while fragments of iron, scattered about the encumbered esplanade, were the only remains of the artillery which had once defended the walls. The immediate conclusion of the soldier was, that while they had been delayed in making their escape down the river, Captain Rous had arrived, destroyed the fortress, and departed from the coast; which opinion was strengthened by the observation of his guides, who discovered, by the appearance of the charred remnants of the barracks, that its conflagration had but very recently taken place.

With unformed plan and baffled prospects, the fugitives sat about furnishing a meal, for they had fasted since the previous evening, ere they commenced the descent of the St. John, and were nearly worn out with extreme excitement and fatigue. Among the ruins of the dismantled fort Edward sat by the side of Clarence, with a cloud of care upon his brow which he endeavoured to shake off in vain; but Dennis wandered down to the sea shore, and strayed listlessly over the rocks and sand, as though there were some cord stirred in his rugged breast by the contemplation of objects to which he had for some time been a stranger, and the spell may have owned a deeper source, for they were closely associated with the recollections of his far island home. Clarence strove, with a woman's creative fancy, to banish the despondency of her lover; building up a fairy castle of hopes that was sure to be speedily demolished, as Edward would shake his head sadly, or with a faint smile, kiss her soft cheek with unutterable fondness. Yet still she spoke so trustfully in the assurance of some favourable circumstance occurring that might assist them in their present need, after the perils they had gone through, that her listener, in despite of his better judgment, felt relieved and enlivened by the hopeful words of the beloved one beside him. Meanwhile the Indians had struck a fire and prepared some venison, which was gratefully received by their fellow travellers. But Waswetchcul partook not of the repast, for she sat apart with her long black hair shrouding her pale features, and though she spoke not, nor gave any stronger utterance to her suffering, yet the chief, as he cast a softened eye occasionally towards her, knew well that she was mourning deeply the recent fate of her relative; for although he had been ever harsh and unfeeling towards her, yet was he still her father's brother and the sole protector of her bereaved childhood. Directly opposite the French fort, the harbour was bounded by a dark, wooded hill, bold and broad, which extended on either hand, from its upper curve to where it gradually terminated the seaward entrance. Nothing could be more devoid of life or human association than its grim loneliness, its unmolested repose; yet the soldier little thought that ere a century's lapse, not a vestige of forest growth would remain upon its side, and that where the spruce and cedar trees then spread their boughs, the habitations of his adventurous countrymen would be thickly clustered; and the clamour of a busy mart with its troubled interests, its wayward vicissitudes, usurp forever the peaceful heritage of the beast and bird, desecrating the simple but majestic solitude. Then, the still shores gave back no echo, save that of a bird's song or a breaking billow; no fluttering pennon gleamed above the solitary wave: the gull flapped its wing with a shrill scream, as it sailed upon the wind, and the savage eagle of the sea held indisputable dominion over its tributary realm.

Chapter XX

While the party lingered within the deserted fort, without having as yet determined upon any mode of proceeding in the unlooked for straits to which they were reduced, by a circumstance over which they had no control; a demand for promptness of action was suddenly presented in the alarming conduct of Dennis, who was observed hastening towards the works, from the shore, where he had been loitering, with violent speed, shouting at the top of his voice, "the salvages! God help us, the salvages!" and the justice of his apprehensions was but too quickly proved; for shooting beyond a point that had obstructed the view of their approach, the fugitives beheld, with unenviable feelings, a perfect flotilla of canoes, urged with desperate haste, apparently to the very spot where they stood, aghast with amazement, by the numerous Indians by which they were filled. The first impulse of the whites was to fly into the woods behind the fort, for concealment; but the Micmacs, assured of its impossibility, when within an arrow's flight of so active and merciless an enemy— stood motionless, without even lifting their weapons from the ground on which they rested, and folding their arms, awaited, with calm fortitude, the doom that seemed so inevitable to their acute minds. But the anxiety of all was unexpectedly relieved; for instead of making directly for the glacis, the hostile fleet swerved from its original course, apparently influenced by a far more serious object than the capture of a few prisoners; for it seemed as the canoes flew past in their passage upward, leaving the fort behind, that they were themselves striving their utmost to escape from a pursuing foe; for so rapid were their motions, that nothing could be distinguished but a multitude of black, nodding heads above the sharp canoes, and the lightning glance of paddle blades, as the river was broken and whirled into countless eddies by their impetuous propulsion. Hark! What deep sound is that which makes the life-blood of the soldiers dance with long-unfelt joy, as it breaks seaward and rolls majestically along the harbour, filling the clear morning air with lingering reverberations? What winged monster tears and skips its thought-like way over the waves and through the very midst of the retreating canoes; throwing them into confusion, and half-hiding, with a shower of spray, the effects of its resistless stroke, as three of the number, with their wild crew, are scattered, piece-meal, upon the tide into which the iron scourge plunged, after its short but desolating career? O that sound!—that message—though the harbingers of Death to the Milicete—"as the music of the storm blast," the fury of its rush are to the homeless petrel; so were they welcome, doubly welcome to the ear and eye that received the delightful impression. Another booming roar, and a second shot, ricochetting along the river, cut its unsparing way among the yelling natives, from whom it culled a fresh batch of victims; then around the headland—

"Walking the waters like a thing of life,"

came gliding into sight a swam-like frigate, her curving canvas shining like pale gold in the early sunbeam. How gloriously that most beautiful creation of man,—the ocean queen,—stalked along over the blue waves, tossing the foam from her sharp prow, as if in scorn of the giant element she alone could tame.

"Huzza!" shouted Edward, throwing his cap into the air with uncontrollable joy,

"'Tis Rous! 'Tis Rous! Look, dearest;—two, three, there they are after all; and we are saved. God guard thee evermore, thou noble battle flag! Well know I thy hope inspiring cross, for I have bled beneath its crimson shade; but never yet when I looked upon thee—emblem of my country—has my faith in thy prosperity ever faltered. Joy, beloved! See—there are friends—red jackets, too, by St. George!—Verily, it were well if I go not distracted with delight."

Such were the extravagant ebullitions of feeling with which Edward hailed the brilliant vision that burst so unexpectedly upon them; as three men-of-war in succession, came rounding into view, with every sail set to catch the light morning breeze; whilst his companions were no less moved by the sudden revulsion from the most gloomy anticipations to a degree of joyful bewilderment, which the prospect of a certain restoration to all that was held most dear, could in their circumstances, be well imagined to produce. The leading frigate, when in front of Fort Bourbon, cast anchor, and as she furled sail, the hollow rattle of a drum resounded between her decks; while the flitting of dark objects in busy motion through the open ports, told that the crew were clustering thickly at their quarters.

The impatient Europeans would delay no longer. Hurrying to the landing with enthusiastic haste—which was singularly contrasted with the cool, collected manner of the stoical Indians,—they quickly embarked, and with a handkerchief of Clarence fluttering on the end of a long spear, as a pledge of their amicable character, indispensible to their safe approach, paddled directly towards the ship. The moments flew, they beheld curious faces peering down from port and bulwark, as the canoe came alongside. Then they stood upon the white deck, and a host of friends, whose honest hands were convulsed with temporary palsy, as they shook those within their grasp, again and again; pouring at the same time, words of heartfelt congratulation into the wanderers' ears. The beautiful Waswetchcul gazed with affright at the strange objects that surrounded her, and pressed closely, with the timidity of a fawn, to the side of Clarence, for protection from the admiring glances of the *pale faces*, as they passed below; and it was curious to note the wonder and awe with which the queer, outlandish looking jack-tars gathered, at a respectful distance, round the stern warriors of the forest; while they would roll their quids about and make their characteristic remarks in a mess-mate's ear. If the red men were a mystery to the amphibious sailors, the latter must have seemed a most remarkable species of the human race—a link between man and the frog—in the eyes of the Micmac warriors.

That day, the naval force under Captain Rous, remained in the neighbourhood of the enemy's fort, completing the destruction which it then appeared, the garrison themselves had commenced, previous to its abandonment; not having sufficient confidence in their prowess to resist the armament which, as they had learned, was about advancing to attack them. With the evening the anchors were weighed, and the ships, spreading their broad wings, bid farewell forever to the banks of the wild St. John.

As they stood across the Bay of Fundy, the twilight was deepening around, and Edward walked the deck in converse with doctor Dickson, whom, it will be remembered, we introduced on a former occasion;—he had acted as a professional guardian to the detachment of troops on board, and seemed greatly astonished at the success of his young friend's scheme; having expressed his firm conviction from the first, that it was one of the most decided cases of monomania that had come within the sphere of his observation.

"My boy," said the doctor, in reply to some remarks of the other, "what you tell me is singular, very singular; but forgive me if I cannot reconcile it with the discrepance of known habits, and a brutish incapability of receiving instruction, or, in fact, a want of perception, and consequently a depreciation of not only the beautiful and exalted in nature, but the incalculable blessings which accrue from a cultivated understanding and the adoption of a more rational mode of living. See yonder savage;"—continued the doctor, pointing to Pansaway, who was leaning with folded arms against the mast, and gazing abstractedly at the waste of waters before him. "See what apathetic disdain he exhibits toward the surprising products of art and science that surround him. Methinks the sight of a British man-of-war might well, were it possible, excite a spark of curiosity and emulation in his cold soulless bosom; '*fas est et ab hoste doceri.*'"

The doctor, having run himself out of breath with his indignant reproachings of the unlettered heathen, appealed to his well-stored snuff-box, which,—like the widow's cruise,—was never empty, and he found its contents to accord that better with the pungency of his feelings, than the loud laugh with which his speech was hailed by his auditor.

"Come, doctor," returned Edward, "spare your abuses of my venerable friend, and let me tell you that you were grievously at fault when you thought yon brave man devoid of observation, or the finer qualities of our nature; believe me, many a man, rich in worldly gifts and unproductive wisdom, might receive a moral lesson of humility and contentment from that poor Indian, ignorant though he may seem to the eye of prejudice. But, as you speak the French, hold discourse with him, and you can judge for yourself; as according to your axiom, one case in point is better than a thousand theoretical deductions."

"Granted," was the pertinacious reply, "'*experimentum crucis*;' I lay my life the result will fully establish the accuracy of my argument."

Upon this intent, the two advanced toward the Indian, and the medico, somewhat with the same tone and manner used in speaking to a child, addressed him thus, in French—

"Brother."

"Ay?" was the guttural reply, as Pansaway turned his head slowly round to the questioner, seemingly loath to be disturbed from his reverie.

"What think you of those things?" rejoined the other, pointing to a shot-rack at his feet; but Pansaway turned away without deigning a reply, and fastened his eyes again upon the curling waves.

"I said so;"—whispered the man of science, triumphantly, to his companion,—"the creature is merely gifted with instinct, and so is a beaver; '*fruges consumere nati*,'" here he took another pinch.

"Forbear," muttered Edward, sternly, while he addressed his faithful ally in a very different style.

"Pansaway, we would learn your opinion of the ball that the big thunder drives; what say ye?"

At the sound of Edward's voice, the warrior turned immediately round and replied, in broken patois,

"Me think him pretty strong, may be more stronger than medicineman's *pelowwey*; sometime he no cure um. But big thunder—s'pose him go through somebody, then certain he never be sick no time any more;" and the Indian's white teeth shone as his lips parted in a quiet grin.

"Confusion!" exclaimed the astonished Dickson: "could he have meant me? How knows he my profession?"

Upon repeating the question to Pansaway, he answered, without looking round—

"Cos him head crazy."

Not understanding the inference, or the reason why the Indian associated an idea of mental derangement, with the practice of medicine, Edward applied for an explanation; upon which Pansaway, turning to him, said—

"Open Hand, listen! Indian medicine-man say, whatever place you be sick, there you must be take something for cure: may be roots, may be drink—may be tye leaves on him spot more better: so he will do.

Then you see, *Boo-wo-win* think a good deal, so he can grow more wiser; but, s'pose his head not strong enough, then he will go crazy, and be no good any more. Then may be he will take medicine in him nose, all same one *Anglasheou Boo-wo-win*. Certain his head must be very sick, so he will take tobacco dirt up his nose all the time. Certain—poor man—he should be very crazy—me sorry."

And the undaunted forrester affected to look with condescending pity upon the chop-fallen object of his provoked sarcasm, 'ere he walked away, while Edward could not restrain his mirth; which irritated the doctor so much, that he made rather a sharp reply, upon which the old forrester, drawing himself up to his full proportions, and regarding the other with an expression of ineffable scorn, raised his arm with the dignity of a sovereign, as he cut short the speaker with this pithy rebuke—

"Show me a warrior and I will talk to him. Go, stranger—Pansaway is no fool."

It was long 'ere Edward attempted to mention the subject again to his medical friend; when he did, however, ask his opinion of the Indian, he shook his head mysteriously, and strove to hide his evident confusion, while he muttered between his teeth, in the pauses of each nasal inhalation—"*rara avis in terris, nigroque simillima cygno.*"

On the following morning the ships of war, entering a narrow passage through the mountainous range that traverses Nova Scotia,—a natural bulwark,—from east to west—from the bason of Minas to St. Mary's bay—swept into a beautiful sheet of water at the head of which Annapolis Royal was situated. To the left the view was bounded by an uniform ridge of mountains, whose several bases were projected boldly into the green meadows beneath, like the bastions of some titanic fortification, in various depths of light and shade; and along their summits the valley's mist sailed slowly, clinging fondly to its native soil in curled and distorted wreaths—having somewhat the appearance of a wild charger's mane—'ere they were torn away by the breeze and melted imperceptibly into the warm blue atmosphere of morning.

In a short time they were at anchor above the town; and Clarence Forbes found an immediate asylum among the many friends by whom she was so well known and so warmly esteemed. There, through the kindness and attention lavished upon the rescued maiden,—which also were extended to her faithful and attached companion—the fair Waswetchcul,—between whom and the former, that pure regard which had sprung up amid scenes of wild excitement and distress, was neither doomed to languish when it was needless as a bond of security on the one part, nor on the other, to pass away with the occasion that stirred it into being; for 'twas the offspring of pity and mutual attraction. Clarence was somewhat restored to her original tranquility and beauty, though it was long 'ere her cheek recovered its wanted richness of bloom, or the impress of anxiety, woven by vicissitude and sorrow, was erased from her young brow. The bud of her sweet life had been chilled by the sharp frost of early grief, and time alone could heal the ravages it had made upon its tender texture; indeed it may be doubted if she ever perfectly recovered that joyous elasticity of feeling, which is so seldom to be seen when we have outstripped our first years, and which takes wing so surely upon the approach of the heart's sad trials. And is not its glorious, star-like ascendancy the sole period of life which may, without exaggeration, be termed our golden age! Like our early love of all things beautiful and true—it may be a simple flower, a song, a wordless thought, a fair young face, pure as the heart it reflects; like the hopes we have buried,—like its painted sign; as the human passion—as the love it seals,—so is the glow that warms, the fresh gladness that plumes the free spirit of our youth, and so surely as the day advances, doth that *life of life* vanish mournfully away; for it cannot bear the noontide heat, the strife and dust of middle age.—Then, when the soul awakes from its brief and pleasant dream, and, as some lone exile from a better land, beholds the rugged and toilsome pathways of the world, is it wonderful that memory,—the urn that holds the records of the lamented past,—should be more fondly treasured than the hope which hath always forsaken. 'Tis a phantom, luring the victim on, ever on, with deceitful smile, until, grown merciful at length, it beckons *truly*, from the heaven that gilds our grave.

With the return of the troops from the frontier, where all hostilities had ceased, Clarence was restored to the arms of her father, who had been apprized of her safety, and as soon as his wounds would permit, hastened to Annapolis. Like the painter who threw a veil over the face of him whose emotions he felt were incapable of delineation, we will not attempt to portray the voiceless depth of those feelings which hallowed the meeting of the father and his child; 'twould indeed be a vain and useless task. A few days subsequently, Edward Molesworth received the hand of her whom he had proved himself so well worthy of possessing;—whose virgin affections had so long been unalterably his. And at the same time the wild flower of the Milicete was united to the Micmac chief, by a rite which thought it might consecrate could not link a firmer bond than that which pure affection had already woven.

A return to his native country being considered necessary to the perfect recovery of Captain Forbes, he took passage in a transport about to leave for England, with invalids, the charge of whom, upon application, Edward was fortunate enough to obtain.

Mournful was the parting between the Europeans and their forest friends; for a community of suffering and peril had bound them to each other. Many were the tears that Waswetchcul shed, as she clung to Clarence, long and sorrowfully, upon her departure for the old world: nor was she alone in the indulgence of passionate regret. Clarence pressed her lips on the clear, soft brow of the Indian girl, and bidding her not to weep, threw a memento round her neck; one brief clasp to the heart that throbbed as if it would break with anguish, and she hastened tearfully away.

O! how often in after years,—whose flight was noted by the successive presents, which each spring was sure to bring as a pledge of fond remembrance from those so far away,—did the faithful squaw sit by the sea shore and muse upon that unknown country which lay a moon's journey over the wide interminable waters, wondering if the *Sunbeam* was thinking in her happiness, of the one that loved her so well—so truly still, and if there were many like *her* among the daughters of the pale-faces. Then would she weep bitterly and gaze upon the pictured resemblance of her friend, which ever hung at her bosom, with every token of fresh, impassioned grief.

Even the stern warriors forgot their habitual self-restraint as they shook the hand of Edward on taking leave. Argimou turned away with strong emotion, and the iron-hearted Pansaway could not meet the sad look of the *Open Hand*, as he bid adieu, without faltering; and his parting words were low and inarticulate to the ear of him he had so nobly assisted in time of need. Nor must we forget to mention that Dennis, inspired by a fit of spontaneous generosity, purchased two hunting knives and presented them to the foresters with these words—

"Here, Sagamy, avic, and yerself, ould sarious, kape *thim* for the sake o' Dennis Sherron; an may they niver want an edge or a male's mate to deal wid, nor—be the same token—an appetite to take a hoult on; divil a thing else, plase God. Amin."

Some time previous to his departure, Edward tried to persuade the chief to return with him to England, but without avail. The answer of Argimou was characteristic and expressive:

"Brother," said he with pathos—"it can never—never be. When you take the moose from the woods and keep it among the settlements of the pale-faces, it will pine away and die. O no! Argimou must go to his people; for they are without a guide. We were born on this ground, our ancients lay buried under it; shall we say to the bones of our fathers—arise and come with us into a foreign land?"

And so they parted. One to his ancestorial abode in a country where life and human happiness was the object of man's mightiest achievements in science and art; where every means of enjoying a paradise on earth, was within reach of those who could command a little yellow dust;—if the world was ever yet capable of yielding, but for a season, aught that could beguile the restless mind of man, ever athirst with an immortal longing for the unattainable, the unknown. The other to his green forest shades, with a store of memories and thoughts to occupy his lonely musings in after years. By the red camp fire, in the still watches of the night; in the hour of trouble, and when his wronged heart was torn with dreadful anguish, he remembered the words of the *Open Hand*, and straightway the curse that was about to issue from his lips, sank powerless and untold. He strove to forget for his *brother's* sake, the cruelty and injustice of the race to which he belonged.

Chapter XXI

To those whose interest may have been engaged in the foregoing page,—an irregular narrative of vicissitude and suffering, not unusual to the early adventurers among the woods and wilds of the new world,—we would address ourselves briefly. If such are impelled by the spirit of old romance, to refuse all further sympathy to the trials of those who have triumphed over the vexatious obstacles ever supposed to encumber the rarely trodden paths of true love; with grateful thanks for their forbearance thus far, we could courteously recommend them to stop here. If we have awakened one genuine feeling, touched one chord of gentle memory, we have our reward. But with those who take a deeper glance at the motives and consequences of human actions, those who are more prone to reflect upon the dark struggle of man, for all he holds most sacred upon earth—the want and woe which results from human oppression—the agony and despair that wring the exile's heart—the sad legend of a nation's downfall,—than to pause at the brief but eventful record of that which forms but an episode in the history of our troubled lives;—we would tarry a little longer. To the moralist, the man of thought, we offer a subject of mournful but not unprofitable meditation.

Argimou went back to his tribe, among whom he acquired considerable fame by his justice and wisdom; and he was conspicuous, throughout the great changes that each year wrought in the destinies of his people, for the calm fortitude and bravery with which he struggled against, and partially retarded the untoward events that, in the end, were fated to crush, evermore, the power and prospects of the tribe. And long the *wild flower* of the Ouangondy bloomed beneath the shelter of his wigwam: while the good Pansaway was honoured for his deeds and his virtues, and 'ere he slept that sleep which knows no dream, he taught his grandson how to be a just man and a brave warrior.

In the progress of time, the tie that bound the native tribes to the interests of the French, was dissolved; for a great revolution had taken place in the concerns of the American colonies; the English having finally become sole masters of the wide realm over which the French had once securely ruled. The strong town of Louisburg had fallen, and of its battlements, its palaces, scarce a vestige remained. The prophetic denunciation of the Jewish temple of old might have proclaimed the judgment that had befallen the fated stronghold; for not one stone remained upon another, and in the expressive language of the historian, the fisherman, as he sails along the now deserted shores, points out to the curious stranger, a few dark mounds, as the place where once stood the proud and flourishing Louisburg.

The reduction of the island of St. John immediately followed, and 'ere long, the British were in possession of the Canadas, from which the last remnants of the French were finally expelled. Though, by flood and forest, blood had been poured out like rain, on the broad St. Lawrence and by the Great Lakes, the "Tri-color" was forever furled, the war-whoop heard no more. A new race dwelt by the majestic streams, and listened with awe to the roar of the giant cataract, from their homes in the deep green solitudes; while the warrior tribes were journeying away from homes and the haunts of the stranger, whose hearth-stones were planted on their ancient soil—whose broad roads led over their father's graves; whose friendship had proved a honied poison—whose presence a destroying curse!—Then, only, was it that the Micmacs entered into a compact with the English; for the Acadians had long since been driven out of their possessions, and ruthlessly torn from home and kindred, to linger and die exiled among strangers; still their faithful allies clung to the doomed peasantry, with unswerving firmness to the last. But it was in vain to resist the sure, though rigorous decrees of fate. The overwhelming tide of civilization rolled from the sea coasts, and though met and contested at every point, with unflinching bravery by the warlike hunters, yet, step by step, they were gradually given back from the shores, and isolated within the woods that were already beginning to vanish away before the axe and firebrand of the settler; so that, wearied with incessant strife and shorn of their bravest warrior, a doubt whether they would be enabled to exist much longer, as a distinct tribe, was the grave motive that induced a reconciliation, with those it were useless any longer to oppose. It was resolved, therefore, to accede to the offer of friendship on the part of the English, which had been ever rejected with scorn whilst there remained a single hope of baffling the invaders of their fatherland. This interesting ceremony—which, at the time, was considered of some importance, as a guarantee for the future peace and prosperity of the colony—took place at Halifax in the year 1761, shortly after the death of Governor Lawrence; when the management of provincial affairs devolved temporally, upon the Chief Justice, Jonathan Belcher, Esquire.

Within a room of far less pretension, in size or decoration, than the chamber from whose walls, at the present day, old England's later sovereigns look down in grandeur upon her descendants, conspicuous among whom stands the pictured donation of *The Sailor King*;—a brilliant throng was gathered, such as had seldom been seen at that day within the infant colony. There were the members of His Majesty's council in antique costume; remarkable for their well bred courtesy of demeanor, mingled with a lofty reserve, befitting their important station; there were the representatives of the people, not—as has been observed at an after period—men possessing neither the polish of cultivation nor the simple dignity of the savage; but men of high toned manner and unquestionable loyalty. There were, also, comfortable, quiet looking citizens of broad build and peaceful dispositions, who came to take a safe look at the grim warriors they had heard so much of, and whom they respected in the same ratio that they were feared; and, in contrast to the burgers, both in dress and air, were to be noticed the officers attached to the military force of the garrison; while, last, not least, many a fair face and form evinced that the curiosity of the softer sex had induced them to venture a peep at the wild men of the woods.

The President, having taken his seat, expressed his readiness to receive the deputation from the Micmacs; upon which the door opened, and, with bold, tearless bearing, the Indians strode into the chamber and walked directly up to the foot of the throne, without deigning to return the innumerable glances directed towards them, from every side. A murmur of half suppressed wonder—it might be apprehension, ran round, as the whites beheld, for the first time, within their palisaded town the fierce warriors who had so long kept them in continual dread by their determined animosity, while many openly expressed their admiration at the noble figures and easy gestures of men, tutored only in the rough schools of nature; whose tall frames were displayed to advantage, by the embroidered tunics in which the chiefs were clothed, with the additional decoration of wampum belts and variegated plumes. But, of all there, the most striking was their leader—he who, by superior rank, was alone qualified to speak the word of his tribe to the *Anglasheou*. This was Argimou, the *Bashaba*. The eventful years that had elapsed since the incidents previously narrated, had wrought some changes in his appearance; for, though his face still retained its ingenious and noble expression, yet was it also possessed of a sterner character than formerly; but there was the same proud fearless lip and eagle glance—the same erect, symmetrical form as of yore; time—though it had robbed it of its youthful curve—its panther-like pliancy of motion,—had imparted a more massive breadth of proportion and a more majestic severity of outline. Half hidden among the group—as if seeking to shun observation—stood Pansaway now a worn, weary-looking man, with iron-grey hair, and furrowed, melancholy countenance. During the whole ceremony he kept his gaze fixed intently upon his son's face, and never, for an instant, suffered it to wander around the thronged and unaccustomed assembly: what were *they* to the old Indian? The child of his manhood—the great warrior chief of his age—was the sole beacon of his heart and eye?

After several introductory ceremonies had taken place, the President made a speech wherein he exhorted the chief to render faithful submission to the Sovereign with whom he was about to enter into a treaty of peace, which, if broken, would never be again tendered, and incur the vengeance of the English government. That as he, the President, now took him by the hand, in token of friendship and protection, it would be incumbent upon his tribe ever to unite in resisting any hostile schemes against the British authority. The treaty was then signed by the President and the Micmac chief; after which, in accordance with the ancient custom of the tribe, they walked in solemn procession to the place where a grave had been prepared, in which, as a pledge of eternal amity, a tomahawk was about to be buried. There the ornamented *pipe of peace* was lighted, and the chief after taking a few whiffs, handed it to the President, who received with courtesy, the propitious emblem, and inhaled a long draught 'ere it was returned. Three successive times the *tomagon* touched the lips of either, after which, the Sachem arose and spoke to the interpreter as follows:—

"Listen! that ye may convey truly, and without deceit, the voice of the Micmac to the ear of the *Anglasheou*. Tell my brother that he hears the nation speak through my word." (Then turning to the President he continued.) "When the *Wennooch* came to *Acadie*, the Indians made a peace with him that might last forever, and the Micmac swore to aid and protect the strangers and fight for *Onanthio*—who was their great King and Father—and they fulfilled their promise, justly, until their brother's hearts were broken—the Micmac could do no more. Alas! the silver chain of our love never rusted or severed; for it melted brightly away. Now, O stranger! the friendship which we once gave to *Onanthio*, I offer to thy king and thy people, with a clean and fearless heart—and an open palm.

"Listen! *Anglasheou*, and think not that I have been prompted by compulsion or unworthy fear, to seek the good will of thy nation;—the Micmac is free—and never made a talk with Fear! O no! I come of mine own accord, to smoke peace and call King George my Great Father and friend. Now, therefore behold, O brother. For myself and in the name of the chiefs and warriors of the nation, I, their *Bashaba*, bury the hatchet forever, as a pledge of peace with the *Anglasheou*; and may it not be troubled; for so long as it remaineth hidden in the ground—so long will the chain be unbroken. In witness of what I have said—look ye! this *belt* will preserve my words!"

Suiting the action to the sentiment, Argimou, as he concluded, dropped the tomahawk into the grave, and afterwards presented a belt of wampum to the President as a record of his alliance. When the earth was carefully smoothed, with the customary observances over the emblem of war, the health of the Sovereign was drunk with enthusiasm, by the assembled multitude, and three tremendous cheers proclaimed that the hatchet was forever buried between the Micmac and the *Anglasheou*.

Chapter XXII

L ong years rolled away, and with them passed the power and happiness of the Indian tribes. The pestilence of the stranger swept them away, like a blighting wind; the *fire-water* wasted with unquenchable fever the strong frames that had once bid defiance to the winter storm and the most harassing toil.—And gradually,—with the introduction of foreign luxuries, and by association with the whites,—the stern hunters of the wild lost that simplicity and virtue, which had once taught them to despise the indulgence of propensities any further than natural wants required, or strict morality justified. The grand old woods were polluted by the clamour and wrangling bustle of greedy adventurers, before whose locust-like progress the green leaves vanished away; and with them came the guileful thought—the cold clutch of Avarice—the scorpion-fangs of Disease. The men of iron—the chainless hearted—whose spirits might break but never bend, said that they could not live by the salt water, for the air was poisonous with the breath of the pale-faces, and they had brought strange ways among them; therefore they rose up in wrath and sorrow, and left their own country, and journeyed to the setting sun, where the white men had not yet penetrated; and they returned nevermore.—Some said that they could not hunt any longer, for the noise of axes, felling trees in the clearings, had driven the game away; so they snapped their bows and became slaves to the fire-water, and thus madly—miserably died. Meanwhile the strangers grew fat and multiplied, like pigeons, in the country of the Indians, and beheld them vanishing away from the groves, without heed, or even a kind word to soften the misery they had brought upon a once mighty people. But the starving native would not beg: he was too proud *yet*, and his heart and hope were not altogether crushed by the heavy woes that had assailed him. Neither had the iron of sorrow's fetter eaten its corroding way into the soul it bound; for he still firmly believed that at some future period, they would be restored to their ancient patrimony and happiness; that hope nourished the diminished spark within their breasts, and it would flash up, at times, when something of the spirit of former days roused them into a brief oblivion of regret. Then the dark void would be illumined with a dreamy vision, a pictured prospect, coloured, by that single ray, with a brilliancy more attractive, even than the memory of the olden time; alas! 'twas as false as the deceitful source from whence it sprung: as the last fitful flicker of the taper 'ere it forever expires! But the Indian never broke his alliance with the English, and bore his sufferings patiently without a murmur.

In the mild glory of a summer eve, when the sun played laughingly, among the leaves, tingling them with mellow gold, and the sky was mantled in a rich flood of rosy light, soft as the blush of a girl's cheek, from her first love-kiss,—an aged Indian stood by a quiet spot in the deep and lonely forest. 'Twas a sad but solemn place, where a man might weep, unseen by aught save heaven, or the viewless spirits of the dead; and purge his soul by earnest communion with Nature's omnipresent God.

A small circle, green and mossy, at a high elevation, had been reclaimed from the woods, centuries ago, and thickly scattered over the area, were innumerable mounds, unadorned and undistinguished, save here and there, by a round grey stone or a wooden cross, half buried in woods and long rustling grass; and on every side, gigantic, hoary pines, with occasionally an elm or white birch intermingling its airy foliage, rose high and gloomy, like a wall, overshadowing with their arms, the mysterious relics below; while through a vista, opening to the west, long sweeping lines of vale and mountain ridge were seen, steeped in the gorgeous colouring of fleeting day, and eloquent with the grandeur of repose. Many a winding river, like a large serpent, might be traced, meandering through glade and forest grave; many a shadowy lake, like a silver mirror, reflected back the heaven from the wide, woodland solitude; and hill and interval, melting far, far away into a mutual tint, were insensibly lost, while the level line that marked the boundary of the sky, denoted that the prospect terminated only with the ocean's broad expanse.

The Indian leaned him on a staff,—for he seemed weary and bent with time,—and uncovered his grey head with reverential awe, as he looked around and felt the dread stillness and solitude of the place creep within his very soul. Who would have recognized in that double, dejected man the fiery warrior who had once made the hills echo with his war-whoop, and hailed with wildest transport the music of the battle or the storm?

'Twas Argimou, at the burial-place of his nation. The last of all those warriors who could not bring themselves to the humiliation of asking assistance from their conquerors, had protracted his departure, partly impelled by the strong love he bore his country, and partly urged by a sense of duty that revolted at the thought of deserting his unfortunate brethren, and enjoined protection to the poor lingerers who still wandered fondly around their desecrated haunts,—like timid birds whose nests have been rifled, and who could not tear themselves away.—At length, with a bursting heart, he had come to look once more at the ancient memorials, ere he left his home forever. At his feet lay three half-obliterated graves, one of which was marked with a mossy cross, rude but expressive, telling that the slumberer died in the faith of the *Wennooch*—a believer in the Son of God;—that was Pansaway's grave. But whose is that where the wild rose is shedding its leaves, as an offering on beauty's early bier; where the blue violets look up to heaven in the semblance of hopeful truth, pure and unnoted.—Whose but Waswetchcul's, and the small mound at the foot contains the ashes of her son. The *Wild Flower* had withered years ago, with the bud that sprung up from its root, in the scourging pestilence of the whites, and they were long since transplanted in "that flowery land whose green turf hides no grave."

Argimou bent down and hid his face within his shrunken hands, while he called to remembrance the beauty and gentleness of his only love; and the time when he carried her away from the Milicete country, with the *Sunbeam* of the *Open Hand*, the only just man he had ever known among the greedy Anglasheou. He thought how lonely and homeless he had been since she and her child died; but when he remembered the dark troubles that had intervened, and then saw how peacefully the flowers and sunbeam shone on the quiet graves, he felt it was better so. Then, the change that had swept over the destinies of his race, shook his soul with a tempest of grief, as he looked abroad upon the country where his fathers hunted; the streams where the white sail glided, and the canoe lay forever moored. Where was their ancient patrimony, their seagirt inheritance? Like the voice of his beloved, the bold warriors of the Micmac, gone—forever gone! Where were the mighty Mohawk, whose war-song so often echoed on the confines of their territory; were they, too, driven away? Ay, the *Bear-tribe*, was very numerous and strong, but *it* also hath vanished, no one knowing whither. Go ask the wind!—perhaps it can tell. And the other nations of the Iroquoi, and the tribes of the Great Abenaci; they were plentiful as the leaves and had strong hearts—yea, hearts without fear,—surely they still dwelt in their old forests; their fathers' country? Go, stranger! Follow the sun from his cradle to his grave, you will see a great land, few red men—but many graves.

While such-like musings suggested themselves to the old chieftain's mind, mournfully, and with trembling limbs, he bowed in hopeless lamentation over the mouldering monuments of the departed; and he would have shed tears, had not their source long since been dry. Shaking off, at length, by a violent effort, the unusual weakness that oppressed him, suddenly he stood erect, and his form dilated with excess of passion. Growing strong with the woe that wrung his soul, as he brooded upon their sorrows and wrongs, in fervent adjuration he raised his voice, filling the sacred burial-place with unaccustomed murmurs.

"Great Spirit of the universe!"—he exclaimed, stretching his arm towards the vaulted sky. "Can this thing be?" And he listened awhile; but no sound, save a low, indistinct moan, broke the deep silence of the woods, and the light bows were unshaken.

Then once more he spoke aloud—that lonely man.

"Shades of my fathers! Will the good time of the Indian *never* return?"

And a sudden wind swept among the funereal pines, and the innumerable leaves seemed whispering to each other in wonder, as the sunbeam vanished away; while dark night lit upon the sacred tumuli, and from the dim, haunted forest, that seemed to tremble at the sound, a dread voice replied: "*never!*" When the echo died away, Argimou lay stretched upon Waswetchcul's grave—the heart of the *Sagamou* was broken. Old Tonea's prophecy was fulfilled: *the white gull had flown over all!*

> Peace to the red men that are gone!
> Their children are the pale strangers' scoff;
> The heritage of their Fathers is a mournful thought;
> The memory of their glory—a broken song!

Afterword

Argimou: *A Legend of the Micmac* first appeared in 1842 as a serialized publication in *The Amaranth*, a literary journal published in Saint John, New Brunswick. Historical fiction was then enjoying wide international popularity. Sir Walter Scott's novel *Waverley* (1814) not only had launched the "Wizard of the North" on a successful career as a historical romance writer but also had consolidated the conventions of a genre eagerly read from Great Britain to North America. "Uniting the attributes of prose and poetry," notes James D. Hart in *The Popular Book: A History of America's Literary Taste* (1963), "[Scott's] historical romances presented the pageantry of the past, the adventure of heroic life, the beauty of spacious scenery, and a dramatic conception of human relations, all more exuberantly and firmly realized than in any other contemporary works of literature" (73). Avid readers haunted British and North American booksellers anticipating the arrival of the latest Scott novel, adds Hart (74–75), and the weekly *Free Press* of Halifax was typical of Canadian newspapers in reprinting serialized excerpts from works by Scott (such as *Tales of My Landlord* on 28 December 1818 and 5 January 1819) to meet reader demand. Sales of second-hand copies of Scott's three-volume novels were advertised locally ("Books"), while subscription libraries—such as those founded in Saint John or St. Andrews, New Brunswick, in 1811 and 1815, respectively—offered an array of Scott's historical poetry and prose. For the price of a library subscription, St. Andrews readers in 1815 had access to *The Lay of the Last Minstrel, The Lady of the Lake, Marmion*, the *Ballads*, and *Rokeby* (*Catalogue*), while in 1835, the Society Library in the larger urban centre of Saint John held volume sets of *Ivanhoe, Waverley, Kenilworth, Rob Roy, Redgauntlet, Quentin Durward, Woodstock, Guy Mannering, Peveril of the Peak, Fortunes of Nigel*, and *St. Ronin's Well* ("List"; see also "Account"; St. John Society). It is perhaps not surprising, then, that when the new Saint John Mechanics' Institute began a lecture series in December 1840 "on the life and writings of Sir Walter Scott," it attracted a weekly audience of six hundred people (Quill, "My Dear").

On a national level, as literary historian Robert L. McDougall has noted, an 1839 *Literary Garland* essay on Scott was politically astute in seeing Scott's work in the aftermath of the 1837 Rebellion in Upper and Lower Canada as being not only a beacon of "Freedom, Charters, Country, Laws, Gods and Religion" but also a palliative to the disruption of the times (17–18). And, like McDougall, Carole Gerson has argued for the impact on Canadian literature of critic Goldwin Smith's 1871 Toronto public address "The Lamps of Fiction" in elevating Scott's literary and social principles as models for binding "the geographically disconnected regions of Victorian Canada into a coherent cultural community" (71–72; see also McDougall 10–13). Thus, the influence of Scott on Canada was enduring, notes McDougall, reiterating that a key time in that impact was the 1840s, "clearly a formative period in the evolution of tastes and values in Canadian society" (21).

Given Scott's cultural ascendancy, it is not surprising that, when the literary periodical *The Amaranth* began publishing in Saint John in January 1841, it should self-consciously appeal to readers' taste for public history and historical romance. Founded in 1783 by exiled Loyalists at the end of the American Revolution and incorporated as British North America's first city in 1785, Saint John had emerged by the 1840s as a mercantile, shipbuilding, and timber-trade centre with a population of approximately thirty thousand. In spite of being devastated in 1837 by a fire that had destroyed over a million dollars' worth of property, the city had become a focal point for advancing the literary and musical profile of New Brunswick. Provincial writers such as James Hogg, William Martin Leggett, Peter Fisher, Walter Bates, and Oliver Goldsmith, Jr., had turned to Saint John as a publishing centre in the 1820s and 1830s, and the opening of the Mechanics' Institute in 1840, replete with a library and a public lecture hall that seated eight hundred comfortably, had enhanced the educational attractiveness of the city. With the launch of *The Amaranth* in 1841, Saint John newspaper correspondent Moses H. Perley, writing under the *nom de plume* Peter Quill, had congratulated Robert Shives, the journal's "enterprising publisher," on establishing "a work which will speedily receive a number of original writers to adorn its pages" and be the foundation of literary publications "destined to be of long continuance and increasing value" (Scrapbook). Having already achieved international success by publishing New Brunswick sporting sketches non-pseudonymously in London, Perley was to set an example for other aspiring provincial writers by demonstrating in his *Amaranth* contributions the universal appeal of exploring one's own cultural background. Thus, much of *The Amaranth*'s fiction by regional writers such as Gaeneye, J.M., or Junius was to draw inspiration from the local, ranging from Gaeneye's ironic exposure of Saint John's class tensions to Junius's satire on a King's College fop. Moreover, the widespread taste for the historical novel influenced by the popularity of Sir Walter Scott was to result in frequent period-based contributions to *The Amaranth*, particularly by upcoming writers such as William Burtis, Emily Beavan, and

215

S. Douglass S. Huyghue.[1] Of the three, Beavan and Huyghue would eventually publish in London and end their professional lives in Australia.

S. D. S. Huyghue: Background to Writing *Argimou*

Born in Prince Edward Island on 23 April 1816, the son of Lieutenant Samuel Huyghue, 60th Regiment, and Isabel Clarke (Totten) Huyghue, Samuel Douglass Smith Huyghue was named after the incumbent Governor of Prince Edward Island and christened on 12 May 1816 in St. Paul's Anglican Church in Charlottetown (St. Paul's). By 1817, Huyghue's father, described in the 1871 census as having been born in the West Indies and as having Danish ancestry, had gone on half pay with the 60th (A. G. Hart 376) and had moved to Saint John to become First Clerk in the Ordnance Department (Chubb, *New Brunswick* 1839, 54). A family christening in Trinity Church, Saint John, on 24 May 1842, correspondence references to religious texts and sermons at "the Stone Church" (S. Huyghue), and Lieutenant Huyghue's supervision of the Male School of the Saint John Church of England Society (Chubb, *New Brunswick* 1844, 24) all point to a staunch Anglican family background. An 1826 real estate advertisement by S. Huyghue, Esquire, for a cottage in Saint John's Lower Cove may further illuminate the family's social status ("For Sale"), as does the presence of three household servants in the 1851 federal census of Saint John County. And while lists of attendees at Saint John's rigorous Grammar School have not survived, the inclusion of Huyghue's brother William on a Grammar School awards list for Classics in 1833 (St. John Grammar) would suggest that Douglass Huyghue, in all likelihood, attended the same upwardly mobile classical high school.

By 1840, the twenty-four-year-old Douglass Huyghue seems

to have been living in Halifax, Nova Scotia. He appears in public records first as S. D. S. Huyghue, 2nd Lieutenant, in the militia lists of the 4th Halifax Regiment in *Belcher's Farmer's Almanack* for 1840, and subsequently as a sometime 1st Lieutenant from 1841 to 1850. Moreover, in 1840, under the pseudonym Eugene, Huyghue began making regular literary contributions to the recently established *Halifax Morning Post and Parliamentary Reporter*, edited by J. H. Crosskill. Crosskill welcomed the contributions of the young writer to his newspaper: "*Eugene* has sent us a dozen beautiful verses, to grace our first page of Saturday," he announced on 3 December 1840, and on 8 May 1841, he declared that "*Eugene* is not forgotten. His *Indian's Lament* is mislaid, or it would have appeared long ago. We must have another search among our papers for the manuscript, and hope to be successful this time, as the lines are to our taste, and true to nature." Dated 1 February 1841, "The Indian's Lament" finally appeared on 25 May 1841. In evoking a sense of the lost independent culture and economy of Indigenous peoples in the Maritime provinces, the poem anticipated the thrust of *Argimou*, Huyghue's more ambitious work, and begins with the Indigenous speaker standing "at the dawn of day" gazing over "[t]he broad expanse of his own loved bay":

> The boom of a gun in the sun's last ray,
> Roll'd peal upon peal through the hills away;
> The leaves are stirred with its moaning breath,
> Like whisperings low at the couch of death,
> An Indian band through the dark pines wound,
> But paused to list to its last faint sound;
> There were sad eyes turned in that twilight beam,
> To gaze once more where their homes had been.
> Oh, the wanderers' hearts throbb'd mute and cold,—
> The grief of the exile may not be told! (1)

Reinforcing the pain of cultural and physical loss in the poem is the motif of the "White Gull's" flying "over all"—a metaphorical articulation of European intrusion into Mik'maw territory that was to be reiterated by Huyghue in the dying Chief Tonea's prophecy midway through *Argimou* and in the concluding lines of the novel.[2]

Whether Huyghue was already writing *Argimou* while still in Nova Scotia is unclear. Little is known of his activities in Halifax prior to his return to Saint John in the early 1840s. However, a December 1838 ink wash drawing signed and dated by Huyghue and showing a Mi'kmaw party launching a canoe from the Dartmouth shore opposite Halifax not only confirms Huyghue's artistic abilities but also suggests in the intricate design of the Chief's coat his possible familiarity with Chief Louis-Benjamin Peminuit Paul of the Shubenacadie Mi'kmaw band. Former Nova Scotia Museum Curator in History Ruth Holmes Whitehead suggests in *Micmac Maliseet and Beothuk Collections in Europe and the Pacific* (1989) that the Mi'kmaw ceremonial chieftain's coat in the S. D. S. Huyghue Collection of Canadian Indigenous arti-facts in the Museum Victoria Archives in Melbourne, Australia, once belonged to Chief Peminuit Paul, and implies that Huyghue knew the chief before the latter's death in 1843.[3] Thus, germane to Huyghue's writing of both "The Indian's Lament" and *Argimou* in the early 1840s may well have been his connection with the venerable leader, who, beginning in 1815, had repeatedly appealed to public authorities to address the conditions of territorial and economic deprivation being experienced by mainland Mi'kmaq. Rhetorically petitioning Queen Victoria in 1841 just two years before his death, Peminuit Paul mov-ingly explained to Her Majesty that

I cannot cross the great Lake to talk to you for my Canoe is too small, and I am old and weak. I cannot look upon you for my eyes not see so far. You cannot hear my voice across the Great Waters. I therefore send this Wampum and Paper talk to tell the Queen I am

in trouble. My people are in trouble. . . . No Hunting Grounds—No
Beaver—No Otter . . . poor for ever. . . . All these Woods once
ours. . . . White Man has taken all that was ours. . . . Let us not perish. (qtd. in Upton; see also Phillips 151)

The poignancy of Peminuit Paul's appeal, coming at a time when
Huyghue seems not only to have had contact with the Mi'kmaw
community at Shubenacadie but also to have been writing poetry and
prose articulating the plight of Indigenous cultures in the Maritimes,
may do much to explain Huyghue's decision to return to New
Brunswick and work on *Argimou*.

Argimou and the New Brunswick Literary Catalyst

Douglass Huyghue appears to have been back in Saint John by the
autumn of 1841, when he began submitting poetry and prose to *The
Amaranth*. In an era described by critic John Gross as hungry for
intellectual guidance (89), this periodical promised readers an eclectic
blend of original and excerpted material. In addition to publishing
selections from British and American periodicals, it reported on
activities of the Saint John Mechanics' Institute, reviewed recent
books, solicited articles and fiction from local authors, and fostered
an interest in provincial history. Editor Robert Shives's review of *An
English Spelling Book, with Reading Lessons, for the Use of the Parish
and Other Schools of New Brunswick* reflected his social philosophy,
arguing the case for making educational texts in the province relevant
to the history of the local constituency:

> We think, however, that had the reading lessons been made sub-
> jects of simple and amusing, as well as instructive details of the
> settlement and advancement of the Province, including historical
> information, arranged in an easy and comprehensive style, it would

have rendered the work a still greater means of imparting a correct and instructive familiarity with something more than plain words—and thus have served a double purpose.

Thus, it is not surprising that Shives's periodical welcomed the historical fiction of local writers such as William Burtis, Emily Beavan, Moses H. Perley, and "Eugene." From September 1841 to the autumn of 1843, Huyghue's poetry and prose were published almost monthly in *The Amaranth*, the climax being the serialization of his historical romance *Argimou* between May and September 1842.

Huyghue had returned to New Brunswick at a time when the land claims, the economic sustenance, and the traditional way of living of the Mi'kmaq, the Passamaquoddy, and the Maliseet (Wulstukwiuk) were as fraught with challenges as the conditions described so lyrically by Mi'kmaq Chief Peminuit Paul in Nova Scotia. Visiting the province in the early 1840s prior to the publication of his *Canada, Nova Scotia, New Brunswick, and the Other British Provinces in North America, with a Plan of National Colonization* (1843), traveller James S. Buckingham noted that in Saint John "there are a very few Indians still lingering about the streets, but these are so poor and feeble, that in a very few years it is probable they will all be extinct" (410). As Brian Cuthbertson notes in *Stubborn Resistance* (2015), conditions such as these impelled newly appointed Governor Sir William Colebrook to seek "betterment for New Brunswick Aboriginal peoples" when he arrived in the province in 1841 (30). Working through Saint John writer, lawyer, and locally appointed "Commissioner of Indian Affairs" Moses H. Perley, Colebrook urged "the necessity of securing to [Indigenous people] their lands, of preventing encroachments on them and of administering them in such a manner as to secure to them all the advantages to be desired from their permanent possession" (30). Colebrook also sought educational facilities for Indigenous children, the consolidation of central villages for the Wulstukwiuk (Maliseet) and the Mi'kmaq, and trust funds set up for Indigenous communities based on the leasing or selling of reserve lands (31).

Embarking on fact-finding missions for the Governor, Perley traversed New Brunswick, often by canoe, visiting Maliseet communities such as Tobique and Madawaska as well as Mi'kmaq areas such as Eel Ground Reserve, Red Bank, and the Little South West Reserve (Cuthbertson 32–34). Honoured by both the Mi'kmaq and the Maliseet between 1839 and 1841 and elevated by the Mi'kmaq in 1842 by being elected "Wunjeet Sagamore" or "chief over all" (Spray; Phillips 139–40), Perley noted in 1843 that he had not slept "in a bed for two months together" (qtd. in Spray). His analytic report on the state of the Mi'kmaq and the Maliseet peoples in New Brunswick was received and debated by the provincial government in 1842. Perley's subsequent opposition to the 1844 New Brunswick Indian Act's sanctioning of sales of Mi'kmaq and Maliseet reserve lands to facilitate immigrant settlement and his challenge to the government's neglect of Indigenous interests culminated in his being removed in 1848 from having any further official involvement in Indigenous affairs (Cuthbertson 42–64; Spray).

In spite of Perley's active professional life as a lawyer, one-time Indian Commissioner, emigrant agent, and government-appointed consultant on railway expansion into New Brunswick, he continued throughout the 1840s to publish fictionalized "Sporting Sketches from New Brunswick" in *The London Sporting Review*, *The Sporting Sketch Book* of London, and *The Amaranth*. In these, he depicted the lure of New Brunswick's impressive wilderness and the skills of the Indigenous guides with whom he had hunted and fished since childhood. Offering a series of Saint John Mechanics' Institute lectures on the history of New Brunswick to an audience of eight hundred to a thousand people between December 1840 and January 1841 ("Amaranth"; "Mr. Perley's"), he also collaborated in 1842 with the recently returned Douglass Huyghue in organizing an exhibition of Indigenous cultural artifacts at a grand bazaar held at the Mechanics' Institute. "This room was fitted up by our native townsman, M. H. Perley, Esq., Indian Commissioner," noted a reporter, "assisted by Mr. Douglas Huyghue, a young gentleman of much taste, who remained in the Room during the exhibition, contributing to the enjoyment of the visitors" ("Grand Bazaar"). As art historian Ruth B. Phillips suggests, "It seems highly likely that one or more of the chiefs' outfits that had been presented to Perley" on the Miramichi in 1839 or 1841 might "have been included in the exhibition" (141). Whether Huyghue also displayed Chief Louis-Benjamin Peminuit Paul's ceremonial coat that "[r]ecords show . . . was sold to a captain in the British military in 1840" ("Nova Scotia") and that Huyghue subsequently took to Australia is purely conjectural, but Phillips notes that, "from his description of the creation of Argimou as a chief" in *Argimou*, it is clear that "Huyghue was very familiar with these outfits and their role" in the ceremonial installation of a *Grand Sachem* of the Mi'kmaq (141).[4] In the novel, she adds, Argimou was "invested with a dress of costly material, heavy with minute embroidery, and leggings of scarlet cloth, beaded and fringed" (141). Thus, while the exact content of the Mechanics' Institute display remains unclear, the linking of Huyghue to Perley in mounting the exhibition not only contextualizes Huyghue's social circle in Saint John but also reinforces a sense of his ongoing interest in Indigenous cultures. That his association with Perley in the Mechanics Institute continued beyond the Grand Bazaar is reinforced by an 1842–43 "Report of the Directors of the Mechanics Institute" indicating that, among the public lecturers "during the season just ended," were "Messrs. Huyghue, Twysom, Gesner, and Perley." Gesner, who was New Brunswick's first provincial geologist and who travelled with Perley to the Miramichi in 1842, shared Perley and Huyghue's concerns about the marginalization of Indigenous cultures, bitterly noting of the Mi'kmaq in the late 1840s: "They have been supplanted by civilized inhabitants, and in return for the lands for which they were the rightful owners, they have received loathsome diseases, alcoholic drink, the destruction of their game, and threatened extermination" (qtd. in Jennifer Reid 36). Bonded by their mutual concern for the future of Indigenous communities in the province, the trio—Gesner, Perley, and Huyghue—represented a focused voice of social conscience in early 1840s Saint John.

Argimou and the Sir Walter Scott Legacy

Building on the note of ancestral loss informing his 1841 poem "The Indian's Lament," Huyghue published in *The Amaranth* the short stories "Malsosep; or, The Forsaken" (October 1841) and "The Unknown" (February 1842), depicting an Indigenous world eroded by colonial settler infiltration. "Malsosep" melodramatically portrays the love of a young Maliseet woman for an indifferent English officer. Set against the wider backdrop of the 1837 Rebellion in the Canadas, the narrative moved from New Brunswick to Halifax to Pele Island, providing a passing insight into Malsosep's larger-than-life Maliseet admirer, Adela, also a victim of social change. Both stories lacked the intimacy between narrator and audience that was to give *Argimou* a sense of immediacy, but, in his description of Adela's demeanour and dress, Huyghue nonetheless captured the warrior's aura of romantic dignity:

In truth he was a noble sample of the native tribe;—tall, firm, and graceful—arrayed in the garb of a hunter, with the blue embroidered tunic descending to the knee, disclosing every excellence of attitude and form; leggins drawn tightly over the calf, and feet encased in moccasins of dressed moose skin; a gun and a knife, with the powder horn slung behind, completed his equipment; while the long raven hair shrouded his broad erect shoulders, and his eye sent forth a gleam so bright, so fearless, so hawk-like, that the beholder trembled to imagine the soul that lit its ray, roused by the fire of anger or revenge. The features were aquiline, probably from a slight mixture of Acadian blood, but the prevailing expression was energy and deep resolve, the evidence of an unshackled spirit. (301)

Huyghue's two stories paved the way for the serialization of *Argimou* in *The Amaranth* in 1842. From the beginning, it was clear that this was a historical work informed by the social conscience of its young author and by Sir Walter Scott's literary philosophy "that the spirit of another age is active in our present lives" (Wittig 224). Thus, the novel opens by briefly valorizing the legends of the great Mi'kmaw warrior, chieftain, and trickster figure Argimou: "swifter" of foot "than the carriboo" with a "voice in battle . . . like the storm in the forest" (3).[5] The narrator then moves quickly from the world of oral tradition to the historical context of the Maritime provinces in the 1840s, self-consciously warning the "[g]entle reader" that, "in a little time" (4) through "the propagation of disease" (5) and "the blighting introduction of . . . the accursed 'fire-water'" and "the axe of the settler" (5), "all traces of the numerous and powerful nations" of the Indigenous peoples "of the New World" will be "obliterated for ever from the face of the earth" (4). "We are the sole and only cause of their overwhelming misery, their gradual extinction," he bitterly concludes this opening section; "directly, by lawless appropriation of their hunting grounds, to utter violation of every principle of justice, human or divine, which is supposed to influence the conduct of a christian people" (5). Urging Victorian "Legislators and Philanthropists" to redeem "the vaunted integrity of the national character" by assisting the province's beleaguered Indigenous communities, Huyghue's narrator concludes his introductory remarks by lamenting that "[w]e rear the germ of a great city without casting a thought upon the generation crumbling beneath" (6).

Having identified the social impetus informing his writing, Huyghue then turns to regional history not only as a context for *Argimou*

Journey in *Argimou:*
A Legend of the Micmac

- Fort Lawrence
- Fort Beauséjour (Cumberland)
- Aulac
- Shepody (Bay)
- Grindstone Island
- Petitcodiac River
- Petitcodiac (Chepody)
- Bay of Fundy
- Kennebecasis River
- Maliseet Village
- Reversing Falls
- French Fort
- Annapolis Royal

Prince Edward Island

Petitcodiac (Chepody)

Petitcodiac River

Baie Verte

Aulac
Fort Beauséjour
Fort Lawrence

Shepody Bay

New Brunswick

St. John (Wolastoq) River

Grindstone Island

Kennebecasis River

Maliseet Village

Reversing Falls

French Fort

Bay of Fundy

Nova Scotia

Annapolis Royal

but also as a demonstration of how the past has shaped the present. The year is 1755. The British Fort Lawrence and the French Fort Beauséjour confront one another across the Tantramar Marsh on the edge of the Bay of Fundy at the intersection of the present-day provinces of New Brunswick and Nova Scotia. With the skill of a topographical artist, Huyghue pulls readers into the bleak majesty of the location and the proximity of the political players, intruding only to assert his narrative reliability based on a "visit to this remarkable spot [some years since] while musing upon the stirring scenes once enacted beneath the grassy ramparts" (28–29). As historians such as Stephen E. Patterson, John G. Reid ("Empire"), Jeffers Lennox, and Andrea Bear Nicholas ("Settler") have noted, for over two hundred years the inhabitants of what are now the Maritime provinces had experienced the alternating tensions of British, French, and Indigenous political aspirations to effect control of mainland *Acadie* (Nova Scotia including present-day New Brunswick), Île Saint-Jean (Prince Edward Island), and Île Royale (Cape Breton Island). This was "a region of movement," notes Lennox, "dependent on patterns of violence and sustenance" (424). Thus, by the beginning of Huyghue's novel, centuries of political and military manoeuvring have finally reached a climax in the destruction of Fort Beauséjour. "[F]or four days the besieged withstood the efforts of the English," notes the narrator in describing the attack, "when, reduced to a state of misery and ruin by the harassing bombardment, they offered terms of capitulation, which were acceded to; upon which the British troops marched into the fortress, and the French laid down their arms" (36).

In describing this pivotal moment of French defeat, Huyghue conforms to the classic formula of a Sir Walter Scott historical novel—a fiction "set in a time of rapid change, with old ways succumbing to new ones against a background of warfare or other civil turmoil" (Frye et al. 227). Not only would the fall of Fort Beauséjour on 12 June 1755 mark the first step in the eventual end of French military hegemony in

Acadie, Île Saint-Jean, and Île Royale, but also it would facilitate the eventual deportation of over eleven thousand Acadian "neutral French" from these regions between 1755 and 1763 (Conrad and Hiller 82–86). Huyghue's description of approximately seven hundred Acadian civilians huddled in the forest seeking solace near their Mi'kmaw allies after the destruction of Fort Beauséjour, Fort Gaspereaux at Baie Verte, and their farms on the Isthmus of Chignecto represents the first depiction in Canadian fiction of what would become the suffering of the 1755 Acadian Deportation. The writer graphically depicts "children, clamouring for food," the elderly "stricken to a second childhood by the event that had befallen" them (79), and desperate men bearing arms who, "with the withering ice of their despair," sat "stern and silent with their straw hats drawn down to cover their hollow eyes" (80).

In the midst of this human anguish, the dying prophecy of the Mi'kmaw chief Tonea that the day was coming when the Mi'kmaq will "have *no* country!—*no* hunting grounds!—*no* home!" (82) because "*The White Gull has flown over all!*" (83) strikes a note of doom in the novel that will be reiterated in its final pages. Patterson has argued that, "after 16 years of almost constant warfare" in which Mi'kmaq and Maliseet had depended heavily on French logistical support for "arms and ammunition" as well as trade, the Indigenous communities had economically "become a dependent people" (52). French-language treaties signed by the Maliseet and the Passamaquoddy with the now dominant British in Halifax in February 1760 after the fall of L'Acadie, Fortress Louisbourg, and Quebec, as well as new "treaties of peace and friendship" that various Mi'kmaw bands concluded with British authorities in Halifax throughout 1760 and 1761, "were those of a conquering power," adds Patterson; they "said what the British wanted them to say" (58; see also Nicholas, "Settler" 28–35; J. G. Reid, "Historical" 58–60). Thus, although Huyghue depicts Argimou proudly striding into the Council Chamber in Halifax before a crowd of Nova Scotia's dignitaries in 1761 to proclaim that "I come of mine own accord, to smoke peace and call King George my Great Father and friend" (206), he also reveals the aged Argimou's despair at the end of the novel when he recognizes that "[t]he white gull" has indeed "flown over all" (211). Reflecting "the clash of different traditions," Argimou ends, as do many of Scott's historical novels, with the recognition that "the actions and fates of men are moulded by their society and its history" (Wittig 223).

Huyghue, Scott, and Conventions of the Historical Novel

In selecting Argimou as the focal point of his novel, Huyghue was clearly aware of the chief's importance as a shaman (*puoin*), a magician, a trickster figure, a warrior, and a hero in Maritime Mi'kmaw oral tradition. Often associated with Prince Edward Island, the Isthmus of Chignecto, and the Petcootkweak (Petitcodiac) area of New Brunswick, Argimou as trickster had allegedly driven the Kwedeches (Mohawks) out of the Tantramar Marshes in the seventeenth century by disguising himself as a chieftain 103 years of age and allowing himself to be captured by the Kwetejk:

[T]he old man was tied, bound to a tree, a quantity of dried wood piled round him, and the torch applied. As soon as the fire began to blaze, he made one spring and was clear of all cords and green withes, tall, straight, young, and active, and ready for fight.

"There!" said [the Kwetej shaman], "didn't I tell you it was Ulgimoo? Will you not believe me now? In a moment your heads will be off." It was even so. One blow dispatched him, and similar blows fell upon the rest; and only three of the whole army of several hundred men escaped. Ulgimoo did not receive a scratch. The three that were not killed he took prisoners; he cut their ears, slit their noses, and their cheeks, then bade them go home and carry the joyful tidings of their defeat, and be sure to tell that they were all slain by one Micmac, one hundred and three years old. (Whitehead, *Old Man* 48)

While undoubtedly privy to such tales of Argimou's extraordinary versatility as shaman and trickster, Huyghue nonetheless chose in the opening line of *Argimou* to focus on Argimou's reputation as a mighty combatant, "as brave a warrior as ever bounded in the war-path of the Micmacs" (3). Captured by Captain Edward Molesworth and British troops while vigorously defending a French blockhouse during the four-day siege of Fort Beauséjour in 1755, Argimou, now a prisoner of war, negotiates to lead the British officer into Maliseet territory to rescue Molesworth's kidnapped English fiancée, Clarence Forbes, and Argimou's own beloved Abenaquis/Maliseet lover, Waswetchcul.

This journey of pursuit becomes the spine of Huyghue's novel, in many respects conforming to the distinctive American genre of the captivity narrative[6] as Argimou and his party track the Maliseet warriors who are wending their way west toward the Saint John River. Whereas the traditional seventeenth-century captivity narrative was informed by a religious thesis underpinning descriptions of trial and survival, Huyghue's novel employs only those captivity conventions that heighten a sense of threat and adventure. The physicality of the battles between the rescuers and the Maliseet brings a dramatic energy to the novel, particularly after Argimou and his companions have plucked Waswetchcul and Clarence from the Maliseet camp at the juncture of the Kennebecasis and Saint John Rivers. The vividly described war-paint of the Maliseet as they pursue Argimou's party invokes a sense of terror for both readers and rescuers ("clothed as with skeleton armour . . . traced in ghastly white, bone after bone, a horrible portraiture of death; the eyes, like bright jewels, glowing, as it were, from deep hollow caverns, and the grinning mouth lengthened and distended" [168]). The suspenseful destruction of the warrior pursuers after a harrowing canoe chase over the churning waters of the

Reversing Falls at present-day Saint John (Menahkwesk) pulsates with the dramatic conventions of the Gothic sometimes found in Romantic-era landscape art:

> Yet they caught one more glimpse of the canoe, but at some distance below the first fall, for it shot up perpendicularly into air from out the whirlpools, as if poised by the weight of one clinging with expiring grasp to the lower end; then it gradually subsided again into the yeast of waves, and as it sank, a cry was faintly heard to penetrate the din—shrill and piercing—such as the last utterance of a strong man's agony and despair;—but the deep thunder of the torrent made reply, and the waters curled and danced over the Milicete's unhallowed grave. (178)

While the graphic nature of this scene emerges out of Huyghue's demographic experience of growing up in Saint John, there seems little doubt that the young author also relied on a number of conventions from Scott's historical novels to further his tale. For example, while Argimou and his father, Pansaway, serve as hero and wise old man figure respectively, Huyghue also adheres to the standard Scott tradition of developing key type figures as fictional facilitators (Wittig 228–29). Thus, Dennis, the Irish batman with his rich country brogue, love of rum, and down-to-earth commoner's sense of irony, offsets the tension of the pursuit by bringing a comic folk-figure dimension to the novel. Moreover, in Edward Molesworth, Huyghue creates a typical Scott hero—the kind that critic Georg Lukács describes as "a more or less mediocre, average English gentleman" who nevertheless "possesses . . . a certain moral fortitude and decency which even rises to a capacity for self-sacrifice" (32).

Introduced by Huyghue's narrator as "a young Englishman of good family and prospects, who had entered the army when only a boy" (37), Molesworth proves to be a brave fighter on the expedition to rescue

Clarence and Waswetchcul. Argimou and Pansaway learn to trust him, nicknaming him "[t]he *Open Hand*" (166). But he also becomes a literary device for Huyghue, enabling him, for example, to introduce conventions of dramatic Gothic suspense as Edward envisages the worst of fates for his beloved Clarence, whom he imagines "bound to the torturing stake . . . her face . . . phrenzied with agony and horror!" (148). As the novel nears its conclusion, Huyghue also employs Molesworth as a facilitator for satire, pitting Dr. Dickson's celebration of British social and scientific superiority against Pansaway's shrewd comic commentary on the physician's consumption of snuff: "Certain his head must be very sick, so he will take tobacco dirt up his nose all the time. Certain—poor man—he should be very crazy—me sorry" (196). Thus, throughout the narrative, Huyghue continues to privilege Indigenous practicality, self-sufficiency, and forthrightness over British self-conscious conventionality. In addition, there is much in Huyghue's valorization of wilderness life that reflects the early-nineteenth-century fascination with Romantic Primitivism, seeing those who "had remained closer to nature and had been less subject to the influence of society" as being "nobler than civilized peoples" (Harmon and Holman 407–08). Accordingly, once Waswetchcul is rescued, she and Argimou, unhindered by Victorian precepts of decorum, graphically lose themselves in the "tumultuous pleasure" (161) of their reunited love. By contrast, the conventional English-born Clarence, once rescued, decorously engages in "a full interchange of thoughts" (162) with her fiancé, Molesworth. She sobs and prays in the arms of the solicitous officer before falling asleep, enjoying "the first unbroken slumber that she had experienced since the fatal morning of her departure from Fort Lawrence" (162). At the conclusion of *Argimou*, the all-too-brief collaboration of the British and the Indigenous couples in the novel unravels except in memory as Edward and Clarence return to a middle-class life in Britain and Argimou and Waswetchcul remain in the Maritimes, facing the increasing loss of fishing sites, the reduction of forest habitat for hunting, and the debilitating impact of epidemics (or what the novel calls "pestilence" [207]). Huyghue's authorial intrusions reinforce his passionate sense of the injustice that European military and settler colonization have brought to the traditional way of life of Indigenous peoples in the region. Invoking terms such as "the cold clutch of Avarice" and "the scorpion-fangs of Disease" to convey a sense of the destructive impact of European "greedy adventurers" upon a traditional Indigenous way of life (207), the narrator concludes the novel by focusing on a grey-haired Argimou grieving over his long-dead family and mourning the "great land, few red men—but many graves" (210) that mark the fulfillment of "Old Tonea's prophecy" that "[t]he white gull had flown over all!" (211).

The Boundary Commission, *Bentley's Miscellany,* and *Argimou*

Huyghue's poetry and prose continued to appear almost monthly in *The Amaranth* until January 1843. An entry on *The Amaranth* in *The Loyalist and Conservative Advocate*, however, noted on 9 February 1843 that it "miss'd our old favourite *Eugene*, this month," whereas a lecture on painting that Huyghue had been scheduled to deliver at the Mechanics' Institute in Saint John in 1843 was cancelled (Harper). An explanation for Huyghue's sudden absence from the cultural scene finally appeared in the *New Brunswick Courier* on 25 November 1843, when it announced that Douglas Huyghue, Esquire, had been made a British Commissary appointment to the joint American–British Boundary Commission settling the northern borders between the United States and "the British Provinces of New Brunswick and Canada" ("North Eastern"). Given the long career of Huyghue's father, Samuel, in the Military Ordnance service in Saint John, it is perhaps not surprising that Huyghue should follow in his father's footsteps. Pencil sketches of Fredericton attributed to Huyghue place him in the capital city in April 1843, but by June of that year he and his provisioning party had left Fredericton to journey up the Saint John River toward the Boundary Commission's Commissary headquarters at "Lake Isheganelshegek, on the north-west branch of the St. John" (S. D. Huyghue, "Winter's" 630). Here, Huyghue's central provisioning station would supply Lieutenant-Colonel Estcourt's survey party scattered along the border between Maine, Lower Canada, and New Brunswick, including maintenance of a direct access to the road to Rivière-du-Loup on the St. Lawrence River.

In two of four essays published in *Bentley's Miscellany* of London in 1849–50, Huyghue vividly describes survival in the vast unbroken forests of New Brunswick in the midst of the unforgiving winter of 1843–44. Caught for fifty-six days in a tented temporary supply station on the Saint John River en route to his destination at Lake Isheganelshegek, he and his companions subsequently pushed northward in spite of icy water, icicle-coated supplies, deep snow, and bitter cold:

> At length we cleared away the snow once more, lighted fires, and threw our weary selves besides them to rest. The men were fagged out. For six days they had struggled on against every disadvantage, until the skin was pealed from their limbs. They had polled and dragged, and cut a way with the clothes continually wet and frozen upon them, and still we knew not how far we had yet to go. The nearest place of refuge was at the forks of the river; now from this we might be twelve miles distant, or only one, for none of us had ever been thus far before, or knew anything of the course we were pursuing. ("Winter's" 633)

Eventually reaching Lake Isheganelshegek, where a store, a stable, and two log houses had been built as Commissary headquarters, Huyghue drew upon his experiences in the great unbroken forests of northern New Brunswick and Maine during his work on the

Boundary Commission—and upon his collateral visits to Quebec City and Ottawa—to inform his reminiscences. As with *Argimou*, Huyghue's use of first-person address in his essays created a sense of intimacy, pulling readers into the passion and immediacy of his experience. In "A Winter's Journey," for instance, he is intrigued by the fishy taste of beaver's tail, by the one-hundred-foot-high stands of red pine reminding him of "the description of Lucifer's spear, in 'Paradise Lost'" (633), by the icy lake's contractions sounding "like the firing of cannon" (634), and by the "tall, silent Indian" on the boat to Quebec standing "apart with his arms folded" "in a worn coat of deer-skin, fringed in the seams" with "no sympathies there" (636).

The fate of Indigenous people like the "tall, silent Indian" caught in the throes of European expansion was to engage Huyghue as much in his *Bentley's Miscellany* essays as it had in *Argimou*. In "The Scenery of the Ottawa," he sees a Victorian world of proactive business and immigrant settlement everywhere he travels. Visiting the Lake of Two Mountains on the Ottawa River, he laments "the tendency of modern improvement to sacrifice landscape to utility" (489), noting that near the ridges that gave the lake its name "is a large Indian village prettily seated on a point of land, with its neat church and thickly-clustered dwellings built close to the water's edge" (490). "Here," Huyghue notes, "reside the feeble remnants of two celebrated tribes, the Mohawks and Algonquins, who obtain a precarious subsistence by hunting on the upper parts of the river" (490). Elsewhere, at a portage at Chats Falls, he encounters an Iroquois family en route to traditional hunting grounds higher up the river. The father's storytelling enables Huyghue to record in his essay the oral history of the battles of the Adirondacks, Yendots, and Five Nations, including a validation of the importance of the wampum bearer in traditional Indigenous culture. Yet "The Scenery of the Ottawa" ends, as does *Argimou*, by revealing the dignity of an Indigenous past being subsumed by contemporary subsistence realities. As his Iroquois tale bearer concludes, "[M]y father told me the story, you see, because it was about the old times and the wars. May be they got married and lived happy: who knows? There was plenty game then, and the old people were not left to starve in their wigwams. All is gone now" (497).

"All is gone now" sounds hauntingly like *Argimou*'s "*The white gull had flown over all*." And, as in the novel, the *Bentley's Miscellany* essays (such as "My First Winter in the Woods of Canada," in which the author interacts regularly with Maliseets, Hurons, Iroquois, Penobscots, Montaguards, and Abenakies while working on the Boundary Commission) reiterate the theme of a lost Indigenous hegemony. "It was strange to think," muses Huyghue, that the Canadians

> were now in possession of what once belonged solely to *them* [Indigenous peoples]; for there was not an individual quality, either of the outward or inward man, that seemed to give priority to the European, or justify his claim to what the other had held as a direct birthright from his Maker. (156)

Observations such as these in the *Bentley's Miscellany* essays act as a gloss on the issues of loss and morality first explored in *Argimou*. In the novel, rivers, forests, and the sea are not only embedded in the spiritual life of the Mi'kmaq and the Maliseet but also factored into every aspect of Indigenous life from identity to sustenance. For example, as the Maliseet in *Argimou* travel "through the wilds" toward their destination at the mouth of the Kennebecasis River, they connect with

> those mysterious signs known only to the native.—The upward glance of the leader at the moss on the trees, the peculiar inclination of certain plants, were as sure guides to those wanderers of the wild as the star and compass are to the voyager on the pathless ocean; the very language of Nature appeared intelligible to her dependent children. (68–69)

This integration of natural sustainability and Indigenous spirituality, whether in travelling the tidal Wolastoq (Saint John) River or penetrating the dense forests above the Kennebecasis Valley, contributes to making *Argimou* one of Canada's earliest topographical novels. Whereas John Richardson's *Wacousta; or, The Prophecy* (1832) draws upon Fort Detroit's dark undergrowth and Pontiac's 1763 bloody uprising as embellishments to a Gothic tale of sensationalistic revenge, Huyghue's integration of rivers, forests, rocky plateaus, and foggy estuaries into his ruminative exploration of the relativity of cultures reinforces a sense of the immutability of time and place. And, like Scott in his novels, Huyghue sees within this context "certain transitional stages of history" (Lukács 35). Thus, in *Argimou*, the fall of Fort Beauséjour in 1755 becomes a key piece in the ongoing chess game unfolding in the relationship between English, American, Acadian, French, and Indigenous peoples. Between the fall of Beauséjour in 1755, the defeat of Louisbourg in 1758, the de facto capitulation of Argimou to the British in Halifax in 1761, the loss of Indigenous lands to settler intrusion, the spread of European diseases (resulting in the deaths of Waswetchcul and her child), and the havoc wreaked by alcohol on tribal life, Argimou is shown by the end of Huyghue's novel to be all but defeated. While the *Bentley's Miscellany* essays were to articulate further the impact of Victorian expansionism on Indigenous life, *Argimou* stands, argues Nicholas, as "one of the first socially conscious novels" about the impact of European hegemony on native culture and independence "written in New Brunswick." Indeed, one could expand that to Canada. "In light of the prevalent racism of the time," Nicholas adds wryly, "there was little inclination for anyone in New Brunswick to heed Huyghue's plea for justice" ("Role" 64).

Post-*Argimou* in Halifax, London, and Australia

Based on a dated sketch of the Boundary Commission depot at
Lake Isheganelshegek now held privately in Australia, it is likely
that Huyghue was still with the Boundary Commission in October
1844 and that he executed the drawing. Moreover, the report of
*Correspondence Respecting the Operations of the Commission for
Running and Tracing the Boundary Line between Her Majesty's
Possessions in North America and the United States* submitted to
the British House of Lords in 1845 indicates that the completion
of the Commission's activities would occur in July 1845, to be followed
by two months of winding down. A reference in the diary of George
Wolhaupter, a clerk in the New Brunswick Surveyor General's Office
and brother of Huyghue's fellow Boundary Commission Commissary
agent Charles Wolhaupter, situates Huyghue in Fredericton on Friday,
28 August 1846, when George Wolhaupter appreciatively noted in
his diary that he had "called on P. Allan about 9½ P.M. and found a
gentleman of the name of Douglas Hughe [*sic*] with whom he made
me acquainted + I sat there till near 11—our conversation was about
poets and poetry—Mr. H. appears to be a very intelligent person + he
was formerly with my brother Charles on the survey of the boundary
line between the States and the British Provinces."[7]

Throughout the 1840s, even while Huyghue was serving on the
Boundary Commission, his name continued to be listed in *Belcher's
Farmer's Almanack* as a 1st or 2nd Lieutenant in the 4th Halifax
Regiment of Militia. However, the republication of *Argimou* in book
form in Halifax in 1847 suggests that Huyghue had probably returned
to the city by that date. Five years had elapsed since the novel was
serialized in *The Amaranth*, at which time *The Halifax Morning Post
and Parliamentary Reporter* published a review entitled "Credit to
New Brunswick" and the Halifax *Times* a commentary that compared
Huyghue's work to that of James Fenimore Cooper ("Amaranth" 294).

Now, in 1847, whether through Huyghue's initiative or that of his former *Halifax Morning Post* editor, John H. Crosskill (appointed Queen's Printer), *Argimou* appeared as a modest paperback published by the *Morning Courier* office, once again under Huyghue's pseudonym, Eugene. Only one copy of the publication, produced on acid paper in simple medium-blue paper covers, appears to have survived, and it is this *Morning Courier* edition that provides the copy-text for this Early Canadian Literature edition.

In 1848, Huyghue's brother W. F. Huyghue also appeared briefly in the Halifax almanac professional columns described as "Clerk in Charge" with the Royal Navy (*Belcher's* 1848, 94–95). Although Douglass Huyghue remained listed in 1848, 1849, and 1850 as being a member of the 4th Halifax Militia Regiment, it is clear from records in the publishing firm of Richard Bentley & Son in London that Huyghue had moved to England by September 1849. A "Memorandum of Agreement" signed between S. D. Huyghue, Esq., of 116 Great Russell Street, Bloomsbury, and Richard Bentley, of New Burlington Street, Publisher, London, on 6 October 1849, arranged for the publication of a new novel entitled *The Nomades of the West; or, Ellen Clayton*. Bentley, who was a sometime publisher of Canadian writers Thomas Chandler Haliburton and Susanna Moodie, drove a brisk bargain with the young New Brunswick author,

> deducting from the produce of the Sale thereof, the Charges for Printing, Paper, Advertisements, Embellishments, if any, and other Incidental Expenses, including the Allowance of Ten per Cent on the gross amount of the Sale, for Commission and risk of Bad Debts, the Profits remaining of every Edition that shall be Printed of the Work, are to be divided into two equal Parts, one Moiety to be paid to the said S. D. Huyghue Esq. and the other Moiety to belong to the said Richard Bentley.

Advertised in *The Athenaeum* on 16 February 1850 as a "New Romance of Canada" ("New Works"), *The Nomades of the West* has been described by Phillips as a historical novel about "the travels of two young white orphans and their Abenaki, Mohawk, and French-Canadian companions, whose adventures take them across the North American continent to a lost utopian community of refugees from the Aztec empire found deep in the Rocky Mountains" (340n24). Huyghue's preface, however, dated January 1850, made it clear that, as with *Argimou*, he had serious intentions when writing his novel. Invoking readers to pay attention to the ongoing destruction of Indigenous cultures in British North America in the face of settler expansion and modernity, he added:

> Now I have lived in the wigwam of the Red Man; I have smoked, talked, and hunted with him; I have trusted him with money; and whenever uncontaminated by intercourse with his white neighbours, I have invariably found him to be a happy and a noble man. . . .
>
> I have stood by his peaceful grave where the trees he loved wept their leaves over the bones of the forest-child, and the mattock of the pioneer had not yet unearthed them to make a highway; and the spirit of the solitude has taught me to be just to my brother man.
>
> The following tale is associated with this extraordinary people,— extraordinary as unfortunate, for they are becoming rapidly extinct. It presents them to the reader as they were before their ranks were thinned, or their spirit broken by aggression. May it awaken his sympathies in their behalf, and would that it might impel the spirit of philanthropy, which is the redeeming feature of the age, to devise some plan to rescue those perishing tribes! (v, vi)

A novel in three volumes, *The Nomades of the West* was priced high at 33s.6d and does not appear to have been a financial success. More

salubrious for Huyghue's immediate financial situation was the publication, in 1849–50, of his four essays in *Bentley's Miscellany*, all of which
appeared under the general rubric "Recollections of Canada." Bentley's
records indicate that, on 29 January 1850, Huyghue received the sum
of "Sixteen Pounds One Shilling and sixpence for Copyright of three
articles in *Bentley's Miscellany*," while for the fourth, "Forest Incidents,"
he received only £4 and was not paid until mid-January 1851 (Financial). In spite of his *Bentley's Miscellany* publications and his designation as "Novelist" in the 1851 census in London, however, Huyghue
clearly realized in the autumn of 1851 that he could not survive in
England as a writer. At age thirty-three and without a fixed occupa-
tion, Huyghue sailed for Australia on the *Lady Peel* early in October
1851, arriving in Port Phillip on 4 February 1852 ("Melbourne"). On
27 April 1853, Huyghue joined the permanent staff of the Civil Service
in Australia and was appointed to the Office of Mines in Ballarat as a
Commissariat Clerk on 27 August of that year.

Huyghue moved to the Ballarat goldfields at a volatile time, becoming a witness to the miners' uprising and confrontation with troops at
the Eureka Stockade between 28 November and 3 December 1854.
His artwork depicting the violent clashes between the military and the
miners has been reproduced in various publications, including Alan
McCulloch's *Artists of the Australian Gold Rush* (1977) and W. B. Withers's *The History of Ballarat* (1890), while a large chalk-and-watercolour
drawing, "The Eureka Stockade," is in the permanent collection of
the Art Gallery of Ballarat.[8] His personal memoir of the experience,
"The Ballarat Riots, 1854," signed Pax, makes it clear in its opening
paragraph that for a long time his assimilation to Australian life was
anything but seamless:

Chance, or fate, or by whatever name we designate the occult law
which rules our destiny, had so ordered it that, after a somewhat
chequered career, the year of grace 1854 found me a member of the

government staff at Ballarat. The duties that fell to my share were sufficiently arduous to occupy the whole time during office hours, and possessed the merit, at the very least, of preventing me from brooding too much over the deprivations then incident to life in the diggings. My feelings of aversion to the country also were very strong. I could not shake off for many years after my arrival, a forlorn sense of exile under strange stars, and failed to recognize in the hard face of Australian nature, the face of a mother. (1)

Huyghue's sense of social injustice, which had been focused on the plight of Indigenous peoples in *Argimou*, found fresh stimulus when he was appointed to the Commissary Service on the Ballarat goldfields. Leading up to the violent confrontation between miners and authorities at the Eureka Stockade, Huyghue witnessed disenfranchised "mud-bespattered and blunt-spoken diggers" bureaucratically managed by "well-bred but lofty" members of a Gold Commission that was both "aristocratic and exclusive" (Pax 13). The tragedy of the bloody clash between frustrated diggers and the military, with all the consequences of death and destruction on both sides, is summed up in his 1857 poem that reappears as an appendix to Huyghue's memoir and that memorializes "The Miner of the Stockade":

> Rear'd where the o'ertax'd nations give
> Their toil to fill the magnate's maw,
> He came to earn his bread and live
> Untrammel'd by patrician law.
> Hopeful he came—and Nature spread
> Her treasures for her sturdy child:
> But misrule rais'd its baleful head
> And then outrang his war cry wild.—
> Stung into strife by outrage keen
> He was no rebel to his Queen. (Pax 68–69)

In the aftermath of the violence, Huyghue was deeply moved by the dead with "their faces ghastly and passion-distorted and their eyes staring with stony fixedness." With a novelist's sense of pathos and irony, he noted a small dog that clung to the corpse of its master—ignorant, noted Huyghue, of "either Cross or Crown" (Pax 33).[9]

Huyghue remained with the civil service at Ballarat until 1872, eventually being posted by the Ministry of Mines, first to Graytown and then to Melbourne, where he retired in 1878 on a pension of £195 annually (Kerr 378; see also R. E. Johns's journal entry dated 4 June 1878). Throughout those years, Huyghue continued to research, to write, to draw, and to paint. His artwork is now held by public institutions such as the Art Gallery of Ballarat, the Latrobe Library, and the State Library of Victoria (McCulloch, *Encyclopedia* 606). His distance from his family in New Brunswick was somewhat alleviated by the immigration in 1860 of his unmarried sister Emma Sophia (sailing on the famed Saint John clipper ship the *Marco Polo* ["Shipping"]) and by friendships with Australians such as Reynell Eveleigh Johns, with whom he shared interests in natural history and ethnology (Griffiths 41). Notes and diary entries in Johns's papers at Museum Victoria Archives indicate the range of their eclectic exchange through letters, magazines, and books (for example, on 21 January 1869, Huyghue had sent Johns extracts "from a most interesting series of lectures on *Man's Origin & Destiny* by Lesley). While a pursuit of social history is consistent with Huyghue's interests in *Argimou* and in his *Amaranth* writing (Griffiths 41), what is also clear is that Huyghue's life was never far from New Brunswick. For example, in a diary entry dated 6 May 1878, Johns notes that he had "[r]eceived a letter from poor Huyghue, whose parents lost everything but their lives in the great fire of St. John's, New Brunswick." And it is in consultation with Johns and Huyghue's sister Emma that Huyghue arranged some time before his death in 1891 to donate his papers and his collection of Indigenous cultural artifacts from Canada, including the ceremonial Mi'kmaw chieftain's coat acquired circa 1840, to what is now the S. D. S. Huyghue Collection at the National Gallery of Victoria in Melbourne, Australia.

Writing of Huyghue, Phillips notes that the "edifice of human cultural evolution" that writers and readers such as Johns and Huyghue constructed in the Victorian period "has now been carefully dismantled by postcolonial critical theorists and students of the history of anthropology" (146). Nonetheless, she adds, in Huyghue's unpublished work, especially his "freethinking" essay "Christ a Myth" housed in his papers in Melbourne, one glimpses how "human creativity and thought can combat xenophobic tendencies and promote openness to difference" (147). And, indeed, it was this very "openness to difference" that had impelled Huyghue, even in his early twenties, to write *Argimou* and to challenge society's marginalization of Indigenous cultures. His plea early in the novel that readers "discard all narrow conception of moral obligation to our fellow creatures" and instead "embrace, within the scope of a comprehensive benevolence, every individual composing the family of the human race" (6) reflected what was to be an informing principle in his career. Promoting "openness to difference" was the raison d'être of *Argimou* and the foundation of his essay on the Ballarat Uprising.

Huyghue's career took him to three continents, each phase broadening his writing on the "family of the human race." Throughout that time, he carried with him the wampum belts, the Mi'kmaw ceremonial coat, and smaller Indigenous cultural objects that he had acquired in the Maritimes and in central Canada early in his career. Like "other antiquarian collectors," notes Phillips, "Huyghue undoubtedly regarded" these items "as 'relics' to be preserved as a record of a noble people and a simple but wholesome way of life that were doomed to disappear" (139). Thus, he would no doubt have been amazed and gratified that, almost a century after his death, his Mi'kmaw chief's coat from around 1840 would journey to Canada from Australia on temporary loan to the Glenbow Museum's touring exhibition *The Spirit*

Sings: Artistic Traditions of Canada's First Peoples in 1988 and would subsequently generate a chapter in Phillips's scholarly book (149–53, 340–42). Nor, indeed, could Huyghue ever have anticipated current interest in Nova Scotia's Mi'kmaw community in having the chieftain's ceremonial coat returned to the province for a more permanent cultural display, and, in doing so, bestowing upon the outfit something that it may always have had, from the beginning, "a kind of ambassadorial function" (Phillips 152). Were Huyghue alive today, Phillips adds, he would undoubtedly "be gladdened by the knowledge that Mi'kmaq culture and identity have not disappeared" as he so feared would happen when he wrote *Argimou*. And, invariably, from everything that we know of the integrity and idealism of Douglass Huyghue, he would "want his chief's outfit to support contemporary Mi'kmaq projects of cultural recovery" (153).

It is within discussions of cultural repatriation and resilience such as these that Huyghue's novel continues to carry resonance. British literary critic Marilyn Butler has noted that

> writing about literature, whether its bias is historical, linguistic, philosophical or psychoanalytic, must aim to pass the test of adding to experience which is still current. The great writings of the early nineteenth century are not merely pieces of historical evidence, fossils in the ground, but living texts that we too are engaged with. Just as they had no first author, they have not found their last reader. To see these works within their cultural context is also to acknowledge their place in a world we still inhabit. (10)

Her observations help to contextualize Huyghue's writing, in particular *Argimou*. One can speculate that, within the parameters of this discussion, Huyghue would have welcomed this reprint of his novel. Published three times (1842, 1847, 1860) in Canada in Huyghue's own lifetime—and reputed to have appeared in the United States in approximately the same period (MacFarlane 46)—*Argimou* not only reflected the social conscience and citizen engagement of its author but also reminds us of the role played by our national literature in heightening our cultural awareness of nineteenth-century Canada. Moreover, at a time when the English-speaking world was enthralled by Sir Walter Scott's historical tales of Highland courage or selfless values, it is significant that Huyghue recognized the adaptability of those literary conventions to chronicle British North America's tense power struggles, capture its romance, and sharpen its voice of social reform.

GWENDOLYN DAVIES, *University of New Brunswick*

Acknowledgements

I would like to thank the following for assisting my research on S. Douglass S. Huyghue:

Mora Dianne O'Neill, Associate Curator of Historical Prints and Drawings at the Art Gallery of Nova Scotia, for introducing me to the signed S. D. S. Huyghue 1838 ink wash drawing *View of Halifax from Fort Clarence* (with Mi'kmaw family), donated to the Art Gallery of Nova Scotia in 2016. The sketch establishes Huyghue's whereabouts in 1838 and the ceremonial chieftain's coat worn in the drawing supports the premise that he knew Chief Peminuit Paul of the Shubenacadie Reserve. I am also grateful to Dianne O'Neill for the information that Douglass Huyghue was listed in *Belcher's Farmer's Almanack* in the 1840s as a Lieutenant in the 4th Halifax Militia Regiment.

Wendy and Alan Taylor of Australia, through Josh Green, Photo Archivist at the Provincial Archives of New Brunswick, contacted me about six drawings of New Brunswick from roughly 1843 that they had inherited through their family. These give every evidence of being executed by Douglass Huyghue while he was serving in New Brunswick on the 1843–45 Boundary Commission between Great Britain and the United States. Probate and public documents link the Taylor family (which, like Huyghue's, had nineteenth-century Saint John antecedents) to Huyghue in Australia and provide provenance for their having inherited the sketches. In the process of authenticating Huyghue's drawings, the Taylors have consulted with the Art Gallery of Ballarat, where a building on the premises is named after Huyghue.

Australian researcher and writer Chris Vening generously sent me newspaper and public venue online sources (including the arrival of Huyghue's sister) and notice of Tom Griffiths's book *The Antiquarian Imagination* with a chapter on R. E. Johns. Mr. Vening, like the Taylors, sent information on Huyghue's burial site in Boroondara General Cemetery in Melbourne with a headstone that prominently reads: "Born in Prince Edward Island Canada."

Over the years, I have been indebted to archivists and librarians at the New Brunswick Museum, Library and Archives Canada, the Provincial Archives of New Brunswick, the Saint John Free Library, the Public Archives and Records Office of Prince Edward Island, the Nova Scotia Archives, the Guildhall Library, and the British Library for their assistance. In Australia, archivists and staff at the Public Record Office of Victoria, State Library of Victoria, Museum Victoria Archives (Melbourne Museum), National Library of Australia (Canberra), the Mitchell Library (State Library of New South Wales), and the University of Melbourne Library have been most helpful both by correspondence and when I was on site.

Finally, I want to express my appreciation to retired Nova Scotia Museum History Curator and authority on Mi'kmaw culture, Dr. Ruth Holmes Whitehead, who, in 1979, after the Ralph Pickard Bell Library at Mount Allison University produced a teaching edition of

Argimou, went through the text, commenting on some of Huyghue's references. She conjectured that Huyghue had read Marc Lescarbot's 1609 book *Histoire de la Nouvelle-France* and Champlain's accounts of his 1604–05 mapping of the east coast for the writing of his novel. She noted anachronisms such as a reference to flint arrowheads or to Mi'kmaw women in 1755 wearing conical caps (which were first mentioned in 1791), but she believed the portrayal of the snake dance to be accurate. She noted in the capture of Clarence that the Maliseet would never have had a prisoner ride a horse while they walked (especially when the prisoner was a woman), and she provided the very interesting piece of information that, at the 1761 signing of the peace treaty in Halifax between the British and the Mi'kmaq, one of the signatories was Joseph Argimault.

I would like to thank Benjamin Lefebvre, editor of the Early Canadian Literature series, for his patience, editorial guidance, and expertise.

Notes

1 Surviving records spell and present Huyghue's name inconsistently. Although several sources list his name as "Douglas"—including his tombstone—or as "S. D. S. Huyghue," this edition relies on surviving payment receipts from *Bentley's Miscellany* and on the title page of his later novel, *The Nomades of the West; or, Ellen Clayton* (1850), on both of which he signs himself "S. Douglass S. Huyghue." Huyghue's surname is thought to be pronounced *Hewg.*

2 Although the second edition of the *Canadian Oxford Dictionary* (2004) prefers "Mi'kmaq" as both a noun and an adjective to refer to both people and language and still accepts "Micmac" as a variant, current usage distinguishes between "Mi'kmaq" as a noun for the nation and "Mi'kmaw" as a noun for a single person and as an adjective. My thanks to Dr. Ruth Holmes Whitehead, Curator of History (retired) at the Nova Scotia Museum, for her advice on this usage.

3 The beadwork design on each Mi'kmaw chieftain's ceremonial coat was unique.

I would like to thank Dianne O'Neill for suggesting the similarity between the chieftain's coat in Huyghue's 1838 ink wash Halifax drawing and the one now held in the S. D. S. Huyghue Collection in the Museum Victoria Archives in Melbourne, Australia. See also Whitehead, *Micmac* 88.

4 Phillips suggests an alternate source to the origins of the Mi'kmaw chieftain's ceremonial coat. She indicates that "Stephen Augustine, curator of Maritime Ethnology at the Canadian Museum of Civilization and a Mi'kmaq elder knowledgeable in oral tradition," has postulated "that the Huyghue chief's outfit could very well be the one presented to Perley on the Miramichi in 1841, a suggestion made all the more plausible by Perley's probable investiture with another fine outfit when he was raised to the rank of 'chief over all' during the year of the exhibition" (140–41).

5 Page references to all quotations from *Argimou* correspond to this Early Canadian Literature edition. Argimou's name has been variously spelled over the centuries as Algimault, Argunault, Aolgimault, Algemoure, Alguimou, and Argimeau. The pronunciation would be "Ulgimoo," the current spelling "L'kimu." See Lockerby 407–17; Whitehead, *Old Man* 9–10, 47–48, 84–85.

6 A captivity narrative is "[a]n account by or about Europeans held captive by American Indians, a popular GENRE during the seventeenth and eighteenth centuries" (Frye et al. 88).

7 Charles Wolhaupter, who served on the Boundary Commission with Huyghue, emigrated, as did Huyghue, to Australia. Sailing from Saint John in 1851, he taught for seven years in Australia before returning to New Brunswick. He drowned by falling from a steamer, the *St. John*, on her evening passage from Fredericton to Saint John in June 1858.

8 Of the items included in the bibliography below, *Eureka Stockade* and *View of Halifax from Fort Clarence* are signed S. D. S. Huyghue, whereas *Anglican Church, Fredericton, BBC Depot Ishegaulshugik Lake, Party Preparing for Line, Oct. 1844, Bridge at the Mouth of the Backaguimic River, Fredericton, Fredericton, 27 April 1843*, and *Grand Falls, 2 August 1943*, are unsigned.

9 Huyghue's allusion to "either Cross or Crown" refers to the symbolic heart of the confrontation between the miners and the government in the Ballarat Riots. The Eureka Flag, representative of the reform movement led by the miners, had an eight-sided star worked into its design. Reputed to have been devised by

a Toronto miner, Captain Ross, who died in the confrontation with the troops at Ballarat, the flag was dubbed "the Southern Cross." As a constellation visible mainly in the Southern hemisphere, the Southern Cross has long been associated with Australia (see McCallum). In a note sent to his friend Reynell Eveleigh Johns after witnessing the Ballarat Riots, Huyghue indicated that "[a] portion of the insurgents banner is pinned to the corner" of the letter ("Account").

Works Cited

I. Archival Sources

J. Russell Harper Collection, Provincial Archives of New Brunswick, Fredericton.

Lawrence F. Hashey fonds, Provincial Archives of New Brunswick, Fredericton.

Library and Archives Canada, Ottawa.

Moses Perley Letters, New Brunswick Museum, Saint John.

New Brunswick Historical Society fonds, New Brunswick Museum, Saint John.

New Brunswick Museum, Saint John.

Provincial Archives of New Brunswick, Fredericton.

Public Archives and Records Office, Government of Prince Edward Island, Charlottetown.

R.E. Johns Papers, Museum Victoria Archives, Melbourne.

Richard Bentley & Son Publishers' Archives, British Library, London.

Robert Hazen Papers, New Brunswick Museum, Saint John.

State Library of New South Wales, Sydney.

The State Library of Victoria, Melbourne.

Ward Chipman Papers, Library and Archives Canada, Ottawa.

Wolhaupter Family Collection, Provincial Archives of New Brunswick, Fredericton.

II. Books, Periodicals, and Electronic Sources

"Account Sale of Books . . . St. John Society Library by Order of Mr. A. R. Truro." 1835, Robert Hazen Papers, New Brunswick Museum, Saint John.

"The Amaranth." *The Amaranth*, Jan. 1841, pp. 29–32.

"The Amaranth." *Loyalist and Conservative Advocate*, 9 Feb. 1843, p. 3.

"The Amaranth." *The Times* [Halifax], 13 Sept. 1842, p. 294.

Anglican Church, Fredericton. 1843, Provincial Archives of New Brunswick, Fredericton.

BBC Depot Ishegaulshugik Lake, Party Preparing for Line, Oct. 1844. 1844, Provincial Archives of New Brunswick, Fredericton.

Belcher's Farmer's Almanack, for the Year of Our Lord 1840. C. H. Belcher, 1840.

Belcher's Farmer's Almanack, for the Year of Our Lord 1841. C. H. Belcher, 1841.

Belcher's Farmer's Almanack, for the Year of Our Lord 1842. C. H. Belcher, 1842.

Belcher's Farmer's Almanack, for the Year of Our Lord 1843. C. H. Belcher, 1843.

Belcher's Farmer's Almanack, for the Year of Our Lord 1844. C. H. Belcher, 1844.

Belcher's Farmer's Almanack, for the Year of Our Lord 1845. C. H. Belcher, 1845.

Belcher's Farmer's Almanack, for the Year of Our Lord 1846. W. C. Manning, 1846.

Belcher's Farmer's Almanack, for the Year of Our Lord 1847. W. C. Manning, 1847.

Belcher's Farmer's Almanack, for the Year of Our Lord 1848. W. C. Manning, 1848.

Belcher's Farmer's Almanack, for the Year of Our Lord 1849. C. H. Belcher, 1849.

Belcher's Farmer's Almanack, for the Year of Our Lord 1850. C. H. Belcher, 1850.

"Books." *Weekly Chronicle* [Halifax], 21 Dec. 1821, p. 1.

Bridge at the Mouth of the Backaguimic River. 1843, Provincial Archives of New Brunswick, Fredericton.

Buckingham, James S. *Canada, Nova Scotia, New Brunswick, and the Other British Provinces in North America, with a Plan of National Colonization.* Fisher, Son, & Co., 1843. *Internet Archive*, archive.org/details/McGillLibrary-130149-5095.

Butler, Marilyn. *Romantics, Rebels and Reactionaries: English Literature and Its Background 1760–1830.* Oxford UP, 1981.

Catalogue of Books in Saint Andrews. 1815, Lawrence F. Hashey fonds, Provincial Archives of New Brunswick, Fredericton.

Census of Canada, 1871. Library and Archives Canada, Ottawa.

Census of Canada East, Canada West, New Brunswick and Nova Scotia, 1851. Library and Archives Canada, Ottawa.

Chubb, Henry. *The New Brunswick Almanack for the Year of Our Lord 1839.* Saint John, Courier Office, 1839.

———. *The New Brunswick Almanack for the Year of Our Lord 1844.* Saint John, Courier Office, 1844.

Conrad, Margaret R., and James K. Hiller. *Atlantic Canada: A Region in the Making.* Oxford UP, 2001.

Correspondence Respecting the Operations of the Commission for Running and Tracing the Boundary Line between Her Majesty's Possessions in North America and the United States, under the VIth Article of the Treaty Signed at Washington, August 9, 1842. London, 1845.

"Credit to New Brunswick." Review of *Argimou: A Legend of the Micmac,* by Eugene. *Halifax Morning Post and Parliamentary Reporter,* 7 July 1842, p. 2.

Crosskill, J. H. "To Correspondents." *Halifax Morning Post and Parliamentary Reporter,* 3 Dec. 1840, p. 2.

———. "To Correspondents." *Halifax Morning Post and Parliamentary Reporter,* 8 May 1841, p. 2.

Cuthbertson, Brian. *Stubborn Resistance: New Brunswick Maliseet and Mi'kmaq in Defence of Their Lands.* Nimbus Publishing, 2015.

Eugene (*see also* Huyghue, S. D.; Huyghue, S. D. S.; Huyghue, S. Douglass S.; Pax). "Argimou: A Legend of the Micmac." *The Amaranth,* May 1842, pp. 129–42; June 1842, pp. 161–77; July 1842, pp. 193–209; Aug. 1842, pp. 225–38; Sept. 1842, pp. 257–81.

———. *Argimou: A Legend of the Micmac.* Halifax, Morning Courier Office, 1847.

———. *Argimou: A Legend of the Micmac.* 1977. Mount Allison U, 1979.

———. "Argimou: A Legend of the Micmac." *Albion* [Saint John], 3 Mar. 1860, p. 1.

———. "The Indian's Lament." *Halifax Morning Post and Parliamentary Reporter,* 25 May 1841, p. 1.

———. "Malsosep; or, The Forsaken." *The Amaranth,* Oct. 1841, pp. 298–306.

———. "The Unknown." *The Amaranth,* Feb. 1842, pp. 33–38.

Financial records. Richard Bentley & Son Publishers' Archives, British Library, London.

"For Sale." *New Brunswick Courier,* 2 Sept. 1826, p. 1.

Fredericton. 1843, Provincial Archives of New Brunswick, Fredericton.

Fredericton, 27 April 1843. 1843, Provincial Archives of New Brunswick, Fredericton.

Frye, Northrop, et al. *The Harper Handbook to Literature.* Harper & Row, 1985.

Gerson, Carole. *A Purer Taste: The Writing and Reading of Fiction in English in Nineteenth-Century Canada.* U of Toronto P, 1989.

"Grand Bazaar." Ganong Collection, Scrapbook C11. 1842, New Brunswick Museum, Saint John.

Grand Falls, 2 August 1843. 1843, Provincial Archives of New Brunswick, Fredericton.

Griffiths, Tom. *Hunters and Collectors: The Antiquarian Imagination in Australia.* Cambridge UP, 1996.

Gross, John. *The Rise and Fall of the Man of Letters: English Literary Life since 1800.* Pelican, 1973.

Harmon, William, and C. Hugh Holman. *A Handbook to Literature.* 7th ed., Prentice Hall, 1996.

Harper, J. Russell. "Mechanics' Institute Lectures for 1843: Photographers/Artists/Saint John." J. Russell Harper Collection, Provincial Archives of New Brunswick, Fredericton.

Hart, A. G. *Hart's Annual Army List.* John Murray, 1851.

Hart, James D. *The Popular Book: A History of America's Literary Taste.* U of California P, 1963.

Huyghue, S. Letter to Miss Waterbury, 11 May 1861. New Brunswick Museum, Saint John.

Huyghue, S. D. (*see also* Eugene; Huyghue, S. D. S.; Huyghue, S. Douglass S.; Pax). "Forest Incidents." *Bentley's Miscellany,* 1 May 1850, pp. 472–77.

———. "My First Winter in the Woods of Canada." *Bentley's Miscellany,* 1 Feb. 1850, pp. 152–60.

———. "The Scenery of the Ottawa." *Bentley's Miscellany,* 1 Nov. 1849, pp. 489–97.

———. "A Winter's Journey." *Bentley's Miscellany,* 1 Dec. 1849, pp. 630–37.

Huyghue, S. D. S. (*see also* Eugene; Huyghue, S. D.; Huyghue, S. Douglass S.; Pax). "An Account of the Eureka Stockade Riot at Ballarat in 1854—Sent to Reynell Eveleigh Johns by His Friend S. D. S. Huyghue." State Library of Victoria, Melbourne.

———. *The Eureka Stockade.* 1882, Art Gallery of Ballarat.

———. *View of Halifax from Fort Clarence* (with Mi'kmaw family). 1838, Art Gallery of Nova Scotia, Halifax.

Huyghue, S. Douglass S. (*see also* Eugene; Huyghue, S. D.; Huyghue, S. D. S.; Pax). Contract for *The Nomades of the West; or, Ellen Clayton.* Richard Bentley & Son Publishers' Archives, British Library, London.

———. *The Nomades of the West; or, Ellen Clayton.* 3 vols. Richard Bentley, 1850.

Johns, R. E. Diary. R. E. Johns Papers, Museum Victoria Archives, Melbourne.

Kerr, Joan, editor. *Dictionary of Australian Artists: Painters, Photographers and Engravers, 1770–1870.* Vol. 1. Power Institute of Fine Arts, U of Sydney, 1984.

Lennox, Jeffers. "A Time and a Place: The Geography of British, French, and Aboriginal Interactions in Early Nova Scotia, 1726–44." *William and Mary Quarterly,* 3rd ser., vol. 72, no. 3, 2015, 423–60.

"List of Books Imported by the Society in 1816." Ward Chipman Papers, Library and Archives Canada, Ottawa.

Lockerby, Earle. "Ancient Mi'kmaq Customs: A Shaman's Revelations." *Canadian Journal of Native Studies*, vol. 24, no. 2, 2004, 403–23.

Lukács, Georg. *The Historical Novel*. Translated by Hannah Mitchell and Stanley Mitchell, Penguin, 1969.

MacFarlane, William G. *New Brunswick Bibliography: The Books and Writers of the Province*. Saint John, 1895.

McCallum, Austin. *The Eureka Flag*. R. Fletcher & Sons, 1973.

McCulloch, Alan. *Artists of the Australian Gold Rush*. Lansdowne, 1977.

———. *Encyclopedia of Australian Art*. Hutchison Group, 1984.

McDougall, Robert L. *Totems: Essays in the Cultural History of Canada*. Tecumseh Press, 1990.

"Melbourne Arrivals: Lady Peel." *Sydney Morning Herald*, 11 Feb. 1852, p. 2.

"Mi'kmaq." *Canadian Oxford Dictionary*. 2nd ed., 2004.

"Mr. Perley's Lectures." *Royal Gazette*, 13 Jan. 1841, p. 4.

"New Works in the Press." *The Athenaeum*, 16 Feb. 1850, p. 189.

Nicholas, Andrea Bear. "The Role of Colonial Artists in the Dispossession and Displacement of the Maliseet, 1790s–1850s." *Journal of Canadian Studies / Revue d'études canadiennes*, vol. 49, no. 2, 2015, pp. 25–86.

———. "Settler Imperialism and the Dispossession of the Maliseet, 1758–1765." Reid and Savoie, pp. 21–57.

"The North Eastern Boundary." *New Brunswick Courier*, 25 Nov. 1843, p. 2.

"Nova Scotia Mi'kmaq Seek Return of Chief's Regalia." *Government of Nova Scotia*, 12 June 2007, novascotia.ca/news/release/?id=20070612003.

Patterson, Stephen E. "Indian–White Relations in Nova Scotia, 1749–61: A Study in Political Interaction." *Acadiensis: Journal of the History of the Atlantic Region / Revue d'histoire de la région atlantique*, vol. 23, no. 1, 1993, pp. 23–59.

Pax (*see also* Eugene; Huyghue, S. D.; Huyghue, S. D. S.; Huyghue, S. Douglass S.). "The Ballarat Riots, 1854." 1884, State Library of New South Wales, Sydney.

Phillips, Ruth B. *Museum Pieces: Toward the Indigenization of Canadian Museums*. McGill–Queen's UP, 2012.

Quill, Peter (Moses H. Perley). "My Dear Post." *Halifax Morning Post and Parliamentary Reporter*, 9 Dec. 1840, p. 2.

———. Scrapbook: Early History of St. John and N.B. New Brunswick Museum, Saint John.

Reid, Jennifer. *Myth, Symbol, and Colonial Encounter: British and Mi'kmaq in Acadia, 1700–1867.* U of Ottawa P, 1995.

Reid, John G. "Empire, the Maritime Colonies, and the Supplanting of Mi'kma'ki/ Wulstukwik, 1780–1820." *Acadiensis: Journal of the History of the Atlantic Region / Revue d'histoire de la région atlantique*, vol. 38, no. 2, 2009, pp. 78–97.

———. "Historical Analysis and Indigenous Dispossession." Reid and Savoie, pp. 58–61.

Reid, John G., and Donald J. Savoie, editors. *Shaping an Agenda for Atlantic Canada.* Fernwood Publishing, 2011.

"Report of the Directors of the Mechanics Institute." *New Brunswick Courier*, 20 May 1843, p. 4.

Richardson, John. *Wacousta: or, The Prophecy.* Cadell, 1832.

Scott, Sir Walter. "Tales of My Landlord." *Free Press* [Halifax], 28 Dec. 1818, p. 1; 5 Jan. 1819, p. 1.

"Shipping Intelligence." *The Argus*, 1 Feb. 1860, p. 4.

Shives, Robert. Rev. of *An English Spelling Book, with Reading Lessons, for the Use of the Parish and Other Schools of New Brunswick*, by William Corry. *The Amaranth*, Mar. 1841, p. 96.

Spray, W. A. "Perley, Moses Henry." *Dictionary of Canadian Biography*, n.d., biographi.ca/ en/bio/perley_moses_henry_9E.html.

St. John Grammar School minutes, 1805–34. New Brunswick Historical Society fonds, New Brunswick Museum, Saint John.

St. John Society Library to William L. Avery, 25 June 1835. Robert Hazen Papers, New Brunswick Museum, Saint John.

St. Paul's Anglican Church Baptismal Register. Public Archives and Records Office, Government of Prince Edward Island, Charlottetown.

Trinity Church Baptisms 1835–60. New Brunswick Museum, Saint John.

Upton, L. F. S. "Peminuit (Pominouet) Paul, Louis-Benjamin." *Dictionary of Canadian Biography*, n.d., biographi.ca/en/bio/peminuit_paul_louis_benjamin_7E.html.

Whitehead, Ruth Holmes. *Micmac Maliseet and Beothuk Collections in Europe and the Pacific.* Nova Scotia Museum, 1989.

———. *The Old Man Told Us: Excerpts from Micmac History, 1500–1950.* Nimbus Publishing, 1991.

Withers, W. B. *The History of Ballarat*. F. W. Niven & Company, 1890.

Wittig, Kurt. *The Scottish Tradition in Literature*. 1958. Mercat Press, 1978.

Wolhaupter, George Philip. Diary. Wolhaupter Family Collection, Provincial Archives of
New Brunswick, Fredericton.

Books in the Early Canadian Literature Series
Published by Wilfrid Laurier University Press

The Foreigner: A Tale of Saskatchewan / Ralph Connor / Afterword by Daniel Coleman / 2014 / x + 302 pp. / ISBN 978-1-55458-944-9

Painted Fires / Nellie L. McClung / Afterword by Cecily Devereux / 2014 / x + 324 pp. / ISBN 978-1-55458-979-1

The Traditional History and Characteristic Sketches of the Ojibway Nation / George Copway / Afterword by Shelley Hulan / 2014 / x + 208 pp. / ISBN 978-1-55458-976-0

The Seats of the Mighty / Gilbert Parker / Afterword by Andrea Cabajsky / 2015 / viii + 400 pp. / ISBN 978-1-77112-044-9

The Forest of Bourg-Marie / S. Frances Harrison / Afterword by Cynthia Sugars / 2015 / x + 258 pp. / ISBN 978-1-77112-029-6

The Flying Years / Frederick Niven / Afterword by Alison Calder / 2015 / x + 336 pp. / ISBN 978-1-77112-074-6

In Due Season / Christine van der Mark / Afterword by Carole Gerson and Janice Dowson / 2016 / x + 356 pp. / ISBN 978-1-77112-071-5

Argimou: A Legend of the Micmac / S. Douglass S. Huyghue / Afterword by Gwendolyn Davies / 2017 / viii + 256 pp. / ISBN 978-1-77112-247-4